TITLES BY TOM CARROLL
COLT'S CRISIS - BOOK 1
COLT'S CROSS - BOOK 2
SHANGHAI PROTOCOL (FORTHCOMING) - BOOK 3

TOM CARROLL

COLT'S CROSS

Book two of the COLT GARRETT series

ISBN: 978-1-947863-15-6 (Hardcover edition)
ISBN: 978-1-947863-16-3 (Paperback edition)
ISBN: 978-1-947863-17-0 (Kindle edition)
ISBN: 978-1-947863-18-7 (Downloadable Audio edition)
ISBN: 978-1-947863-19-4 (CD-Audio edition)

Library of Congress Control Number: 2021952305

This book is a work of fiction. Names, characters, dialogue, places, incidents, and opinions expressed are the product of the author's imagination or are used fictitiously. Any resemblance to actual persons, living or dead, business establishments, events, or locales is entirely coincidental and should not be construed as real. Nothing is intended or should be interpreted as expressing the views of the US Department of Defense or any other department or agency of any government body.

The US Department of Defense's Prepublication & Security Review cleared this manuscript as amended for public release on September 17, 2021. The appearance of US Department of Defense visual information does not imply or constitute DoD endorsement.

Printed and bounced in the United States of America.
First printing December 2021.

Cover art and design by bookcoverart.com

Visit www.tomcarrollbooks.com and www.facebook.com/ TomCarrollBooks for more information.

Writing a book is more challenging than I thought and more rewarding than I could have ever imagined. None of this would have been possible without the help of a large group of friends, old and new, that took the time to help me when I needed it most. That is true friendship.

Copyreading team. I'm eternally grateful to the group of friends that agreed to read through the pre-publication edition to help me find my errors: Amanda Rowe, Chris Hall, David Stocks, Jim Carroll, Laurie Carroll, and Michael Evans.

The Experts. A special thanks to the group of naval, military, intelligence, medical, and aviation experts who tolerated my endless questions and attempted to ensure the novel's technical elements approximated reality: Captain Kurt Storey, Captain Darren Glaser, and Commander Bill Webb, USN; Captain Roger Spealman, Federal Express; Lieutenant Colonel Gene Vey, USAF; Chief Warrant Officer 4 Jeff Brandsma and Chief Warrant Officer 2 Chris Dowling, USA; Former Deputy Chief Glenn Cramer, Washington State Patrol, and Randy Moller, MD.

My family. To Laurie: for always being the person I could turn to for encouragement while creating the novel's first draft. She allowed me to take over our dining room table with my research materials, and she quietly listened when I shared my excitement about writing novels with our close friends. To my grown children, Amanda and Sean: thank you for letting me try out possible plot lines and for letting me know when I was off base.

And to Ivan Zann at BookCoversArt.com for the great cover.

For the more than 82,000
American service members
who were prisoners of war
or who are missing in action.

You are not forgotten.

You have no enemies, you say?
Alas! my friend, the boast is poor;
He who has mingled in the fray
Of duty, that the brave endure,
Must have made foes! If you have none,
Small is the work that you have done.
You've hit no traitor on the hip,
You've dashed no cup from perjured lip,
You've never turned the wrong to right,
You've been a coward in the fight.

Charles Mackay, 1915

RANK INSIGNIA OF THE U.S. ARMED FORCES
OFFICERS

Prologue

Saigon, South Vietnam, April 29, 1975

"You planning on sleeping the entire morning, Spence? Don't you have to be at work in an hour?"

Spencer Hale groaned and then squinted at his bedside clock. "Crap," he thought. "It's eleven!" The young American had been working as a case officer for the CIA for the past five years, a prime position after graduating from Boston College with a degree in international studies. The recruiter had told him it was his minor in French that had attracted the CIA's attention. As it turned out, that was one reason why, after he completed field operations training, Langley assigned him to Saigon. The Vietnam War was becoming a lost cause. The chief of station had drastically reduced the agency's staff in Saigon as President Ford withdrew US forces from the city. The reduced staffing gave Spence an opportunity to develop closer relationships with the chief of station and his deputy, which he hoped would serve him well when he returned to Langley. He was always on the lookout for ways to advance his CIA career. He rolled out of bed and stumbled into the bathroom.

"I said, don't you have to be at work in an hour?" Leyna shouted from the apartment's kitchen. Leyna Tran, assistant manager at Saigon's Hotel Continental, these days spent more and more nights at Spence's apartment in downtown Saigon than in her own place. For the past two months, the couple had been sleeping together. Leyna, he knew, had developed strong feelings for the person she called, "the tall and handsome American," whom she had been led to believe worked at a travel agency downtown. Spence knew she definitely wanted to take their relationship to the next level and last week had asked him to give her a key to his apartment. But Spence also knew something that Leyna didn't: Saigon would fall within days, and it would be desperate, dangerous, and unpredictable. He would be leaving the city without her.

"Thanks," answered Spence from the apartment's tiny bathroom. "Gonna take a quick shower and then head out!" He shaved and stepped into the shower, enjoying the hot water as it filled the bathroom with steam. The last few days had been chaotic, as staff worked nonstop to plan for the evacuation. Over 6,000 Americans remained in Saigon, and nobody knew exactly when President Ford would order the final evacuation, or what option would be selected, or who would leave with the Americans and how. Spence hoped Saigon's Tan Son Nhut Airport would remain open so that US C-130 Hercules cargo planes could land and evacuate the Americans. But the CIA chief of station thought the airport would close soon or be overtaken by the Northern troops already in the purlieus of the city, so a frenzied helicopter evacuation to US Seventh Fleet ships in the South China Sea was much more likely an option. Spence toweled off and had just finished dressing when he heard Leyna shout, "It's going to be hot today. The radio announcer just said it's already 105!"

"What?" he said as he sat down on the bed, the CIA officer part of Spence's brain now fully alert.

Lenya walked into the bedroom. "I said, it's going to be very hot, already 105. And the ARS station is playing 'White Christmas' in April! DJ must be stoned."

Spence silently stared at Leyna. She asked, "Hey, babe. You okay?"

Spence offered an awkward smile at his girlfriend and gathered himself before responding. "I was just thinking if it's going to be that hot today, I better change into a short sleeve. And I think I'll take my gym bag with me. Been weeks since I worked out." Lenya returned to the kitchen while Spence grabbed his gym bag from the closet. He was definitely not okay. The phrase, "the temperature in Saigon is 105 degrees and rising," and the playing of White Christmas on the American Radio Service were the two prearranged signals for Saigon's immediate helicopter evacuation. The green evac booklet listed fourteen assembly points in the city, but Spence knew his assignment. He grabbed his prepacked "Go Bag," containing two changes of clothing, a shave kit, and some personal mementos. Bag in hand, he walked into the kitchen to say goodbye to Leyna. Forever.

He startled Leyna when he tightly hugged her from behind as she washed the dishes from last night's dinner. "Hey! I don't think we have time for that! I'll see you when you get home!"

Spence walked to the door, stopped for a moment before turning back to remember this moment. "I love you."

She smiled and kept washing the dishes without looking up. "If you loved me, you'd give me a key!"

Spence paused, looked at Leyna one last time, and silently placed his apartment key on the table as he left through the front door.

US Government Building, Saigon, April 29, 1975

Spencer Hale walked past the French Embassy on Thong Nhut Boulevard and then down several side streets and through the travel agency's back entrance. A nervous Marine checked his ID, after which Spence hurried to the CIA's secure wing looking for the deputy chief of station, Leon Dupont. Leon was considered an old hand, working behind enemy lines with the French Resistance during World War II while in the Army's Office of Strategic Services. In his late fifties, with a receding hairline and horn-rimmed glasses, he looked more like a law professor than a spymaster.

"Spence! Glad you made it so quickly!" Leon looked at the ancient Hamilton watch he'd worn since his OSS days. "It's been less than an hour since Ford ordered Operation Frequent Wind, and choppers are already inbound. Ford wants Ambassador Martin out tonight."

Spence looked around the room as agency employees furiously shredded documents and destroyed computer equipment. "What can I do to help, sir?"

Leon leaned closer. "I need you to do something special for me." He took Spence by the arm and walked him to the side of the room.

"Son, there's a small safe in my sleeping quarters over at Pittman where I keep some extremely sensitive information. The North Vietnamese and their Russian buddies cannot get their grubby hands on the files inside that safe. I have to stay here with the boss. I need you to run over to Pittman right now, destroy all those files, and get up to the roof and get your ass on the next chopper out. Just a half dozen or so files. Use the shredder in my room and scatter the mulch. I know this sounds like errand crap, but if those files get into the wrong hands, people will definitely die." Leon scribbled a series of numbers on his business card's back and pressed it into the young man's hand. He pulled Spence closer. "This is extremely important, son. Don't let me down."

Spence raced the few blocks to the apartment building and quickly climbed the stairs to the top floor. Helicopters were already landing on the roof as the words of "White Christmas" blared through speakers throughout the city on the humid Spring day. Locating the safe was easy enough, and Spence quickly spun the combination lock in the sequence Leon had written on the business card. He opened the small safe's door, reached inside, and grabbed a stack of paper files. As Spence turned to the paper shredder at the end of the room, the lights suddenly went out, and he tripped over a chair and hit his head on the hardwood floor. When he finally came to, the power was back on, and he heard people yelling on the roof above. Disoriented, he collected the files, not noticing that one thin file with the words "SOG BASE PYTHON—TOP SECRET (SPECIAL ACCESS)" stamped in red ink on the cover had slid under a table. He hastily shredded the other classified files and dumped the paper mulch out the open window before running to the stairs and then to the roof above.

A crowd of American and Vietnamese people pushed and shouted to get a place in line for the next helicopter. A Marine sergeant directed Spence to the front when he saw his agency identification. Before long, a gray Bell 205 helicopter hovered over the building and slowly descended until just the front of the aircraft's landing skids rested on a 20-foot structure atop the roof.

The Marine motioned to the improvised ladder leading up the awaiting helicopter. "You're next, sir. Your ride back to the world!" Spence climbed the unsteady metal ladder and through the aircraft's open door.

The pilot in the right front seat shouted over the engine noise in a heavy Texas accent, "Welcome aboard, son! Ever flown Air America before?" Spence found a seat near the front and watched as more than a dozen more people boarded, all without luggage. The sergeant slid the large cabin door closed as the helicopter lifted into the air and headed directly out to sea, back to "the world."

Leyna Tran walked to the door and saw the key Spence had left on the table. She giggled, picked up the key, and locked the door behind her on the way to work. She was thrilled with the prospect of starting a life with Spence and maybe even moving to America, but soon enough she first heard and then saw dozens of helicopters, all heading to the east. She stared at the swarm, looked down at the small brass key in her hand, and began to cry.

SOG BASE PYTHON, Cambodia, May 4, 1975

Engineman Second Class (SEAL) Luke Gallo was in an upbeat mood as he cleaned his CAR-15 rifle while sitting on a wooden pallet near the base's ammunition dump. The United States had evacuated Saigon earlier in the week. The SOG BASE PYTHON team had received orders to immediately break camp and be ready for airlift home at first light the following morning. He hadn't seen his family in almost a year. When he returned home, he planned to leave the Navy and attend college using the G.I. Bill. Luke's sister Leslie was ten years younger than he was and wrote him weekly letters ever since he had left for Vietnam. She made him promise to come home to her soon, and he wanted to keep that promise.

The Military Assistance Command Vietnam, Studies and Observation Group (MACV-SOG) units had been in Vietnam since the early 1960s, created to wreak havoc against the North Vietnamese. With bases in North and South Vietnam, Cambodia, and Laos, the SOG units included warriors from the US Navy SEALs, Air Force, Army Green Berets, Marine Corps Force Recon, and the CIA. The United States had disbanded all top-secret SOG units in April 1972, except for SOG BASE PYTHON. Luke had been ordered to the top-secret base in Cambodia in 1974 as a part of a thirty-person team that directed covert operations in and around the Ho Chi Minh Trail as American forces withdrew from Vietnam. The trail ran through Laos and Cambodia and provided a steady stream of trucks, troops, and ammunition for Northern forces and sympathizers into South Vietnam throughout the war. Because it was challenging to observe the route from the air, the PYTHON base provided the best real-time intelligence. Luke enjoyed working with the local troops, mainly Montagnards, Cambodians, or Vietnamese. They were brave soldiers under fire and extremely loyal to the Americans at the small hidden base.

Luke had just finished cleaning and reloading the last of his rifle magazines when he heard several choppers fly into the densely forested valley. Shielding his eyes from the bright afternoon sun, instead of the familiar American-made "Huey" helicopters, he was shocked to look up and see three heavily armed Soviet Mi-8 "HIP" attack helicopters making a low strafing run on the base. He grabbed his rifle and the stack of ammo mags and dove for cover behind a Jeep. The attack helicopters relentlessly poured rocket and automatic weapons fire into the American positions, virtually obliterating the unprepared ground forces. Luke emptied magazine after magazine at the helicopters until one spun around and barreled directly for him. He watched with horror as the attack helicopter fired two rockets at him, and his world went black.

Phnom Penh, Cambodia, May 5, 1975

Kiri Phan was exhausted and wanted the long day to end. The teenager considered himself lucky to have avoided his parents' fate: forced relocation from Phnom Penh to a state-run farming collective. Pol Pot's Khmer Rouge regime had just seized power in Cambodia and purged scholars and professionals to better engineer the country's return to an agrarian society. Kiri's older brother, Kosal, had just graduated from medical school and had fled the country into Vietnam. That had been two months ago. The only reason Kiri had been allowed to stay in the city was that he was the high school's photographer, owned a camera, and could operate the school's darkroom. The totalitarian regime needed him to take photographs of political prisoners held in his former school, now called Security Prison 21, or simply S-21. The Khmer Rouge had a near-fanatical obsession with thoroughly documenting the wretched souls held in their prisons.

Kiri sat at a wooden desk in his combination office/darkroom when the prison commandant walked in. The man had a reputation for taking sadistic pleasure in the prolonged torture of prisoners. He had insisted on creating complete files on each prisoner so that he could detail his efforts for his superiors.

The commandant ordered, "Phan, another truck just arrived. Grab your equipment and document the new batch before you leave!" and then he stormed out of Kiri's room.

Kiri Phan loaded a roll of film into his camera, grabbed a worn green ledger, and raced out of the room and down the prison's main hallway. He watched as armed guards carried two stretchers into the cell at the end of the hall and shackled two severely wounded men to the rusted metal bed frames bolted to the cement floor. Kiri focused the lens of his Canon FX 35mm camera on the prisoner's face in the bed on the left and let the camera lower when he realized the man was an American. Since working at S-21, Kiri had only photographed Cambodians. The American's shirt was gone, and he had bled profusely from a crudely bound wound on his right shoulder. On his left arm was a faded tattoo of a playful seal wearing a sailor hat. Looking to his right, Kiri Phan saw the other prisoner, also an American, who had severe burns over half of his body. Both men were breathing heavily and barely conscious.

After forcing himself to take the photographs for the prison record, Kiri asked the first man his name. "Luke Gallo, Engineman Second Class, US Navy," whispered the wounded man, and he gave his serial number. The American grabbed Kiri's arm and desperately pled, "Help me!" Kiri stepped back, looked at the man more closely, and entered his information into the ledger. As he carefully jotted down the information, he thought, "What can I do? I'm just a boy! I have no power." He finished with the journal entry then stepped over to the other man to get his name, rank, and serial number. Kiri was walking back to his office when a group of soldiers wearing camouflaged uniforms stopped him in the hallway.

"Hey, kid," one of them said in broken English with a heavy Russian accent. "You take our picture?"

Kiri had seen small groups of Russian soldiers around the prison in the past, but nobody had told him why they were there. Kiri positioned the three camouflage uniformed Russians against the wall and took their photograph while they posed smiling with their automatic rifles. The tallest one said, "Go and develop pictures while we finish here."

He stepped into his darkroom and developed the roll of film. Alone now in his private space, Kiri was surprised at how much he had been affected by the American's plea for help. He had become increasingly hardened to the despair expressed by prisoners, and after a few weeks, he had begun to observe the people in the cells only as objects to photograph. But the look in the American's eyes as the man begged for help shocked him out of his trance-like indifference and forced him to see the prisoners for what they were: victims of genocide. He resolved to find some way to help.

He printed several copies of the Russian soldiers' photos from the negatives and reloaded his camera with a new roll of film as he waited for the prints to dry. A few minutes later, Kiri walked out of the prison building, looking for the Russian soldiers. In the courtyard at the rear of the building, he saw the Russians burying two bodies in the ground next to the prison's water well. Without thinking about what he was doing, Kiri lifted the camera's viewfinder to his eye and took several photos of the incident. The soldiers saw him standing next to the building and approached him, and Kiri feared they had seen him taking photographs of the nighttime burial.

"Boy! Do you have the pictures?"

Kiri stared at the soldier and then realized the man was asking about the photos he had taken earlier. He reached into his pocket and handed the prints to the tall Russian.

"Thanks. This is for you," said the Russian soldier as he passed Kiri a round embroidered patch. Kiri looked down into his hand and saw the patch depicted a human fist grasping a rifle beneath a red, five-pointed star with a hammer and sickle, the official emblem of the Soviet Spetsnaz, the special operations section of Russia's military intelligence service.

Several hours later, well after the prison commandant and the other camp officers had gone home, Kiri walked back to the cell where he first saw the two wounded Americans. It now held five terrified people in the cramped, damp room: a middle-aged man, his wife, and three small children, all shackled to the cell's bed frames. They reminded him of his own family. He was thankful now that they had been relocated to a farming collective rather than suffer the torture and ultimate death that awaited the family in the cell. Kiri thought about the American and the haunted look in the man's eyes after returning to his office. He didn't understand everything he had just seen but knew something was wrong with killing the two Americans and then the hurried burial in the courtyard. Kiri crossed the room, picked up his prison ledger, and opened it to the last page. Looking at the entry with the American's names, Kiri knew he wanted to keep a record of the things he saw. He took several pictures of the ledger and then developed the second roll of film. He placed all the negatives of the Russians and the Russian patch into his canvas bag and then finally left for his wooden house.

Day One

Phnom Penh, Cambodia, Present Day

Forty-five years later, a frail and dying, sixty-year-old Kiri Phan returned to the S-21 prison. But instead of taking photographs of prisoners while waiting to be interrogated, tortured, and likely murdered, Kiri now took tickets from tourists as they visited the former prison, renamed the Tuol Sleng Genocide Museum. The former jail now preserved evidence of the infamous Cambodian tragedy. Seven days a week, Kiri watched visitors file through the prison gates and into a series of cells that once held political prisoners awaiting their fate. But the cells now featured thousands of photographs of the victims of Pol Pot and his infamous Khmer Rouge. Each day, Kiri walked with tourists past panel after panel displaying faded black and white photographs and looked into each victim's hopeless eyes. While most tourists experienced a profound sense of horror at the genocide's human cost, Kiri experienced deep personal guilt. These were his photographs.

After one of his daily walks through the museum, Kiri sat down on a wooden bench in the museum's courtyard and ate his lunch. He watched as tourists posed in front of the former prison and then as they stood in lines to meet and purchase books from the regime's survivors. Kiri thought, "These are the lucky ones!" Broken and lonely from a rush of memories, he stared at the water well across the courtyard. Tears streamed down his face as he let his mind wander back in time to his terrible experience at the prison so many years before.

In 1975, Young Kiri had continued to take photographs of each prisoner after their arrival. But when a new commandant, Kang Kek Iew, arrived at S-21, Kiri had an additional duty: prison truck driver. Kang Kek Iew was known at S-21 as Comrade Duch. He seemed to enjoy the torture and killing of prisoners more than other commandants. He needed Kiri to help transport the prisoners to a nearby longan grove outside of Phnom Penh. Each day, Kiri drove an old military truck the seventeen kilometers to Choeung Ek, where the prisoners were to be "re-educated"—executed.

After the Khmer Rouge had come to power earlier in the year, Cambodian citizens looked forward to years of peace after the Vietnam War. Instead, most were forcefully gathered and moved to the countryside as an element of Pol Pot's desire to transform Cambodia into a farming society. Personal property was nationalized, currency abolished, families separated, and people forced to farm the land under horrendous conditions. Those who resisted or whose relatives resisted were arrested and sent to makeshift prisons throughout the country, including S-21. Prison S-21 detained over 12,000 people during its operation, and only seven survived.

Kiri remembered driving the trucks crammed full of doomed prisoners to the Choeung Ek Grove, where the terrifying journey always ended with the same result. Guards, some as young as seventeen, blindfolded the prisoners. Then, not wanting to waste ammunition, the guards crushed the prisoner's skulls with shovels before shoving them into giant pits containing thousands of fellow Cambodian men, women, and children. Kiri watched, first with horror and eventually detachment, as guards crushed young children against the trunk of what would become known to the world as "the killing tree." Kiri spent five horrifying years at S-21 and at the Choeung Ek longan orchard that would ultimately become known as "The Killing Fields." More than 17,000 people were executed at the site.

Kiri thought back to the day S-21 closed. On January 7, 1979, five trucks carrying a platoon of Vietnamese soldiers arrived at the front gate. Ten minutes later, Comrade Duch told the prison staff they should return to their homes and never return. The Vietnamese soldiers were surprised to discover the former school displayed a red sign with yellow letters proclaiming, "Fortify the spirit of the revolution! Be on your guard against the strategy and tactics of the enemy so as to defend the country, the people, and the Party." Kiri remembered silently watching as the soldiers entered each building, becoming sick after seeing the horror inside. Before he left the prison, Kiri gathered his camera and a box containing his developing equipment and left S-21, praying that he would never return.

Several weeks after the Vietnamese liberated Phnom Penh, Kiri, now nineteen, wandered the streets looking for food and a place to live. Soldiers slept in the wooden shack on raised poles he had called home. He carried on his back a small canvas pack containing the few treasures he could still call his own. After a close call with a roving band of bandits and with no other options, Kiri found himself at the door of an ancient and weathered Buddhist temple. A short, bald, middle-aged man in a long, saffron-dyed robe greeted Kiri with a thin smile.

"Young traveler, how can I be of assistance?"

Several of Kiri's childhood friends had lived with and been educated by Buddhist monks in monasteries. He felt he would be safe here. Kiri looked down at the Buddhist monk and asked, "Please, sir, I need a place to rest for a few days, and perhaps something to eat. I have no money, but I know how to work hard to repay your kindness."

"You may stay with us for as long as you desire," began the

monk. "Our food is your food. You may call me Khemera, and although you owe us nothing, hard work is always welcome." Khemera smiled broadly at the exhausted young man and led him gently by the arm into the monastery.

Buddhist Monastery near Phnom Penh

Wat Dhammapada sat outside of Phnom Penh and was the spiritual center of the small Cambodian village. It also was one of the few Buddhist monasteries that the ruthless Khmer Rouge regime had not yet purged. Buddhist monks all over the country had been dragged from the wats (Buddhist temples) and forced to perform manual labor. All religious ceremonies were banned, temples either ruined or destroyed, and the Khmer Rouge eventually killed over 50,000 monks.

Kiri enjoyed living with the monks, but he remained emotionally damaged by the brutality he had witnessed at S-21 and Choeung Ek. Within a few months, he decided to become a novice monk and start his formal education in Theravada Buddhism. Buddhists believed that life was a cycle of change and that the world and its living creatures were continually reborn. Depending on how one lived, one's reborn form could vary from a human to any other living creature. The cycle would continue until a person reached a state of nirvana—attained by performing acts of service to others. This desire to gain good karma directly led to the public support of the monks who lived and studied at the monastery. With a shaved head and wearing the same style long, saffron-dyed robe Kiri had seen the day he first entered the monastery, he slept on the floor, ate simply, and spent most of the next few years studying Buddhism and the 227 rules guiding his monastic life. The rules were difficult to learn and follow, but one bothered Kiri most. It forbade any interaction with women. He tolerated the prohibition for several years, but something happened at the monastery that made following the rule almost impossible for him. In 1985, the monastery admitted women into the wat, not as monks but as nuns.

The first time Kiri saw the beautiful Veata, he knew he was in love. He was now twenty-six, and she was five years younger. The Khmer Rouge had killed Veata's parents, and she had survived by agreeing to be the mistress to a farming camp officer. When the Vietnamese troops liberated the farm, she fled into the mountains and lived with other refugees. She eventually realized she couldn't remain there forever and returned to Phnom Penh in search of work. When that failed, she found her way to the gates of the monastery in search of a new life.

Before long, Kiri and Veata started stealing glances at one another during meals and other wat activities. Over the next few months, the flirtatious behavior developed into forbidden touches and then into secret midnight rendezvous in the nearby fields. After nearly a year, the romance had fully blossomed, and it became apparent even to the celibate monks that Kiri and Veata were in love. In the fall of 1986, Kiri and Veata left the Buddhist monastery. They married two months later.

City Apartments, Phnom Penh

The newlyweds were truly happy for the first time in their lives. Kiri had learned to speak and write English in the monastery. This helped him to secure an advantageous and well-paying position as a guide for a tour company that offered excursions from Phnom Penh to Angkor Wat, the world's largest religious monument and near Siem Reap. Although Veata wanted to start a family, Kiri couldn't imagine bringing a child into a world where something horrific as S-21 could exist. He couldn't escape his shame and guilt in having a role in the genocide.

He told Veata about what he had seen at the prison in chilling detail and how he strongly felt the world needed to understand what happened there. Kiri was glad that The Killing Fields movie had publicized the Khmer Rouge's horrific atrocities. Still, his weekly contact with American tourists caused Kiri deep anguish. They reminded him of the young American prisoner pleading for his help and the memory of Russian soldiers burying the Americans in the prison courtyard.

He looked at each tourist couple, wondering if their son or brother was in the shallow grave next to the prison's water well. Throughout their twenty-one years of marriage, Veata begged Kiri to bring the matter to the Cambodian government's attention. But Kiri continually refused, convinced the report would reveal his involvement in S-21. And then Veata fell ill.

In early 2007, Kiri rushed a feverous Veata on the back of his scooter to the local clinic. Two days later, doctors told Kiri that Veata suffered from stage four oral cancer, likely caused by her daily habit of chewing tobacco leaves. Unable to treat the tumors, the small clinic sent Veata home. Her health gradually declined until one day, Veata pulled Kiri close.

"I believe this day is my last, husband," and then she began a long series of deep coughs.

"Quiet, my flower," Kiri whispered. "You cannot leave me yet!"

Veata finally stopped coughing and smiled at her husband. "This decision is not yours to make, Kiri. And now I have something to ask you."

Kiri held his wife's tiny hand and said, "Anything."

"Kiri, I ask you to find a way to share your story about the American boys in that prison. Your guilt is slowly killing you, as sure as this cancer is killing me. Promise me!"

Kiri could refuse her nothing. "I promise," he whispered as his wife took one more breath and quietly passed away.

That was thirteen years ago. Sixty-year-old Kiri Phan finished his lunch and took a sip from a plastic bottle of water. Today, the newspaper proclaimed that the former commandant of S-21 had finally died. Kang Kek Iew (Comrade Duch) died of lung cancer at 77 after serving a ten-year prison term. Kiri found it ironic the same cancer that was slowly killing him had also killed the former prison commandant. When he first learned that Comrade Duch had died, he wondered if it was some sort of sign that Kiri should finally fulfill the promise he made to his wife. His failing health meant that even if Cambodia held him accountable for his involvement at S-21, Kiri would never live to see the inside of a prison. He reached into his pocket and removed a letter he had received from his older brother Kosal's daughter notifying him of his brother's death. Kiri's niece Michele worked in America's capital and had included her email address in the letter. Kiri had never spoken to Michele, who appeared to work for the American government. Perhaps she could help him keep his promise to Veata. Kiri stood up from the bench, walked out to the street, and headed to the internet café at the end of the road.

Day Two

1510 Longworth House Office Building, Washington, DC

United States Representative Michele Phan looked up from her chair at the faded wedding photo on her desk showing her parents the day they married in 1978, a year before her birth. Michele's father, Kosal Phan, had emigrated to the United States from Cambodia to escape the Khmer Rouge and its purges of professionals and scholars. Kosal met Michele's mother, Elizabeth, while Dr. Phan pursued a residency in emergency medicine at the Harborview Medical Center in Seattle. Nurse Elizabeth Montgomery was immediately attracted to the quiet young doctor, and the two quickly fell in love and soon married. A year later, Michele was born, but a complicated pregnancy and difficult birth led to the young mother's tragic death in a Seattle hospital, leaving the young Cambodian doctor to raise his daughter on his own.

A talented high school gymnast, Michele excelled at her studies and received a full-ride Air Force ROTC scholarship to attend the Washington State University. Her father had hoped she would pursue a career in medicine. Still, his pride at being a naturalized American citizen made him thrilled at the thought that his daughter would serve as a commissioned officer in the United States Air Force. Michele became interested in politics and decided to major in political science, but she still found time to compete and win the Miss Seattle beauty pageant during her freshman year. A petite 5 foot 2, she had a stunning smile and dark, piercing eyes. An Air Force career as a helicopter pilot followed her college graduation and commissioning. After the Air Force, a failed marriage, and work as a congressional staffer for several years, she eventually became elected as Washington State's 7th Congressional Representative. She sought committee assignments that allowed her to work on the issues that interested her most: those that involved people who had served their country.

Today's agenda included the House subcommittee on National Security's hearing on the Defense Prisoner of War/Missing in Action Accounting Agency. Michele had a personal interest in the subject matter because her father emigrated from Cambodia, and many Americans who fought there had not returned home. She felt an obligation to help find and bring home the bodies of those American servicemen left behind in Southeast Asia. The agenda listed three witnesses for the morning's meeting: Mr. Ralph Tasby, the director of the Defense POW/MIA Accounting Agency, Ms. Kimberly Zechmann, chair of the National League of POW/MIA Families, and the Honorable Colton S. Garrett, United States secretary of defense.

Michele had first met Colt Garrett during a White House reception after his Senate confirmation. She had been charmed by his smile and gracious manner, and he left her with a positive impression. She wasn't alone. In just two years in the job, the new defense secretary had developed a solid reputation on both sides of the political aisle. Most agreed he ran the massive defense department efficiently, and he even managed to gain bipartisan admiration when testifying before congressional oversight committees.

As Representative Phan walked through her congressional office suite and headed for the door, her chief of staff, Kari Decker, handed her a brown envelope.

"Michele, you need to take a look at this email," advised Kari.

COLT'S CROSS

"The man claims to be your uncle."

Vietnam Veterans Memorial, Washington, DC

Located northeast of the Lincoln Memorial are three memorials dedicated to those who fought in the Vietnam War. The Three Servicemen Statue and the Vietnam Woman's Memorial comprises bronze sculptures representing those who served in Vietnam. More than three million people visit the three memorials each year, but most are profoundly affected by the third memorial, the Vietnam Veterans Memorial Wall. Dedicated in 1982 by President Ronald Reagan, the "Wall" was not without controversy. The memorial's black color and irregular shape led some to call it "The Black Gash of Shame." Nevertheless, it has become one of the most visited memorials in the city, and each day, thousands visit to show their respect for those who gave their lives and, in some cases, to remember lost friends.

"You see, sweetheart, each one of these names represents a person who gave their life during the war. It's important to remember their names; more than 58,000 are engraved on this wall."

The twelve-year-old girl looked at the long wall of names and then up at her grandfather. "Grandpa, why do you wear your old army shirt when you come here? Is it so that people will know that you fought in the war?"

The grey-haired man looked down at his green army shirt with several medals pined to the left pocket. "No, Stephanie. I wear it to remind me of my time with some of these men. And who knows, maybe they're looking down at me right now. I wear it for them." Stephanie noticed a man standing a few feet away as he placed a white piece of paper against the wall and rubbed a pencil across the top, creating an image of the name beneath that he could take home. The man wore a grey suit and smiled at the young girl as he placed the piece of paper into his suit coat pocket.

"Good morning, young lady," the man began, "is this your first time visiting the memorial?"

Stephanie looked up at her grandfather and then at the stranger. "Nope. Grandpa brings me here whenever we come to visit. Why did you rub your pencil on the piece of paper?"

Stephanie's grandfather shrugged his shoulders and smiled at the man as if to say, "Sorry."

The man paused as if he had just remembered something or someone. "My older brother Scott flew Navy jets during the war and was shot down over North Vietnam. His wingman saw him eject and parachute to the ground, but he was never heard from again. That's why there's a plus sign in front of his name rather than a diamond. It means he was listed as Missing in Action rather than killed. I was about your age when the officers came by our house to tell my parents. It still hurts when I remember the look on my parents' faces." The man paused for a moment and then continued, "I stop by now and then to remember him and to make one of these rubbings. It helps me somehow."

Stephanie's grandfather was surprised to find his eyes misting after hearing the man's story, and he reached out and placed his hand on the man's shoulder. "Sorry for your loss, son. I hope someday you learn what happened to him."

The man nodded and then noticed the decorations on the older man's uniform shirt. "Two Bronze Stars and a Combat Infantry Badge. It looks like you saw some action when you were in-country?"

Stephanie's grandfather beamed with pride. "You're damn right we did! And my platoon leader put me in for a Silver Star too, but I never got it. Probably just got lost in somebody's in-box at the Pentagon."

At that moment, a woman in a dark windbreaker approached and whispered to the man in the suit, "Sir, I need to get you back in time for your testimony."

The man turned to go, but then stopped and faced Stephanie's grandfather. "Sir, my name's Garrett; here's my card. Please give my office a call, and perhaps we can track down what happened to that Silver Star nomination."

The man in the suit followed the woman in the windbreaker to a waiting black Suburban. Stephanie pulled on her grandfather's shirt to get his attention. "Grandpa, who was that?"

The elderly veteran stared first at the business card in his hand and then at the large black SUV as it raced away. "That, Stephanie, was SECDEF!"

"What's SECDEF, Grandpa"?

"Sorry, dear. SECDEF is short for the United States Secretary of Defense."

Rayburn House Office Building Tunnels, Washington, DC

Colt Garrett walked briskly through the Rayburn House Office Building's underground tunnels on his way to appear before one of the many legislative committees that exercised oversight of defense department programs and functions. The US Constitution gives the president complete executive authority over government agencies but reserves budget and oversight authority over those same agencies to the legislature. For this reason, Secretary of Defense Colton Garrett and his department reported directly to the president, but he was also required to respond to legislative briefing requests.

Colt and his small group of staffers turned left down the corridor and passed a group of Senate pages on a break from their courier duties. The teenagers didn't give Colt and his team a second glance as they continued down the tunnel. And why should they? Colt was an average-looking man in his late sixties, average height, average weight. And with a receding hairline that caused him to constantly ask his daughter if she thought he had committed the fashion sin of "the comb-over." Today he wore a grey, finely tailored wool suit, a crisply pressed white shirt, and brightly polished black cap-toe oxfords. His necktie displayed several small multi-colored signal flags, which spelled out the message Vice Admiral Horatio Nelson sent to the British fleet before the Battle of Trafalgar: "England expects every man to do his duty." Colt chuckled each time he wore the tie, fondly remembering that former Secretary of the Navy Gordon England habitually wore the same tie while serving in the George W. Bush administration.

The necktie was also a nod to Colt's past as a naval officer. He worked in special intelligence on several highly classified assignments before resigning his commission and transferring into the Naval Reserve. He entered graduate school at the University of Washington and earned a doctorate in international studies. He then worked in the technology industry before founding his consulting firm in the Pacific Northwest. And that's when the call from President Harrison changed everything. He moved to DC as the undersecretary of defense for policy. Good at the job, he was eventually appointed as the 29th secretary of defense after his predecessor unexpectedly died. Being appointed to serve as a member of the president's cabinet was an exhilarating and proud moment; even his wife Linda had relocated to DC to help him move into his stately official residence in the Potomac Hill complex, across the street from the State Department. The couple had been living separately for several years. Colt's confirmation as secretary had given them a new chance to start again, and things were going well between them until Linda learned of the medical condition that would end her life within a few short weeks.

That had been over a year ago, but Colt vividly recalled the intense pain he felt that comes only with a spouse's or child's death. He was actually surprised that he could feel such anguish, and ironically, the only good that came from his loss was learning he could care for someone so deeply. Looking back, Colt realized he was probably clinically depressed for the first few months after the death. Choosing not to seek professional counseling because of its potential impact on his security clearance, he found himself attending church services for the first time since his school days. Talking with the local parish priest about his feelings, first in the sanctuary of the confessional and later in less formal settings such as on long walks and in local pubs, Colt slowly began the long climb back to what some would call normalcy. During one of his talks with Father Leeds, Colt reflected on his relationship with his older brother.

Scott Garrett had been everything young Colt wanted to be when he grew up. A graduate of the Naval Academy at Annapolis, Scott became a naval aviator and flew an F-4 Phantom II fighter-bomber off an aircraft carrier during the Vietnam War. Scott's plane was shot down by anti-aircraft fire while bombing an enemy weapons depot in North Vietnam. Young Colt watched out his upstairs bedroom window when two naval officers in dress blues stepped out of a sedan and solemnly approached his house. He knew all too well what that meant. Everything changed after that. The Navy said Scott had successfully ejected from his airplane, and they assumed he had been taken as a prisoner of war. But after the war was over, there was no additional information on Scott, and Colt's parents died, not knowing what had happened to their oldest son. The loss of his brother was why Colt decided to attend this morning's hearing on MIA service members in Southeast Asia and why he had stopped at the Vietnam Veterans Memorial.

Colt's special assistant and close confidant, Len Wilson, walked at his side as Len attempted to brief his boss on the upcoming legislative hearing. "I need to remind you again, sir, that you're not required to appear today. The House subcommittee on National Security just wants an update on the MIA numbers and the objectives for next week's trip to Cambodia. It's not too late to cancel," Len informed him.

Colt reached into his jacket vest pocket and touched the white piece of paper he had placed there earlier. "Let's just say I consider the MIA topic an important issue, Lenny, and leave it at that. Oh," he continued, "I'd like you to see what you can find out about a missing Silver Star nomination for a veteran. I met him and his granddaughter this morning and gave him my card with our office number. He was in-country with the Army in '68 when an officer submitted the nomination. It would be nice if we can find it and let a young woman see her grandfather get the medal he deserves."

Lenny nodded. It wasn't the first time that the defense secretary took a personal interest in a current or former service person's affairs. He seemed to take a great deal of satisfaction in righting small wrongs as if they were as important as running the massive Department of Defense. Lenny had been working for Colt Garrett since the secretary had joined the Harrison administration, acting as his guide and closest advisor as Garrett navigated the complexity of Washington's bureaucracy and politics. Frustrated with Garrett's insistence on simplifying issues down to their fundamental elements and then acting on the most appropriate course of action, Lenny couldn't believe that anyone could survive within the beltway as long as Garrett had. It wasn't that Lenny didn't understand the concept of doing things for the right reason. A graduate of the US Merchant Marine Academy at Kings Point, Lenny was well-versed in the value of an honor-based philosophy. But after graduation and then several years sailing as a licensed deck officer on the world's largest container ships, he learned that the realities of the business world were slightly different than those he had practiced as a midshipman. After grad school, Lenny decided to pursue a government career and had quickly moved up the Pentagon ladder by the time he met Colt Garrett. Lenny immediately grew fond of the senior policy analyst and soon angled a way onto his staff. The two were on a policy mission in the Pacific when the president appointed Garrett secretary of defense. The trust between the two men grew as they worked through national security issues.

"Yes, sir. I'll expect his call. I hope we can find the award nomination." Changing subjects, Lenny asked, "You are aware that Representative Carlisle will be chairing this morning's committee meeting?"

"Yes, fully aware the former admiral will be asking the questions today. I do read the agendas you provide."

Ignoring the ribbing, Lenny continued. "Yes, sir. It's just that the last time you saw him, he'd just been relieved for cause, and you left him standing on the tarmac in Japan. I'm pretty certain he blames you personally for what happened, and I suspect his recent election to Congress hasn't changed his opinion of you."

Colt paused at the door to the hearing room and placed his hand on Lenny's shoulder. "Mr. Wilson, I think I can take whatever Joe Carlisle has to dish out." With that, he opened the hearing room door and stepped inside.

Rayburn House Office Building, Committee Room 2154

Colt and Lenny walked into the impressive room and made their way to the small table positioned in the center of the room. Colt sat down in the single chair and adjusted the microphone while Lenny placed a thin binder on the desk. "Remember, sir. You're here just to provide your perspective of the department's MIA program, not to respond to questions regarding program details. Director Tasby will present the program update following your testimony, and Ms. Zechmann will speak from the families' perspective. We should be out of here in twenty minutes."

Lenny filled a glass with water from a pitcher sitting on the table and looked up as committee members began sitting down at the two raised rows of wooden desks at the room's front. "And there's my favorite retired admiral, sir."

Colt looked up and made eye contact with the subcommittee's chairman, Representative Joe Carlisle. The two men nodded to one another while Lenny quietly whispered to his boss, "Remember, just talk about your concern for the MIAs and their families, regardless of the question." Lenny turned and sat down in one of the chairs a few feet behind Colt as the chairman called the hearing to order.

"Good morning, everyone," began Representative Carlisle. "This hearing of the Subcommittee on National Security is in session. I'm looking forward to hearing what the Defense POW/MIA Accounting Agency is doing to bring our nation's heroes home. This hearing will inform the public about the DPAA's accounting efforts and allow this subcommittee to oversee the agency's performance. I'm pleased the secretary of defense has found time in his busy schedule to visit with us for a few minutes this morning, but before we get to his testimony, I'll first recognize myself for some opening remarks."

As Joe Carlisle started to read his prepared statement into the record, Colt thought back to his time on the USS Ronald Reagan in the western Pacific just two years ago. Carlisle had been a rear admiral then, commanding the Reagan battle group, and during Colt's visit, the president appointed him acting defense secretary. Carlisle complained to the press about Colt's interference in his operations, and as a result, was relieved for cause and immediately retired from the Navy. Senator Emmett Carlisle, Joe's influential father, ensured his son was elected to Congress the following year and even pressured the party to seat the former admiral as chair of the House subcommittee on National Security. Joe Carlisle's appointment as chair instead of more senior members caused extreme discontent within the party, and Senator Carlisle's reputation and influence greatly suffered. Colt Garrett had no illusion regarding his standing with either of the Carlisle men.

"Mr. Secretary, before you give your opening remarks, I'll ask you to stand and raise your right hand." Colt stood and repeated the same oath he had sworn on countless occasions and then sat back down, took a sip of water, and adjusted the mic.

"Mr. Chairman, Ranking Member, and committee members. I am humbled and honored to appear before this committee today to update our POW/MIA efforts. The DPAA is the government agency that accounts for and repatriates American servicemembers' remains from prior conflicts. To achieve its mission, the agency coordinates with federal agencies, foreign governments, and non-governmental organizations and conducts international negotiations. For example, in fiscal year 2019 alone, the DPAA recorded 218 identifications, the highest yearly total reached by the agency or its predecessor organizations, bringing necessary closure to family and loved ones. As of today, 82,045 service members remain unaccounted for from World

War II through Operation Iraqi Freedom. We estimate that 39,000 of these remains are recoverable. On a personal note, my older brother Scott is one of those unaccounted-for, so I am well aware of the families' pain and anguish. Ms. Kimberly Zechmann, chair of the National League of POW/MIA Families, will be testifying a bit later, and I'd like to thank her for taking the time to come to Washington to appear today. That concludes my prepared remarks."

Joe Carlisle picked up a report and pressed to button to turn on his mic. "Thank you, Mr. Secretary. I didn't know your brother was MIA. Was he lost during the Vietnam War?"

"Yes, Mr. Chairman. He was a Phantom pilot shot down while on a bombing mission over North Vietnam."

Joe Carlisle looked at Colt for a moment. "Thank you. And speaking of Vietnam, can you bring the committee up to date regarding unaccounted-for Americans lost in that war? We're particularly interested in those missing in Cambodia, given next week's Joint Field Activity trip to the region."

Colt considered suggesting that the DPAA director answer the question but decided to respond himself. He reached for the binder that Lenny had prepared and opened it to a green-colored tab.

"Mr. Chairman, as of January 2021, of the forty-eight Americans still unaccounted for in Cambodia, seven are considered non-recoverable. As a result of our investigations, we believe those individuals died, but it's impossible to recover their remains. That leaves 41 in an active status, and they will be the focus of this year's Joint Field Activity to Cambodia, which, as you mentioned, will commence next week."

"The chair recognizes Ms. Phan."

"Thank you, Mr. Chairman," responded Michele. "Mr. Secretary, can you give me an overview of how you conduct

JFAs? I'm new to the committee."

Colt looked to his right at the attractive representative.

"Sure. Each of our annual JFAs includes 25 to 40 US personnel plus their Cambodian counterparts. Together, they work on investigations and excavations throughout the country for one to two months, depending on what they find. Recovered remains believed to be Americans are then sent to our labs in Hawaii for further analysis by forensic anthropologists. We have a POW/MIA investigator stationed in Phnom Penh full-time. He works on leads associated with the remaining individuals still unaccounted for in Cambodia. Last year US and Vietnamese specialists met in Hanoi to discuss Last Known Alive cases in areas of Cambodia controlled by Vietnamese forces during the war. This JFA will be following up on those leads."

"What about the Khmer Rouge wartime atrocities in Cambodia? Is there any information that indicates Americans may have been victims of the regime?"

Colt referred to the briefing binder once again. "Well, my notes indicate the agency has been reviewing materials in Cambodian archives. I think Director Tasby might be able to provide more information during his testimony."

Joe Carlisle looked to his left and then to his right. "If there are no further questions for Mr. Garrett, on behalf of the Subcommittee on National Security, I'd like to thank the Secretary for his comments here this morning. Without objection, we'll take a fifteen-minute recess."

Russian Military Intelligence HQ, Moscow.

On a typical Friday afternoon, Igor Korobov would be at his estate on Moscow's outskirts enjoying a glass of vodka as he

worked his way through Winston Churchill's six-volume series
The Second World War. He enjoyed reading Churchill's history
of the period from the end of the First World War through
1945, primarily because the series helped him to understand
the Western perspective regarding fascism and communism.
He knew that Churchill had deftly avoided official regulations
against the use of government records by having documents
copied and then labeled Prime Minister's Personal Minutes. He
had to hand it to the big man; use your power to change the
rules. And Igor Korobov knew more than a little about using
influence to change the rules because, as the chief of Russia's
military intelligence organization, he had turned the practice into
an art form. Russian military intelligence, or more commonly, the
GRU, was the country's largest and most powerful intelligence
agency. Considered more ruthless than its sister service, the
SVR, Korobov's GRU had broader reach and considerably more
resources

   But today wasn't a typical Friday afternoon. Korobov had
been reviewing an intelligence report on his desk when he
arrived earlier that day that confirmed previous information
regarding Secretary of Defense Colton Garrett. For the past
two years, Garrett had been pushing the O'Kane Doctrine,
a comprehensive set of policies designed to reduce Russia's
influence throughout the world. Garrett had developed
the doctrine when he was the Department of Defense's
undersecretary for policy. With his confirmation as defense
secretary, Garrett appeared determined to implement the
O'Kane Doctrine throughout US foreign policy. The GRU had
made two unsuccessful attempts to assassinate Garrett when
he visited the USS Ronald Reagan while in the Western Pacific
Ocean. That was when Garrett was the acting secretary of
defense. In the two years since the Senate had confirmed him, he

had, if anything, increased his determination to implement the O'Kane Doctrine completely.

Korobov stood up from his ornate oak desk and looked out through the bullet and bomb-proof glass windows of his expansive corner office. He gazed across the grass field below to the adjacent Khodinka Aerodrome, the former site of Russia's National Aviation and Space Museum. Mikoyan-Gurevich MiG-21s and MiG-27s rested near Sukhoi SU-17s and SU-27s as the forgotten relics of an extinct regime lay rusting in the afternoon sun. The three-star general murmured, "Soon, I will join those old warriors in the field . . . but not today."

Because today Korobov had learned that Colton Garrett was about to recommend that the American president push to codify the O'Kane Doctrine in US law. "And that," thought Korobov, "could not be allowed to happen."

The LeDroit Society, Northwest Washington, DC

Becci Quinn gave every impression of being completely attentive and thoroughly engaged as she looked intently into her laptop's camera. The COVID-19 pandemic had initially convinced Becci to hold her weekly staff meetings via video conference. Becci decided to continue the practice after the pandemic ebbed because the staff preferred the remote format. She suspected the team liked the Zoom meetings because they could participate from their homes, but Becci felt she should come into work and take the call from her office as the society's executive director. This morning's meeting agenda focused on the upcoming spring gala, the organization's primary fundraiser. Local business leaders and other wealthy donors gathered at the black-tie affair and mingled with the city's elite. When adequately lubricated with their favorite beverage, Becci goaded her guests to bid on donated items so that the LeDroit Society could continue its mission of serving the needy children of the neighborhood. In fact, most of the society's revenue came from federal and city grants. Although the gala did raise some funds, its primary purpose was to ensure strong community support through relationships created and nurtured at the event. LeDroit's gala was the event of the year, and if you wanted to be seen by the community's rich and powerful, you went. And the LeDroit neighborhood needed support.

LeDroit Park was one of Washington's first suburbs, built in the late 1870s. Famous for its Thomas McGill-designed Victorian homes, the section was once considered an exclusive place to live. But like most inner-city communities, the neighborhood had long been in decline. The area became dilapidated, and some blocks turned into drug markets. In 2005, a few prominent citizens formed the LeDroit Society to return the community to its previous reputation and make it a safe place to live. The non-profit organization applied for grants to repair public roads and infrastructure and eventually hosted social events to bring attention to the neighborhood and increase support to the local schools. Over fifty original McGill homes still stood, some renovated, others converted into modern condominiums. Urban professionals began to relocate to LeDroit Park, and they credited the LeDroit Society for the positive change.

As executive director, Becci Quinn received the lion's share of the credit. As a result, she received many invitations to social and community events. Influential people wanted to be seen and photographed with her, and she agreed to serve on boards of other non-profit corporations. Young, fit, and extremely attractive, Becci Quinn seemed destined for a bright political future. Yet anytime the subject of her political career came up,

Becci politely declined to discuss any plans, stating she'd prefer to work behind the scenes to improve the lives of local children as a community organizer.

Becci spent the rest of the day working on the gala's invitation list, paying particular attention to those who were elected officials. She knew that developing relationships with politicians was relatively easy compared with the more senior officials and bureaucrats and could yield significant results as they progressed in their careers. With her work done for the day, she changed into her running clothes and headed home as the sun went down.

The West Wing, the White House

When people think of the White House's West Wing, most recall television images of the Oval Office with the president sitting at the Resolute Desk in front of a large picture window with an American flag on one side and the president's flag on the other side. And while it's true that the Oval Office is in the West Wing, the three-floor structure also provides office space for the president's senior aides in what some have referred to as the most coveted offices in Washington. The first floor, near the president, is the most exclusive, and where one would find the Oval Office and other offices for the president's most senior advisors. One of those advisors, Jonathan Unger, sat at his desk in his impressive corner office, pondering his future. As the president's national security advisor, Unger was responsible for the National Security Council, created in 1947 to integrate US foreign and defense policy. The council was initially composed of just four members: the president, vice president, secretary of state, and defense secretary. Over the years, the NSC had become a high-level staff of foreign policy experts headed by the national security advisor, who had been a critical foreign policy advisor since the early 1960s. The NSC staff had grown to a more than a 200-person organization over the years and operated much like an independent agency, including legislative, communication, and media-relations functions.

Jon Unger was more than qualified for the position, having previously served as secretary of state. In his mid-seventies, he was diagnosed with post-acute COVID-19 syndrome. He grew easily tired and unable to perform even small physical tasks. When he approached President Harrison a year ago about resigning as the country's chief diplomat, the president had countered with an offer to serve as national security advisor. Jon Unger accepted the appointment, rationalizing that the NSC responsibilities were nothing compared to the massive state department. He agreed to serve through the end of the Harrison administration, just another 18 months. But he had started feeling weaker recently and privately wondered if he would leave the West Wing before President Harrison's term expired. A knock on his door caused him to look up.

"Sir, you have a moment?"

"Sure, Travis. What do you need?"

Travis Webb, the deputy national security advisor, walked into Unger's office and sat down. "Boss, you feeling okay? Diane said you looked a little shaky when you came back from lunch. Things are pretty dead right now, and I just heard the press secretary announced a press lid for the day. I can handle things here. Why don't you head home for the weekend? I'll call for your car."

"I bet you'd like to handle things here," thought Unger. His body might be failing him, but his mind was sharp as ever. Jon Unger's only misgiving about accepting the appointment as national security advisor was that Travis Webb was the deputy. Webb had previously served as deputy secretary of defense under Pat O'Kane. When Pat died of a heart problem, Washington insiders assumed that the president would select Webb as the next defense secretary. But that was before some damaging photos of Webb in blackface went viral, and President Harrison appointed Colt Garrett as acting defense secretary. Webb quietly resigned with the understanding the administration would find a place for him somewhere.

Jon Unger didn't trust Travis Webb, even before the scandal. When he tried removing him from the NSC staff, the president's chief of staff clarified that Travis Webb would stay where he was. Unger would just have to find a way to work around him. Or over him.

"I'm fine, Travis. Thanks for your concern, but I still need to review the Chinese aircraft projections before leaving. I want to be ready to meet with the president on Tuesday. You can go ahead and clear out. I see you already have your briefcase packed."

Travis looked down at the trendy, cotton twill messenger bag in his hand. "Yes, sir. I thought I'd review our human resources policies over the weekend. The chief of staff wants any changes submitted early next week." With that, Travis left Jon Unger's office and headed for the exit.

Jon Unger waited a few moments and then walked out to the receptionist's desk.

"Diane, I'm curious. Did you tell Travis you thought I looked shaky when I returned after lunch?"

Diane Considine had worked for Jon Unger for several years, including during his term as secretary of state. She was very fond of the aging diplomat and had voiced her concern about his health on several occasions.

"Of course not! You do look tired, but I haven't seen him since this morning's staff meeting. And besides, I haven't forgiven him for those photos. Why?"

Jon Unger smiled and walked back to his corner office. He went back to reviewing the Chinese aircraft projections while also thinking of how to remove Travis Webb.

Colt Garrett's Residence, Potomac Hill Complex

The large brick house didn't seem like home anymore, particularly after Linda had died. A few weeks after the couple moved into the stately government house, Colt's wife was diagnosed with hypertrophic cardiomyopathy. The specialist at Bethesda said the wall between Linda's two bottom heart chambers had become enlarged, and it was restricting the blood flow out of her heart. She died on a Sunday morning of sudden cardiac arrest, and within a week, Colt held a memorial service to celebrate her life. The kids had helped with the arrangements and were with him as he scattered their mother's ashes on a rocky beach near Annapolis.

Colt's daughter, Allie Garrett, made her home in Washington State in the small town of Gig Harbor. She and her husband Kyle co-owned a boutique consulting firm that helped companies select and implement cloud-based financial and human resources systems. Allie provided the systems technology expertise, while Kyle led the firm's sales force. The young couple had just purchased a home with a view of the harbor and thoroughly enjoyed the outdoor activities available to those living in the Pacific Northwest. Allie liked that she and Kyle could be together both at home and at the office. But the challenges of running a business had started to strain the young couple's marriage, and Allie had confided in her mother about her problems. With Linda's sudden death, Allie felt more isolated than ever.

Allie's younger brother Dan worked at Naval Air Station Patuxent River, where he flew as a test pilot for the US Navy. Pax River was the home of VX-23, the Navy's test and evaluation squadron for fixed-wing aircraft. Lieutenant Commander Dan Garrett was initially detailed to test fly Boeing's EA-18G Growler, the Navy's electronic warfare jammer, but recently he had been flight testing Lockheed-Martin's F-35C Lighting II. The fifth-generation fighter integrated advanced stealth technology into a highly agile, supersonic aircraft that provided the pilot with unparalleled situational awareness and unmatched lethality and survivability. If things went wrong and you found yourself in harm's way, the best place to be was in the cockpit of a Lighting II. Navy test pilots were the best pilots in the service, and many found their way into the space program.

More than a year had passed since Linda had died, and Colt had begun dating again. He first met Jillian Murdoch when the professor requested that he speak to Georgetown's graduate government policy class. The university prided itself on securing prominent government officials as guest lecturers, but Jillian considered herself lucky when the defense secretary agreed to speak to her students. She was surprised to find he had earned a doctorate in international relations and watched with interest as her usually skeptical grad students appeared mesmerized by the cabinet member's country-by-country lecture on current world events. Blond, 5'6", and about ten years younger than Colt, Jillian also worked as a cable news network contributor. She found it ironic that her occasional appearances on the news program sold more copies of her book on politics than her decades as a college professor. Watching Colt interact with her students during his presentation gave her time to think about this man, and she decided she wanted to get to know him better.

Coffee at the faculty lounge and then dinner at a quiet Italian restaurant a week later developed into a romantic relationship, leading to the problem with Allie. Colt remembered his daughter's reaction when he mentioned in passing he was seeing someone.

"Don't you think it's a bit soon to be dating, Dad?" asked Allie. "And I don't understand why someone your age even needs to be thinking about that!"

"I'm not dead yet!" Colt had answered, quoting a line from a Monty Python movie. Allie wasn't amused, though, and had hung up on her father. Allie's attitude bothered Colt because he also felt conflicted about the new relationship. Linda and Colt had been married for decades, and despite challenges in their marriage, he still loved his wife. Even after finding the letters.

4th Street NW, Washington, DC

Becci Quinn didn't care that her friends thought she was crazy to run at night in Washington, particularly in the LeDroit neighborhood. It was the only time she could exercise, and she needed the activity to clear her mind and not be interrupted by the constant phone calls and other office hassles. During these runs, she could let her mind wander back to the life she had left behind, in a different city with different sounds and smells. Becci passed the LeDroit Market and turned right on T Street when she first heard the footsteps. She ignored the street noises, listened carefully to the sounds behind her. She thought, "running shoes, street clothes, breathing hard, light jacket. It's coming very soon." The teenager was shocked when his intended victim suddenly stopped and faced him. He pulled a four-inch knife and hissed, "Give me that watch, bitch!"

"Okay, okay. Just don't hurt me!" Becci pleaded as she made herself visibly shake. Becci raised her hands in front of her face and then began to unstrap her smartwatch as she looked into the young man's face and recognized the telltale signs of cocaine eyes: bloodshot with dilated pupils. When he smiled at the thought of an easy grab, Becci could see his decaying teeth, and she decided to act. During that cold Russian winter, her close combat training at GRU's Hatsavita Mountain had stressed speed when defending a knife attack. "Always watch the hands," Sergeant Koslov had warned, "and then move!" Becci brought her left hand down and trapped the boy's right hand and knife against his thigh while simultaneously swinging her right hand quickly down and back, and forward and up as she drove her palm into the teenager's nose. She heard the nose cartilage crush as she slammed her right knee into his groin and then gently cradled his bleeding and limp body to the ground. She quickly looked up and down the street and threw the knife into the bushes. She leaned down and placed her mouth close to the teenager's ear and asked, "Who's the bitch now?"

Day Three

Gordon Courte, Washington, DC

In 2010, developer Lowell Gordon renovated several
of the LeDroit Victorian homes into upscale two-bedroom
condominiums that attracted government workers who wanted to
avoid a long commute into the city. Gordon, widely known for his
creative television advertising campaign, "Everyone's a Winner,"
was one of the city's most successful developers. Becci Quinn
had met him at a fundraiser and had jumped at the opportunity to
purchase a luxury home within walking distance of her office.

Becci got up early on Saturday and immediately put everything
she wore on last night's run (top, shorts, socks, and shoes) into
her washing machine. After running the load twice through the
washer's sanitizing cycle and then through the dryer on high,
Becci folded everything and placed them into a plain paper sack.
That done, she spent the subsequent hour scanning online news
and social media outlets to verify there was no news of last night's
assault. Most coffee shops were not yet open as Becci walked the
few blocks to the shelter on Fourth. She set the paper bag down
next to the wooden box marked "donations" and continued down
the street and around the block to head back to her condo.

After a long, hot shower followed by her usual breakfast of
Greek yogurt, granola, and coffee, Becci finally had a moment
to replay the assault in her mind. She felt confident that there
weren't any witnesses, but she knew there were security cameras
everywhere. She thoroughly washed her clothes to remove the
teenager's DNA, and she donated the items in case the police

TOM CARROLL

decided to search garbage cans for evidence of the crime. These
precautions came automatically to her because, in addition to
leading a local non-profit in Washington, Becci Quinn was a
major in Russia's military intelligence service, the GRU.

Russia had discovered the best way to infiltrate deep cover
operatives into the United States was also the most direct:
through Canada. Becci arrived in the Port of Vancouver after a
circuitous journey that began in Moscow and continued with a
ride on the Trans-Siberian Railway to Vladivostok on the Pacific
Ocean. A housekeeping job on a visiting cruise ship was easy to
obtain, and three weeks later, Becci arrived in Vancouver, British
Columbia. She walked off the ship by simply flashing a cruise
ID card stolen from a passenger with similar features. Crossing
into the United States at the Aldergrove border proved pleasingly
uneventful. Her perfectly forged Canadian passport, her story of
coming to America to seek medical treatment, and her stunning
figure combined to make the rookie Customs and Border Patrol
officer smile and say, "Welcome to the United States. Best of
luck to you."

One advantage of working for one of the world's most
professional intelligence agencies was that one received
impeccable documentation and a well-researched legend to
back it up. Becci's new American identity included a birth
certificate, Virginia driver's license, and a US passport that she
could confidently present to anyone to establish her life in the
United States. She found her first job working as a YWCA donor
relations specialist in Virginia Beach. After this, she moved
to Baltimore and worked as manager of donor relations for a
small university. Two years later, Becci secured a position as the
deputy executive director for a large food bank in Annandale and
impressed the board of directors by attracting a slew of wealthy
donors. The board's chair wasn't surprised when Becci told her

she would be leaving to accept the executive director job at the LeDroit Society in downtown Washington.

Becci glanced at her watch and walked into her bedroom to change into her bike gear. Her GRU controller had created a complex schedule of dates and times to conduct video chats over a virtual group exercise session. The next one started in just ten minutes, so she filled her water bottle and tightened her shoelaces. She climbed onto the exercise bike, pressed the button on the back of the display screen, and waited for the virtual spin class to start.

Colt's Garrett's Residence, Potomac Hill Complex

"Hot, moist breath, and the smell of rotting fish. What a terrible dream!" Those were the thoughts that crossed Colt Garrett's mind as he slowly woke Saturday morning. He rolled onto his right side to go back to sleep, but the queen size bed shook, and the mattress springs groaned as the huge golden retriever leaped on the bed.

"Good morning, Drake," said Colt as he pushed the dog to the floor and started to make the bed. The Navy staff assigned to his residence included housekeeping staff and a cook, but Colt preferred to do some of the housework himself. Father Leeds had said that it would help his depression if he started doing simple daily tasks, and now it had become a habit. He put on a pair of blue jeans and a sweatshirt before walking downstairs to let Drake outside.

Dan had found Drake at a military dog adoption service a month after Linda died; Colt's son thought he needed a dog. Dan believed everybody needed a dog. "I just think that having a dog makes people more human," Dan always said. His life as a single Navy pilot prevented him from having a dog of his own, and Colt suspected that the primary reason Dan brought him Drake was that Dan could come visit them both. Drake had served as a working dog, highly trained to detect marijuana, but the drug's legalization meant Drake had been retired. Now, Colt noticed the only thing that "alerted" the dog was the smell of a cheeseburger. Most evenings would find Colt sitting on the living room couch eating his dinner, with 120-pound Drake leaning his entire body weight onto Colt's side, hoping for a bite.

Finished with his breakfast, Colt stood to search for Drake's leash when Chief Petty Officer Higgins announced, "Sir, you have a phone call. It's Ms. Murdoch. Do you want to take it in your office?"

Andrew Higgins was a Navy culinary specialist, and the Navy chief was proud to serve as the defense secretary's chef.

"Thanks, Chief. I'll take it here," answered Colt as he reached for the phone.

"Jillian, I'm glad you called. Weren't we going to see a movie last night after work?"

"Sorry about that, Colt. I had to go over to the network, and some of us went out for drinks and dinner. I should have called."

"Some of us? I suppose that includes Chase as well?" Chase Farley was the network's anchor of Washington Day, a primetime recap of the day's news.

The phone line went quiet before Jillian responded. "No, Colt. Chase wasn't there. When are you going to give that a rest?" She soon hung up the phone.

Jillian was referring to Colt's recent jealousy of her relationships with other men. She knew men found her attractive, and she liked being the center of attention. Her relationship with Colt wasn't exclusive, and she had grown increasingly bothered by his lack of trust. She liked the man, but he had some issues regarding his former wife, and she wasn't sure she wanted to take on all that baggage.

After the call, Colt walked into his office and sat at a large oak desk. Looking at the tall bookshelf near the window, he stared at a shoebox on the second shelf. After Linda had died, he found the box when he finally got around to sorting through her clothes and personal things into two groups: one for the kids and one for the homeless shelter. Most of the sorting was simple. Allie would get Linda's jewelry, Dan her travel souvenirs, and her clothing would go to the homeless shelter. Colt gathered the stack of photos and made copies so that each of the remaining Garrett family members could have a photo album.

When Colt had opened the shoe box, he had found a set of romantic letters to Linda from a man. The letters were dated from a period that Colt was in Washington while Linda remained in their Olympia home. The affair had lasted a few months and then abruptly ended, but it was unclear who had ended it. Colt felt devastated after reading the letters and had several reactions, ranging from anger and betrayal to pain and despair. He didn't know who to turn to for help, leading him to the church and Father Leeds. It was working through his feelings with the priest that Colt understood the real impact of discovering the affair because it caused him to question everything. And perhaps worst, he felt he couldn't trust anyone again, particularly when in a close personal relationship.

"Colt, you'll need to work this out," Father Leeds had advised. "Don't make the mistake of learning the wrong lesson from this experience. Your error was letting your marriage fail, not that you trusted your wife."

Colt was worried that his trust issues were ruining his chances with Jillian, and he knew, somehow, he'd have to find a way to deal with this. Chief Farley found Colt sitting in the office looking through a photograph album.

"Sorry, sir. Another call. This time it's Mr. Wilson. Line two on the desk phone."

Colt closed the family album his wife had made for him when he first moved to Washington. "What's up, Lenny?"

"Sorry to bother you on a Saturday, boss. Do you remember the issue in the Seventh Fleet with the contractor bribing Navy officials and officers? The last case will be coming to trial soon, and the lawyer who's defending Commander Leach wants you to intervene in the case. The lawyer says the trial has done enough damage to the Navy's reputation, and if his client testifies, more dirt will come out. He wants you to instruct the convening authority, Admiral Shaffer, to stop the court-martial and publicly state that Commander Leach is innocent of all charges. In exchange, his client will agree to resign immediately at his current rank and make no further comments to the press."

Still bothered by his call with Jillian, Colt snapped, "Remind me again, Lenny. Who the hell is this guy?"

He could hear Lenny page through his notes. "Commander Ronald Leach is the commanding officer of the USS Robert McNamara, an Arleigh Burke-class destroyer. The ship's underway in the South China Sea, part of a multi-national force tracking Chinese naval exercises off the southern coast of Vietnam. After the operation, the McNamara will be heading to Japan so that Commander Leach can testify at his court-martial."

Colt remembered and grew irritated. "No, Lenny. It's blackmail, and I won't let this guy walk in exchange for getting the Navy off the hook. Look, Lenny, the Navy and others made some mistakes. The court-martial will sort it all out. Tell that lawyer to let Commander Leach know that I consider this offer a breach of protocol, and I will share their offer with his entire chain of command. His communications with his lawyer are privileged, but I'm not his lawyer."

Lenny Wilson whistled softly and quickly changed the subject.

"Hey, is your interview with 60 Minutes going to be aired tomorrow evening? I'm interested in what you had to say about me!"

Colt relaxed a bit and replied, "Yep. Tomorrow night. I hope you like it!"

After the call with his executive assistant, Colt grabbed the leather leash from the hook on the wall and walked to the front door.

"I'm taking Drake for a walk," and he turned the latch. At that moment, two men in dark windbreakers exited a black suburban parked at the curb and started following Colt down the sidewalk. The tallest man quietly spoke into a microphone attached to his wrist. "This is WHISKEY ONE. PATRIOT is on the move."

Gig Harbor, Washington State

Allie Garrett, still angry at herself for hanging up on her father, looked out her corner office window overlooking the picturesque Gig Harbor. In 1840, Navy Lieutenant Charles Wilkes brought a small ship's boat, or gig, into the small harbor to avoid a storm. Later, on his 1841 map of the Oregon Territory, he named the bay Gig Harbor. Gig Harbor Consulting's offices occupied the entire second floor of the marina's warehouse, and Allie had been thrilled when her husband Kyle secured the lease. Their small consulting firm helped mid-sized companies transition their back-office business applications onto the internet, making them more secure.

Moving applications to the cloud also helped businesses focus on profit-generating activities rather than maintaining legacy information technology infrastructures. Allie and Kyle moved the company from Olympia after Linda's death. Allie wanted to avoid seeing the places she had visited with her mother, and Gig Harbor was closer to Tacoma's and Seattle's population centers.

She tried talking with her brother about their father's new girlfriend, but Dan said the same thing as Kyle had when Allie expressed her feelings: "It's probably time for him to move on." Allie watched as a small tugboat pushed a rusted barge loaded with gravel across the bay while small sailboats tacked back and forth in its wake. "Perhaps I'll call Lenny Wilson," she thought. "He knows Dad really well; maybe he can talk some sense into the man."

Potomac Hill Park

Drake raced toward the park's small pond after Colt removed his leash. Colt loved to watch the massive golden retriever leap into the water and scatter the ducks that had made the mistake of resting near the pond's southern end. Drake ran back and sat perfectly still as he watched Colt reach into his jacket pocket and remove a yellow tennis ball. Colt threw the ball as far as he could and laughed as the dog tore across the park in pursuit of the treasure. Drake returned with not one but two tennis balls in his mouth in less than a minute and dropped them both at Colt's feet.

"Excuse me, sir. I think one of those balls is ours."

Colt turned to see a woman walking toward him, carrying a small fluffy dog in her arms. He handed a wet tennis ball to the woman, saying, "Sorry. Drake sometimes does that."

"Mr. Secretary, the ball belongs to Klaus." She set the tiny Pomeranian down on the grass.

"Excuse me, have we met?" asked Colt as he tried to keep Drake from stealing the ball from the much smaller dog.

"Just once, a White House reception. But I did ask you a question at the National Security hearing yesterday. I guess I look much different today."

Colt looked closer at the woman and then replied, "Of course! Representative Phan! Sorry. I suppose we all look different when we're not at work."

"Well, Mr. Secretary, you're kind of obvious with your security detail surrounding you."

The four-person team of agents had stepped closer to Colt when they first saw Michele Phan approach him but then started moving back once they determined her identity.

"Sorry about that, Representative Phan. It's been a few years, and I'm still not used to having a team of babysitters follow me everywhere." Colt reached down and snapped the leash onto Drake's collar.

"Please, call me Michele. And this is Klaus." She attached a leash to her dog's collar. She looked at Colt for a few moments and then said, "I'm curious about your interest in the MIA issue. I listened to your story about your missing brother. Is he the only reason why you decided to attend the hearing? You must have other, more pressing demands."

"Well, Michele," Colt began, "I guess I hate the fact that everyone didn't come home. I think we owe those soldiers and their families everything we can do to find them and bring them back. Really as simple as that."

Michele thought about what he said and then asked, "Are you free for lunch tomorrow, Mr. Garrett? I think it might be fun to share a meal and get to know one another."

"Call me Colt. And I'd love to meet you for lunch. How about the Wok and Roll on H Street at 12:30?"

"That's perfect. See you tomorrow! Come on, Klaus!"

Michele and her dog walked back through the park while Colt, Drake, and the security detail headed back to Colt's official residence. A black suburban with tinted windows followed a short distance behind the group, and an agent spoke into the vehicle's radio, "This is WHISKEY ONE. PATRIOT is heading back to CITADEL."

Colt's Garrett's Residence, Potomac Hill Complex

It's strange how much better lasagna tastes on the second day, thought Colt as he finished the main course and reached for his second piece of garlic bread. Chief Higgins would have prepared for him a freshly cooked meal every day, but Colt had insisted the chief cook enough food during the week so that he could have leftovers on Saturday and Sunday. It just felt more normal to grab a plate from the refrigerator and eat in the kitchen rather than have Chief Higgins waiting on him every night. Colt poured himself another glass of merlot and turned on his laptop. Within a few minutes, he joined a video call with his son, Dan.

"Hey, Dad! How are you and Drake?"

Dan could see the large golden retriever had joined his father on the living room sofa and was coming dangerously close to spilling his glass of wine. Colt let Drake get comfortable on his lap. "We're learning one another's habits, Dan. Drake's discovered that I get up in the morning earlier than him, and I've learned he can't rest if there's a plate of food left on the table."

Dan knew the distraction of a 120-pound dog would be a good thing. "Any plans for tomorrow? I'm going to get my boots and skis out of the storage locker and start getting ready for another year on the slopes. East Coast ski runs can't compare with the hills out west, but they're better than nothing."

"I'm meeting Representative Phan for lunch downtown. We'll probably discuss the MIA program funding. Then later, I'm going to force myself to watch my 60 Minutes interview. I just hope I didn't say anything stupid."

"That's right! That segment is airing tomorrow! Rebecca and I are catching a movie tomorrow night, but I'll make sure to catch it on stream afterward."

"You've been seeing quite a bit of Rebecca recently. Any chance I'll get to meet her?"

"Funny you should mention that. She'll be coming as my date to the squadron dining-out on Tuesday evening. And thanks again for agreeing to come. The skipper is jacked to have the defense secretary at his gala. The only downside is that we have to sit with you at the grown-ups' table. Are you bringing Jillian?"

"Yes. I don't think she's thrilled to accompany me to another formal event, but I know she's looking forward to seeing you."

"Say, Dad. I spoke with Allie, and she's pretty bent about you starting to date again. She's concerned it may be too soon after . . .well, just too soon. I promised her I'd mention it to you."

"Okay, son. You can tell her you talked with me. But I think I'm in the best position to know how to move forward with my life. Let's leave it at that?"

Dan Garrett figured he had taken the subject as far as he should. Besides, this was Allie's concern, not his. "Roger, Dad. Understood. I'll see you Tuesday."

After the video call, Colt spent a few hours reading a novel and then prepared for bed. He understood both his children were concerned about him and only wanted to protect him. They were just going to have to accept that his life had not ended with his wife's, and Colt needed to find someone with whom to share the good things that remained. He climbed into his bed and turned out the light, looking forward to a whole night's sleep.

Four hours later, and drenched with sweat, Colt got up from his bed and carefully stepped over his sleeping dog on his way to the kitchen. He ran the water for a few seconds before filling a large glass and walking to the dining room table. The nightmares had started again after Linda died, and he realized that it was very likely they would keep him from ever getting a full night's rest. Always the same dream, still the same ending. And why should it ever change? The sounds and smells of automatic gunfire at the service station, seeing Peter get cut down and Traci getting hit. And then the look on Russ's face. He could never forget that look. Or the day.

Drake strolled into the kitchen, rested his large head on Colt's thigh, and rolled his eyes up. Colt was amazed that the kind animal seemed to know when he was troubled and needed companionship. He scratched Drake's ears and gave him a treat before changing into a dry set of pajamas and climbing back into bed. He picked up a novel and started reading, hoping to grow drowsy and fall back asleep.

Day Four

One Observatory Circle, Washington, DC

Since 1894, a wide variety of federal officials have lived in the white brick nineteenth-century three-story home on the grounds of the US Naval Observatory. Built initially for the observatory's superintendent, the home's beauty led the chief of naval operations to evict the superintendent in 1923 so that he could move in. Congress funded the home's refurbishment in 1974 as the permeant residence of the vice president of the United States. Walter Mondale was the first vice president to live there, followed by every other vice president, including the current resident, Vice President Maria Hernandez. Maria, the former governor of Texas, joined President Harrison's ticket for the election leading to his second term. At the time, the party pushed the president to add Hernandez as his running mate because of her popularity in the South, not to mention the political advantage of nominating the first Latina to serve as vice president. After the election, it became clear that Maria Hernandez was a competent executive, communicator, and practiced politician.

Maria's father owned Hernandez Petroleum, headquartered in Corpus Christi. He taught his only child the inner workings of the gas and oil business and was pleased with her decision to pursue an economics degree at Rice University. He even supported her decision to move to Great Britain to earn a graduate degree from the London School of Economics, believing she would return from her studies abroad to join him at the family business. But after a few years, Maria became interested in local politics and ran for a seat on the city council. Two terms serving District 32 in the Texas House of Representatives were immediately followed by four terms representing Texas's 27th Legislative District in Washington, DC. She surprised the beltways pundits with her successful campaign for governor, and the national news media began to take notice. Maria showed strong leadership during several national disasters, and her two terms as governor demonstrated her ability to work across party lines to bring prosperity to the state and a healthy environment for the citizens.

Maria had married Ethan Davis shortly after returning home from London, and he had been a strong supporter of her political aspirations. Working for Hernandez Petroleum, Ethan's career progressed quickly through the company as Maria moved up the ladder of the state and federal governments. He became president of the company just months after Maria was elected the governor. After Maria was sworn in as vice president, Ethan moved the company's headquarters to Houston and lived there running the company while Maria lived in the large home at One Observatory Circle.

Party leadership had approached Maria last month about when she would be announcing her candidacy for president. They were very clear that it would be advantageous to have a team of advisors ready to build her campaign's policy platform. She had identified domestic policy experts for the team but had not finalized the national security members. President Harrison strongly advocated for including Secretary of Defense Colt Garrett as an advisor and inviting him to serve in her administration should she be elected. But she had her doubts about Garrett. He seemed competent and well-regarded, but he didn't fit her idea of a typical cabinet member. The man appeared to have a foreign policy of his own rather than following the president's desires. Personal loyalty was crucial to her, and she wasn't sure that Colt Garrett would serve as an advisor to her campaign or, if she was elected, if he would be reappointed as her secretary of defense.

Maria walked into the large living room and sat down in one of the overstuffed chairs. When she voiced her concerns about Colt Garrett to Bill Harrison, the president had replied, "Tell you what, Maria. 60 Minutes is airing a segment on him Sunday evening. Watch that, and we can talk again. He's no yes-man, but I've found it's good to have people like that around."

Four Seasons Hotel, Washington, DC

Becci Quinn sat at her favorite table in her favorite restaurant, Seasons, the power breakfast spot within the exclusive Four Seasons Hotel in Georgetown. She liked the restaurant because it featured farm-focused main dishes and exquisite salads. But she loved the restaurant because of its reputation for a clientele that included the city's most influential people, and it gave Becci a natural place to develop relationships with wealthy donors. Perhaps most importantly, the restaurant provided the covert Russian intelligence officer with the perfect cover to talk with people she recruited as assets to betray their country. Becci knew that talking with a contact over an expensive meal was much less suspicious than meeting with them on a park bench. Besides, the food at Seasons was spectacular.

Becci could see her hybrid-powered Prius parked near the entrance through the restaurant's front windows. The car and the rest of her life were all part of a carefully crafted persona she had created after entering the country. It really wouldn't do for the executive director of a non-profit organization to drive a high-performance, gas-chugging sedan. Her Prius and its strategically placed bumper stickers proclaiming liberal causes of the day completed her image as an ardent, civic-minded advocate for the luckless and disadvantaged. There were times Becci wished her covert persona worked as a high-priced corporate lawyer—BMWs were more fun to drive.

"Good morning. It looks like it's going to be a beautiful day!" Travis Webb pulled out a chair and joined Becci at her table. Travis was one of the American assets in Becci's espionage cell that she ran for Moscow. His lavish lifestyle had first brought him to the attention of Moscow's talent spotters, and he didn't disappoint. Eager for money to cover his substantial gambling debts, Travis was initially willing to share only classified information he considered insignificant. Over time, his concern for the importance of his stolen information decreased as his gambling addiction became more costly. He looked forward to these meetings with Becci because they usually meant he was about to receive another assignment, which meant more money.

"So, Becci, I assume you're having your usual French potato omelet? I'll try the roasted quail, and I'd like to add a side of apple-smoked bacon. Thank you!" Travis let his eyes follow the attractive server as she returned to the kitchen.

"How was your week?" asked Becci as she poured herself a cup of coffee from a carafe. "How're things at work?" Travis Webb was the principal deputy to National Security Advisor Jonathan Unger, which gave Webb access to all National Security Council information.

"It's tough to say. Jon's cut me out of anything important since he came aboard. It's difficult to be his deputy when he goes around me and works directly with the policy advisors. I don't think he likes me, and I'm pretty sure the man doesn't trust me. I told you he tried to fire me after he came over from the state department. I've been thinking about finding something in the private sector."

"Not a good idea, Travis. The Council is the right place for you. By the way, how's Jon been? The last time we spoke, you mentioned his health seemed to be declining."

"Well, I think he's getting worse. He won't admit it, of course. I'd like him to take some time off. I know you want me to start attending those high-level NSC meetings in the Oval Office."

Becci casually scanned the room to make sure others were not within earshot. "Perhaps you may get your chance sooner than you think. And speaking of the others, what are you hearing about the defense secretary. We're very interested in anything you can get on the man and will be very generous if you're successful."

"I'll see what I can do. To be frank, it wouldn't bother me if something unfortunate happened to him. I think we both know I would have made a better defense secretary."

"And Moscow would have preferred you'd been appointed as well," thought Becci as she continued eating her omelet. She wanted to end the meeting soon so that she could craft, encode, and send her report back to Moscow. She had the feeling that Travis Webb might have a promotion in his immediate future.

The Bridge, USS Robert McNamara (DDG-145), the South China Sea

Commander Ronald Leach focused his binoculars on the warship the bow lookout had reported ten minutes earlier. The ship sighting came as no surprise to Ron Leach because one of his helicopters had been tracking the Chinese navy destroyer for several hours. Before he left port, Leach read intelligence reports warning the Changsha was operating in these waters. The commodore was direct when he handed him his orders.

"Watch yourself. I know the court-martial has your attention, and I don't blame you. But I need you to put all that aside for the next thirty days while you're tailing this Chinese exercise. The PLAN has been building up in the South China Sea for some time, and this Spratly Islands exercise is just another chance for them to flex their muscles. Just observe the exercise and try not to get involved in an incident. I should be able to get a relief out to you in three weeks."

PLAN was short for the People's Liberation Army Navy, the official name of the Chinese navy. The court-martial that the commodore referenced was on Leach's mind because it likely meant he would be reduced in rank and dismissed from the Navy before reaching the required twenty years of service to retire with half pay. The evidence against him was damning—video of him receiving a large sum of money from a Singapore shipyard contractor for inside information. Bank records, eyewitnesses, and the unlimited investigative resources of the Department of Defense combined to make him almost sure he would be convicted after his ship returned to port. Even if he escaped a jail sentence, he would be a convicted felon and unable to work as a naval officer, the only job he ever had. His wife, children, and even his Annapolis classmates shunned him after he had been charged with several felonies, and the crew's morale had plummeted. His only hope to avoid the court-martial's guilty verdict was the long shot proposed by his civilian attorney.

"It's all we have left, a direct appeal to the secretary of defense. We know the DOD hates the negative press, and the last thing they want is for you to take the stand in front of all those cameras and share the rest of the dirt. It's pretty straightforward: they drop the charges, and you keep your mouth shut. You retire early, and the whole mess goes away."

Ron had reluctantly signed the letter authorizing his lawyer to approach Secretary Garrett, and he hoped it would work. He knew Garrett had served as a naval officer; maybe the man's affection for the Navy would cause him to do the right thing.

"Captain, here's your laptop. Comms has downloaded your message traffic, and they updated your personal email, too. We finally got our internet link fixed. It turns out it was the same problem with the antenna."

A commanding officer of a commissioned Navy ship was by tradition addressed as captain, regardless of their actual rank. It was just another custom inherited from the Royal Navy that confused everyone who served in the Army or Air Force. Lieutenant Commander Kathy Robertson was the ship's second-in-command and officially called the executive officer, or more simply, the XO.

"Thanks, XO. You see, our friend has joined us," Ron commented and handed his binoculars to her.

"So that's the Changsha," she replied while focusing the binoculars. "Luyang II-class guided-missile destroyer. She displaces 7,200 tons, 515 feet long, twin screws with gas turbines; 130-millimeter gun forward and two 32-cell vertical launch cells forward and aft. I don't see a bird on the helo pad; maybe it's in the hanger. Those three flat radar array panels make Changsha look a lot like "The Big Mac," Captain, only smaller. Kind of gives me the creeps."

The Big Mac was the McNamara's nickname, first coined by a junior sailor the day he stepped aboard the large Arleigh Burke-class destroyer. The same length as the Changsha, The Big Mac was a much larger ship, displacing more than 9,500 tons.

Ron twisted in his chair so that he could directly address Lieutenant Sara Baddeley. As officer of the deck, she was responsible for the navigation and safety of the ship for a four-hour watch. "OOD, please tell me I don't have to remind you of what happened the last time a Chinese Luyang-class destroyer approached a USN combatant in these waters. Would you agree it might be prudent to refresh the bridge team's memory of the incident?"

Sara Baddeley, the Officer Of the Deck, had already briefed her team and the Combat Information Center watchstanders on the incident. But she decided it would be in her best interest not to tell the captain she already did that two hours ago. "Aye, aye, Captain." In a tone and volume that she called her command voice, Sara said, "In 2018, the Decatur was operating near the Gavin Reefs, conducting a freedom of navigation operation. The Lanzhou, a Chinese destroyer, closed from the Decatur's port quarter until it came inside fifty yards. Even though Decatur had the right-of-way, and therefore, had the responsibility to maintain course and speed, the US destroyer commanding officer decided a collision was imminent, and he altered course."

"Very good, Lieutenant," commented the captain in a sarcastic tone.

Sara Baddeley raised her binoculars to her eyes to check the Chinese destroyer's range and bearing and thought, "What a prick! The entire wardroom can't wait until you leave this ship!" The captain initially paid close attention to Sara after she had first reported aboard the McNamara, and she thought he was a pervert.

"Captain," asked Ron's second-in-command, "do you have time to talk about that other matter? It can wait if you want to stay on the bridge while the Chinese ship approaches."

Ron Leach climbed down from his oversized bridge chair and placed his binoculars into the rack. "No, XO. Let's talk now. I'm certain Lieutenant Baddeley will let me know if I'm needed."

COLT'S CROSS

Captain Ron Leach led his XO off the ship's bridge and heard someone shout, "Captain's off the bridge," while a sailor recorded the event in the ship's logbook. When the captain was out of hearing, another Sailor muttered, "Dick!"

Wok and Roll Restaurant, Washington, DC

Colt Garrett had been surprised when Michele Phan asked him out for lunch, and he wasn't sure why she had done so. He had become used to people trying to find a way to get close to him to seek support for some policy or legislation. Washington was that kind of town. So maybe that was it. The congresswoman from Seattle probably had several reasons to spend time with a member of the president's cabinet, and he assumed today's lunch would reveal her motive.

He watched Michele as she looked through the menu and then take a sip of oolong tea. Despite her jeans and an expensive hoodie, it was apparent why the judges selected her as Miss Seattle decades earlier. With medium-length brown hair and blond highlights, large brown eyes, and a perfect complexion, Michele had the features of a fashion model, and she smiled when she caught Colt staring.

"Do you come here a lot?" she asked, then giggling at her question. "Sorry, I didn't mean it to sound like a pickup line. I just wondered how you found this place. A Chinese and Japanese restaurant by day and a karaoke bar after dark. It's not exactly the type of place I'd expect to find the defense secretary."

Colt looked around the casual dining room. "When I'm not working, I like to find small places to catch a decent meal and not have to worry about running into the press. Drake and I were wandering around Chinatown one weekend and stumbled upon this place. I checked out the menu in the window, and that's when I saw the historical society plaque on the building."

"This place is a historical site? You're kidding!"

Colt liked the way Michele's face lit up as she tried to tell if he was making this all up.

"No, I'm serious. You, Representative Phan, are sitting in the exact spot where Mary Surratt sat when federal agents arrested her on April 17, 1865, two days after Abraham Lincoln's assassination. This building was the infamous Mary Surratt boarding house, where the woman plotted President Lincoln's assassination, as well as those of Vice President Andrew Johnson, Secretary of State William Seward, and General Ulysses S. Grant, with Confederate sympathizers."

Michele leaned forward in her chair and rested her chin in her hands as Colt told the story. "You mean that John Wilkes Booth planned Lincoln's assassination in this room?"

"Yes, as well as Lewis Powell, George Atzerodt, and David Herold. Booth was found and killed while hiding in a tobacco barn in Virginia. A military tribunal tried Mary and the other conspirators. They hanged on July 7. She was the first woman executed by the US government."

Michele knew Colt had a doctorate in international relations but was impressed by how passionately he described the building's history. And then a thought occurred to her.

"Wait a minute, wasn't that tobacco barn owned by someone named Garrett? Any relation to you?"

Colt smiled and replied, "Unfortunately, no relation whatsoever. But I have to admit I researched that as well!"

The two enjoyed their lunch, and Michele asked, "So, how does the defense secretary spend a typical Sunday afternoon? Not working, I hope."

"Unfortunately, I focus on work on my weekends. You got

me there. I'll be watching 60 Minutes this evening because they're airing a segment featuring me and my role as SECDEF. I hope I didn't say anything wrong. I didn't even get the opportunity to review the tape."

"I'm sure you did fine," said Michele. "I hope you don't mind me asking, but I wonder how you're doing after your wife's death? I can't imagine how difficult that must have been. My father died more than ten years ago, and I still miss him."

"You know," Colt responded, "I think better. I'm still working through things, but I guess making progress. I've started dating again, but that still feels pretty strange."

Michele picked up the check and placed a credit card on the table as Colt reached for his wallet. "No, Colt, my treat. After all, I invited you!"

Outside the restaurant, a black suburban with darkened windows waited. Two men in dark glasses opened the doors while Colt turned to Michele and asked, "Can we give you a lift?"

"No thanks. I think I'll do a bit of shopping first before going home. Enjoy the rest of your Sunday."

Michele watched as the large SUV pulled away, accelerated up H Street, and turned the corner. She thought, "It might be interesting to watch 60 Minutes this evening." She crossed the busy street and headed for her favorite Asian market.

Captain's Stateroom, USS Robert McNamara (DDG 145)

Lieutenant Commander Kathy Robertson hesitated for a moment and then knocked twice on the cabin door. "Enter," said a gruff-sounding Ron Leach as he watched the ship's executive officer step into his cabin and sit down in the chair next to his desk. Both naval officers wore the Navy's at-sea uniform: dark blue fire-retardant coveralls. Above the left pocket of each officer's uniform was a black leather patch with a gold Surface Warfare insignia above the officer's name and rank. On each collar was their embroidered rank insignia: a silver oak leaf signifying commander or a gold oak leaf indicating lieutenant commander. Leach's uniform had one additional patch above his right pocket: the command-at-sea insignia. The small insignia included a five-pointed star superimposed on an anchor and a scroll with six stars, representing the Navy's first six ships. But the command-at-sea insignia had a more important significance. It meant that Ron Leach was the ship's commanding officer, its captain.

"Before you start, Kathy, I'd like to say I'm sorry you have had to deal with this issue. I know how difficult it's been for you, and I want you to know I'll do everything I can to get this thing resolved as quickly as possible. These things can destroy morale, and the commodore's counting on us to do our job out here."

"Thank you, sir. I appreciate that. Perhaps I should start by presenting the facts, and, after reviewing the regulations, we can determine the next steps?"

"Sure, Kathy. Let's get this over with." Ron poured a cup of coffee from the carafe on his desk and leaned back in his office chair while his executive officer opened a dark brown file containing several sheets of typed notes.

"I have formal written complaints from a female crew member who's claiming that you sexually harassed her on numerous occasions. She documents several inappropriate comments she alleges you made in private and in the presence of others, and she also alleges you physically assaulted her in this stateroom. The complaint includes written statements by several witnesses, and she's specifically requesting that I initiate an Article 138 formal complaint against you as her commanding officer."

Leach knew this was coming, but he had put it out of his mind with the upcoming court-martial. The XO had mentioned yesterday that she had a sexual harassment complaint she was dealing with, but he was surprised to find that he had been the complaint's subject. He saw the look of concern on Kathy's face as he carefully crafted his response. "Well, obviously, this is bullshit. You've seen Petty Officer Lewis flirting with most of the crew. And she's probably still upset about not making second class during the last advancement cycle. You know me. Do you think I'm capable of this? Okay, I know sometimes I make jokes that I think are funny. I don't mean any offense; I'm just trying to add some fun to the serious job we have to do. I think she's just misinterpreting things. I would never do something inappropriate." He paused and then asked, "Do you think you can talk her out of it? Maybe suggest we command-advance her to second class petty officer?"

Kathy Robertson didn't know what to say. Everybody on the ship, including its commanding officer, had taken sexual harassment training and knew that any complaint required a thorough investigation. The captain placed her in a difficult position, directly asking her to convince a Sailor to withdraw a sexual harassment complaint without due process. She understood the man sitting next to her had the sole power to determine her readiness for command. She knew she had to tread carefully.

"Sir, I'll talk with her to make certain she understands the seriousness of her accusation. But if she wants to move forward with the process, the regulations clearly state we must report the complaint to the squadron commander. No choice, sir."

Ron Leach put his coffee cup down and grabbed his copy of Navy Regulations from the bookshelf above his desk. "I thought we had thirty days to respond to the complaint," he said as he leafed through the thick publication.

"Sir, I've checked the Navy Sexual Harassment Prevention and Response Program Manual and Article 138 of the Uniformed Code of Military Justice. If the complaint is against the commanding officer, the ship can't perform the investigation. We have to forward it to your immediate superior, the commodore."

The ship's captain tried another approach. "Look, Kathy, I need a personal favor here. You know I'm under a lot of pressure with the upcoming court-martial. Can't you try to slow things down for about ten days so I can deal with this after we return to port?"

Kathy Robertson picked up her notes, stood up, and put her ballcap on her head. "I'll talk with her, Captain. And I'll interview the witnesses to make sure they'll confirm their written statements. But I doubt this will go away, sir. I can take a few days to make certain everyone is sure about what they said happened. But I must tell you, to be blunt, sir, that I believe this will be going to the commodore no later than early next week."

After Kathy left the stateroom, she walked down the passageway and entered her quarters. She hung her cap on the hook behind the door and sat at her desk. Thinking about her conversation with the captain, she did two things. First, she developed a rough timeline for interviewing Petty Officer Lewis and her witnesses. Second, she started a personal journal to document her conversations and actions regarding the sexual harassment complaint. She knew others would scrutinize everything she was doing from this moment on because she realized the harassment accusation was valid and a court-martial was certain. One other thing bothered her. She never showed the complaint form to the captain, yet somehow, he knew that Petty Officer Lewis had filed it.

60 Minutes, CBS Television Network

"Colton Garrett is the twenty-ninth person to serve as the United States Secretary of Defense. Since 1947, some of the most well-known men in government have held this cabinet-level position, including Robert McNamara, James Schlesinger, Donald Rumsfeld, Leon Panetta, and Dick Cheney. But the incumbent of what many believe to be one of the most powerful jobs in the world is comparatively unknown. Mr. Garrett's responsibilities are vast and include managing the massive defense department and its 1.4 million people on duty throughout the world. With an additional 718,000 civilians, the DOD is the nation's largest employer. The immense agency operates under an annual budget of more than 700 billion dollars in addition to all those people. Since the demise of the Soviet Union, the United States has been the world's sole superpower, and the defense secretary is the person with his hand on its helm. I'm Carissa Curtis, and this evening we'll interview this man who, until his Senate confirmation, has maintained a relatively low profile in the nation's capital. We'll ask him about his DOD priorities and even get to know a bit about him personally. And we might even get a bit of insight into his political future. That and more on this week's edition of 60 Minutes."

After a commercial break, the program returned to show Carissa Curtis and Colt Garrett standing in the center of his impressive Pentagon office. Carissa considered herself lucky to be interviewing Garrett. Only the most seasoned and accomplished reporters worked for the iconic television news magazine, and the network had only employed Carissa for five years. But when the producers asked Garrett to grant the interview, he just had one condition: Carissa Curtis had to be the person who interviewed him. The two had met when Colt was conducting a policy review in the Pacific and Carissa was on the USS Ronald Reagan. The president appointed Colt as acting defense secretary in the days following Secretary O'Kane's death. Carissa took advantage of the opportunity to get the first interview with the newly appointed cabinet member. The young reporter was also present for two unsuccessful attempts on the life of the defense secretary. The experience created a trust that didn't typically exist between senior government officials and a journalist.

"Mr. Secretary, I've never been in this office before. I wonder if we could take a few minutes, and you would be kind enough to give us a tour?"

Colt nodded his head. "Sure, Ms. Curtis. Where would you like to start?"

Carissa walked over to a framed, black and white photograph of an ancient three-masted ship. "How about we start with this photo? I assume it was one of ours?"

"That's a photograph of the USS Constitution when it visited Seattle in 1933. My dad took that picture when he was just ten years old with a Kodak Brownie box camera. After he died, I had the picture enlarged and framed. It reminds me of him."

"I saw the Constitution when I was visiting friends in Boston," Carissa commented. "Why was it in Seattle?"

"That's an interesting tale," began Colt. Carissa could tell he had forgotten about the camera and bright TV lights as soon as he started to tell his story.

"Back in 1924, a marine survey declared the ship unseaworthy. Congress approved the ship's restoration by public subscription, and the Navy sponsored a campaign to raise the funds. Civic groups and school children had raised more than two-thirds of the money, and Congress authorized the remainder needed for the repairs. The Oliver Wendell Holmes poem "Old

Ironsides" became popular again, and the Navy decided to send the ship on a tour of all America's coastal states."

Carissa observed, "You sound as if you're still lecturing in a college lecture hall! I believe you have a doctorate in political science?"

Colt paused for a moment and remembered the television camera. "No, international relations. And sorry about the lecture, I just really enjoy history."

The pair continued the office tour and stopped at a framed print of two Chinese characters in red ink.

"And what is this, Mr. Garrett? Are you a languages expert as well?"

Colt shook his head. "Not even close," he began. "One of my favorite presidents was John F. Kennedy. Not so much for what he accomplished during that short three years in the Oval Office, but more for his ability to communicate ideas and concepts. This print depicts the two Chinese characters for danger and opportunity. JFK said that together, the two characters represent how the Chinese people write the word crisis. He went on to explain how we need to recognize that every crisis contains both elements, and leaders should pay attention to the danger and the opportunity. Scholars have questioned Kennedy's interpretation of the characters, but who cares, I prefer to focus on what Kennedy was trying to say. Good leaders see opportunity when others cannot." The camera focused on Colt's face for several seconds, then panned to his office window as the program paused for a commercial.

When 60 Minutes returned, the television camera framed Carissa and Colt sitting in facing chairs in front of his large office desk, flags and windows framing the shot.

"Mr. Secretary, I understand you have a personal interest in the Missing In Action tragedy. Why do you feel so strongly about the issue?"

"I'm sure you know that enemy troops shot down my older brother during the Vietnam War. Our family was just one of the tens of thousands who suffered the dread of watching a military car stop in front of their house. We experienced real terror as two officers approached the door to deliver terrible news. The experience changed my life. When I first learned that Scott was missing, I was sure we'd see him again. I did everything I could to make sure my brother would be proud of me when he finally came home. But he never did. I know there are thousands of families in this country that feel as I do, and I'm determined that this department never stops looking until we bring each son or daughter home."

The camera focused first on the framed picture on Colt's desk of a carefree Lieutenant Scott Garrett proudly sitting in his F-4 Phantom II cockpit and then back to Colt Garrett's solemn face as he waited for Carissa's next question.

"Thank you for sharing that," said Carissa. "On a different topic, what can you tell us about your politics? I've researched your background, published works, and what you've said publicly. I can't determine if you're a Democrat or a Republican. Where do you stand politically?"

Colt clasped his hands together and answered, "I'm not certain that's anyone's business." He chuckled awkwardly before regaining his composure. "You see, I'm not the Democratic secretary of defense or the Republican secretary of defense. I'm the United States secretary of defense. The job needs to be above politics; too many lives depend on that. I'm not naive, and I understand politics run this town. But when I accepted the president's nomination, I promised him I'd do my very best in the time I'm here. And we both swore the same oath to defend the Constitution."

"Speaking of the president, his second term will be coming to an end. Have you had any conversations with Vice President Hernandez about continuing to serve as her defense secretary should she be elected next November?"

"Well, I won't share any private conversations I may or may not have had with the vice president or any other person for that matter. I will say this, though. When President Harrison waves goodbye as he leaves Washington at the end of his term, I'm pretty certain I'll be driving back to the other Washington to spend some time with my daughter and her family."

The television shot faded to an image of the Pentagon and then to the face of the famous 60 Minutes stopwatch as the second hand continued to tick down.

Colt Garrett's Residence, Potomac Hill Complex

Colt turned off the television after the 60 Minutes show ended and poured himself two fingers of Heritage's Brown Sugar Bourbon. He slowly swirled the amber liquid around the base of a Waterford tumbler as he tried to assess his interview performance objectively. All in all, Colt thought the interview had gone reasonably well. At first, he thought his comments about Scott were too personal to share with the television audience. But on further reflection, Colt felt that Carissa's question had allowed him to talk about the MIA issue and why the country should prioritize bringing those lost patriots home, making it clear why it mattered so much. He wished the interview had explored his priorities for the upcoming defense appropriation and why the DOD needed to replace some legacy technologies. "But that's not how networks get ratings," he thought. "I guess most viewers are more interested in personal stuff than programs and policy." He was surprised by the question regarding a conversation with the vice president about his future in her administration. They hadn't talked about the possibility, and he thought he could sense the vice president's distrust of him in cabinet meetings. "Oh well, it's probably good to get out of town before some congressional committee decides to reorganize the DOD, yet again. And besides, I'd like to take some time off before deciding how to spend the next chapter of my life."

Colt laughed when he realized he'd been pacing back and forth in the formal dining room as he thought about the television program. Linda used to give him grief about the habit he had developed many years earlier. Pouring himself another drink, he thought about looking through his library for another book to start when his mobile phone rang.

"Dad! We just saw you on 60 Minutes, and we thought you were great! Kyle wanted to know why you didn't mention him!"

"Allie, just tell your husband that I did talk about him at length, but the network must have edited that part out!"

"Funny. I'll tell him. By the way, I spoke with Lenny Wilson earlier today. I was just making sure that he's checking up to see you're eating real food. I know how you like junk food, and nobody's living with you to stop it."

"I've been good. And speaking of meals, I had a great lunch today at Wok and Roll. I took you there the last time you visited me."

"I remember. And I recall you spent most of the lunch talking about the Lincoln assassination. Were you there with Jillian?" Allie wanted to bring the conversation back to talk about her father's dating the college professor.

"No, I met a congresswoman there for lunch today. She serves on the national security subcommittee, and I testified there on Friday."

"Another date?"

Colt could hear the tension in his daughter's voice and replied, "Calm down, Allie. It was just business. And I don't think you need to worry about me seeing Jillian anytime soon. Maybe you were right. It's too soon."

After the call, Colt started rereading Ewen Montague's The Man Who Never Was, the true story of a British secret plan to conceal Normandy invasion details. He was looking at some of the book's photographs when he learned he had a guest. He was surprised to find Representative Phan standing in the doorway.

"Good evening, Mr. Secretary. I hope I'm not intruding. I saw your segment on 60 Minutes and decided I need to share some information with you."

Colt put down his book and invited the congresswoman into the living room.

"Please, take a seat. Can I get you something to drink?"

Two hours later, Lenny Wilson answered his mobile phone.

"Mr. Secretary. What can I do for you?"

"Sorry for the late hour, Lenny. My apologies to Margaret. I'd like you to reach out to Special Operations Command at MacDill and see if they can arrange a briefing for me tomorrow, at noon, if possible. I know it's short notice, but I'm interested in getting a complete brief on US covert activities in Cambodia in April and May of 1975. Something has come up that might impact next week's POW/MIA Joint Field Activity."

Day Five

Defense Secretary's Office, the Pentagon, Arlington, Virginia

Many people assumed the Pentagon's five-sided design reflects the nation's five armed services: the Army, Navy, Air Force, Marine Corps, and Coast Guard. But that would be an incorrect assumption because planners designed the immense structure to sit in a location with borders on five sides. The government eventually built the Pentagon on a different lot, but there wasn't time to change the design. It's probably good that the building's design wasn't associated with the number of services because, with the creation of Space Force as a sixth service, a hexagon would now be a proper design. Designed and built in only sixteen weeks during World War Two, the immense structure provides office space for more than 30,000 civilian and military personnel in the twenty-acre complex. The Pentagon's design includes five massive concentric rings connected by ten intersecting corridors and numerous hallways. A five-acre outdoor courtyard, informally known as "ground zero" on the assumption that several Soviet missiles were targeted there during the Cold War, comprises the structure's center.

Just getting to work remains a challenge for those assigned to the Pentagon. Only the most senior employees receive the coveted executive parking pass; exclusive access to the best parking spaces located closest to the building. Location, location, location. Passes for other Pentagon parking lots are considered a privilege, not a right. Most employees travel to work via DOD shuttle bus, private bus service, or mass transportation. On their way to and from work, Washington Metro riders could find themselves sitting next to a Navy petty officer or an Air Force brigadier general.

With its dedicated police force, fire department, shopping mall, food courts, athletic center, medical facilities, dental clinic, banks, library, worship services, and a wide selection of memorials and art exhibits, the Pentagon functions more like a small town or village than a government building. The building gained national and international attention during the 9/11 attack when American Airlines Flight 77 struck the Pentagon's Navy Operations Center, killing 184 people. Outside, visitors can sit on memorial benches dedicated to each of the victims. The memorial's architect organized the benches in a timeline of the victim's ages, from the youngest victim, 3-year-old Dana Falkenberg, to the oldest, 71-year-old John Yamnicky. The Navy Reflection Room, formerly the destroyed Navy Operations Center site, provides a quiet place for people to remember those killed during the attack.

Lenny Wilson sat across from his boss in the impressive office of the defense secretary. It featured large windows on the Pentagon's E-Ring, a perk reserved for only the building's most senior officials.

"It was sort of weird watching you on 60 Minutes last night, sitting where I am now. I thought it went well. Have you heard anything from the White House communications director?"

Colt removed his reading glasses and set them on his desk. "Yes. Breanna called earlier to pass on her congratulations. She was pleased I didn't stray from the talking points her staff had provided, and she thought the part of the interview that showed my personal side was . . . effective. I guess it fits within the administration's efforts to show a softer side to the voters. I am surprised they're still focused on image, given the president is in his second term."

"Presidents are always concerned about their legacy. The party is worried about the mid-terms, and the president will be a major player in keeping the Senate's majority." Lenny noticed that Colt wasn't listening to him as the cabinet member leafed through a document on his desk. He knew Colt wasn't interested in politics or those who were obsessed with it, but Lenny continued to be amazed by how someone in Colt's position could remain so politically ambivalent. Washington insiders thought that Colt Garrett's political indifference was some sort of act to make him appear above the political posturing and infighting, but Lenny knew better. Colt just didn't care.

"Lenny, I'm eager to hear what Special Operations Command has to tell us about US operations in Cambodia. You scheduled that for noon in the tank?"

"Yes, sir," replied Lenny as he referred to the day's schedule. "We'll meet them in the Joint Chiefs of Staff conference room at 12:15, and I have you scheduled to head out to Quantico to speak at the Marine Officer Candidate School graduation. Your draft speech is on your desk. I've arranged for you to meet up at the Quantico range with your Army CID protection detail. They're eager to show you up again at the small arms range."

Colt enjoyed shooting his pistol when his schedule allowed, and he was very good at it. A skilled marksman from his service as a naval intelligence officer, Colt liked talking with his personal protection detail about their weapons. He had challenged the team to another shooting competition.

Lenny opened his mobile phone and asked Colt, "Hey, boss, does this song sound familiar to you? It was released the same year you were commissioned." He pressed a button, and the phone played a few lines from the song "Jenny" by the group

Tommy Tutone, ending in "8675309".

Colt and Lenny played a practical joke on one another for years that involved playing a classic song and then seeing how long the other person would have the song stuck in their brain. Colt laughed and replied, "Okay, you got me!" and then he started humming 8675309, over and over. Looking at his watch, Colt asked, "How about some coffee? I'd like to stretch my legs, and I think we have time before the budget briefing."

Courtyard Café, the Pentagon, Arlington, Virginia

"I'll have a skinny triple tall flat white, with one raw sugar, please. And Mr. Secretary, what can I get for you?"

Colt shook his head and replied, "I'll just have a cup of black coffee, Lenny."

Colt would occasionally order a latte or cappuccino, but whenever he joined Lenny at the café, he ordered a black coffee in subtle protest to Lenny's high-maintenance selection. The two friends had been arguing about coffee for years.

"Why can't you just order a plain cup of coffee? It seems your coffee orders get more complex by the day."

Lenny silently stirred his drink, enjoying the banter with his older friend. "Boss, I do it just to watch the look on your face, to be honest."

Colt laughed and said, "Okay, let's see who the master chief has for me today!"

Colt first started the practice of sitting down with servicemen and women and listening to their concerns when he was on the USS Ronald Reagan a few years earlier. He had asked Navy Master Chief Jim Halderman to offer those stationed in the Pentagon an opportunity each Monday morning to informally meet with the defense secretary over coffee to share their perspectives. Colt felt the brief sessions kept him grounded with what the troops were experiencing day to day, with the added benefit of getting him out of his office for an hour or two.

"Secretary Garrett, this week's group wants to talk about uniforms. May I present Navy Lieutenant Jake Procter, Air Force Staff Sergeant Lindsey Stocks, and Army Corporal Troy Krumland."

Colt motioned to an empty table in the food court. "Please, have a seat." The secretary of defense pulled up a chair, and the three somewhat nervous junior service people joined him at the table while Lenny Wilson and Master Chief Halderman stood nearby. After first getting to know the Sailor, Soldier, and Airman a bit better, Colt asked, "What did you want to share with me regarding uniforms?"

Each service had a standing committee to identify uniform challenges and opportunities for improvement. Still, there were always things that service people thought needed changing. Colt wasn't surprised that uniforms had resurfaced as a topic for one of his weekly meetings.

"I'll start. My beef is that each service has a different camouflage uniform. It's getting ridiculous." Staff Sergeant Lindsey Stocks had stood up from her chair and was facing Colt. He smiled at the fit and attractive young woman. "At ease, Staff Sergeant, this is an informal discussion. Please take a seat." She hesitated for a moment and then sat back down in her chair.

"Sorry, sir. It just doesn't make sense. All the services used to wear the same camo uniform, and it was great. I was working on an Army base in California and could buy working uniforms at their post exchange. And Sailors could buy camo uniforms on an Air Force base. Then the Marines developed a unique digital camo pattern. And then the Army did too, followed by the Air

Force. The Navy had that weird blue camo uniform, and then they changed to a green one that's similar but different from the Marine uniform. The Air Force finally adopted the Army pattern, but we use nametapes with blue thread. I guess I just think we should all wear one camo uniform."

"I think it's kind of stupid that we wear camo uniforms in a building," offered Lieutenant Procter. Colt glanced at the lieutenant's uniform and noticed he wore the gold dolphins of the Submarine Service. "I mean, if I were a terrorist, I'd just shoot all the things that look like trees. If we were serious about effective camouflage, we'd wear shirts and pants in the same colors as the corridor walls."

Colt chuckled and asked, "Lieutenant Procter, what did you want to talk about?"

"Sir, I think the Navy should follow the Royal Navy's example by having naval officers wear shoulder boards on all uniforms. Get rid of the collar insignia, use shoulder boards, soft or hard, on everything we wear, even flight suits. They look great, and those of us who serve on ship or subs wouldn't have to deal with the problem of losing metal collar insignia around machinery and the damage it can cause."

Lenny was making notes on a yellow pad while Colt remained focused on listening to the suggestions. He knew most of the suggestions probably weren't workable, but Colt had insisted that everything he heard at these meetings was fully documented and forwarded to the Joint Chiefs.

"Corporal Krumland, what suggestions do you have to share?" The tall Army ranger looked to his left and right and then said, "Sir, I think these berets are bizarre. Most of the guys are proud of their tan beret, but we used to wear black ones before the Army decided to let everyone wear a black beret. That's when they changed the ranger beret's color from black to tan."

Colt looked around the table and took another sip from his coffee. He always thought the beret was a useless hat for the military and made the wearer look as if they served under Che Guevara. It lacked a brim and didn't shed the rain, but he realized the elite Army units prized the distinctive headwear. "Thank you for sharing your concerns. Mr. Wilson will type these up, and I'll share them with the Joint Chiefs. Don't worry. We won't include your names."

Lenny and Colt walked back toward the E-Ring. "Sorry, sir. That wasn't one of our better Monday coffee meetings. I suppose it's just the luck of the draw."

"Don't worry about it, Lenny. I still think it's worthwhile to meet with the troops to hear their concerns. It does seem ridiculous that each service has its own camo. And why do sailors need to wear camo uniforms unless they're in a ground combat environment? I did like Lieutenant Procter's idea for the Navy to ditch the metal collar devices and, instead, use shoulder boards on every uniform. Remind me to mention it to the secretary of the Navy."

The West Wing, the White House

It wasn't until Maria Hernandez became vice president of the United States that she learned her new job had three offices in addition to the study in her official residence at the Naval Observatory. As president of the US Senate, Maria maintained an office in the United States Capitol. Office S-214, also known as the Vice President's Room, provided Maria with a private space to conduct business while working at the Capitol. S-214 had been the location of many historical events, including the death of Ulysses S. Grant's vice president, Henry Wilson. In 1875, he succumbed to a fatal stroke. The Eisenhower Executive Office Building, located across the street from the White House, included a ceremonial office for the vice president's use when hosting receptions and other formal events. This lavish office featured a spectacular view of the Washington Monument and a desk signed by every vice president since the 1940s.

On the West Wing's first floor, her third office was where the vice president worked every day and where Maria found herself on this Monday morning. She looked at the photograph of her husband, Ethan Davis, and thought back to when they first met. She had just returned from London and had accepted her father's offer to work for him at Hernandez Petroleum. Ethan's reputation as an exceptional petroleum engineer landed him a job in Hernandez's exploration division, and within a few months, he asked Maria out to dinner. A quiet man, Ethan impressed Maria with his passion for the industry and her father's business. The relationship developed over the summer and fall, when Ethan proposed marriage. Raoul and Mrs. Hernandez were thrilled their daughter had found someone who worked for the family business. Raoul believed Maria's marriage to Ethan would ensure she would remain working for his firm and, eventually, succeed her father when the time was right. But he couldn't have been more mistaken.

After a successful campaign for a seat on Corpus Christi's city council, Maria became hooked on politics and embarked on what had become a thirty-year career in public service. At first, her marriage with Ethan thrived, and the young couple proved inseparable. They enjoyed sharing work stories, and the fact they no longer worked together only served to improve their sex life. Things were going great until they discovered that Ethan was unable to father children. A severe case of the mumps due to a missed vaccination during Ethan's youth had left him sterile, and the couple started down the long path to adoption.

Maria thought bringing an unwanted child into their lives was the perfect solution to their situation and expressed her excitement at the prospect of finding a child during the adoption interviews. The counselors could feel Maria's commitment, but Ethan evidently didn't project the same interest level. His reluctance became apparent, and the adoption agency informed the couple they had been deemed not eligible to adopt a child. Maria was devastated by the decision and rightly blamed her husband. Their relationship grew strained after this, leading eventually to resentment and finally to tolerance. Divorce was out of the question; both were practicing Roman Catholics. Maria found excuses to stay overnight at her apartment in Houston, and Ethan seemed to always be on a business trip when she returned to their home in Corpus Christi. She had to acknowledge that Ethan was a good sport making campaign appearances and attending important fundraising dinners. He made speeches on her behalf and even found time to knock on doors during the campaigns. But when their front door closed for the evening after they prepared to go to bed, Ethan and Maria slept in separate bedrooms.

Ethan began seeing other women when Maria represented the 27th district in Congress. Eight years of spending six months of the year in Washington, DC, further distanced the still-married couple. Maria maintained her separate life in Washington, while Ethan maintained his life in Corpus Christi. Then Maria was elected governor of Texas. Eight years in the governor's mansion made continuing their marriage of convenience a challenge. When Maria was elected vice president, both realized they could return to living in separate cities. Maria needed to live in Washington, and Ethan's recent promotion as President of Hernandez Petroleum meant he would have to live in Houston. The only problem was that because the press followed her everywhere, Maria Hernandez seemed destined to live a social life like those led by the Catholic nuns who taught her during elementary school so many years ago.

The nation's first Latino vice president knew about living an isolated existence. Growing up as the only child of a wealthy oil tycoon meant she lacked nothing in the way of material possessions. A lavish home with a domestic staff fulfilled her needs even before she became aware of them. Family vacations to exotic destinations throughout the world provided Maria with a lifestyle most would envy. But from an early age, she became aware that, somehow, she was different from the other children in the private Catholic school. One afternoon, her mother explained the family's Hispanic heritage and that some people would treat her as someone who wasn't quite as acceptable as others. In Houston, attending Rice University broadened Maria's understanding of racial and cultural inequity after volunteering at the local homeless shelter. Located in Houston's Third Ward, the shelter sat at the intersection of McGowan and Dowling Streets and served a population considered one of the most economically depressed in the state.

The neighborhood's condition was the primary reason she decided to run for the city council. Her determination to make a real difference in the lives of people who looked like her drove a desire to seek positions of broader authority and impact. Maria thought her election as governor was the end of her journey until she received President Harrison's phone call to join him on the party's presidential ticket. Four years as vice president had taught her that young girls of color saw her as an example of what they might one day achieve. She felt proud that, soon, she might become the first Latino to serve as president of the

United States of America. It was a lot to live up to. But she had no choice but to continue on her path.

The vice president began to pace the floor in front of her desk as she analyzed her impression of Colt Garrett's 60 Minutes performance. After watching the program live last night and then twice earlier this morning, she distilled her reaction into two distinct impressions. First, Maria no longer saw Garrett as someone moving a national defense plan of his own and different from the president's. She realized that the president appointed Garrett because their views were closely aligned. Garrett's conviction in the strategy was what had made him successful in its implementation.

Second, she began to understand what the president had said regarding surrounding oneself with advisors who told you what they thought, regardless of the current political winds. She quietly laughed at her previous concern that Garrett's defense policy experience intimidated her.

"Of course, it did, and that's okay," she thought. "I have no national security background, and I need people like him to help me govern effectively." She stopped pacing and sat down at her desk to make a few notes for tomorrow's meeting in the Oval Office with the president and Eric Painter to resume their discussion of potential candidates for her cabinet. She wanted to hear what the chief of staff had to say about her national security candidates, but she had a feeling she knew what her final decision would be. Maria looked once more at the photo of her husband and decided she needed to talk with him.

His active and visible support would be necessary for the upcoming presidential campaign, and she knew it would be a lot to ask of him. But it was time to get on with their lives and stop the charade. She hoped her elderly parents would understand, but a few months after the election, she would divorce Ethan

Davis, whether she became president or not.

Air Test and Evaluation Squadron Two Three, NAS Pax River, Maryland

Lieutenant Commander Dan Garrett was in the one place in the world he most wanted to be: the Navy's most significant test and evaluation squadron that conducted research, testing, and evaluation of fixed-wing tactical aircraft and unmanned aerial vehicles, or simply, UAVs. VX-23 provided aircraft, pilots, maintenance, safety oversight, and operations. But Dan did more than work for VX-23. Dan Garrett was a Navy test pilot, assigned to the F-35C Lightning II flight test program. Pax River was where only the very best Navy pilots flew, and they tested every fixed-wing and UAV airframe the Navy fielded. Pilots pushed aircraft beyond their designed capabilities, purposely making them fail. And when they were successful, test pilots earned their pay by recovering the planes from potential disaster and landing them safely. It was hazardous work, but Dan loved the challenge and the superb aviation skills he developed every day on the job. One day he might even be accepted into NASA's astronaut program and find a way to Mars.

Dan was in the ready room performing his operations officer's duties when the duty phone rang.

"Squadron ops, Lieutenant Commander Garrett. How can I help you?"

"Commander Garrett, this is Petty Officer Kappes at squadron admin. There's a Lieutenant Commander Pierce here asking to see you, sir." Dan raced out of the ready room, dashed down the passageway to the squadron admin office, and crashed through the door. He shouted when he saw his guest.

"Hurricane! What're you doing here?"

Lieutenant Commander Katrina (Hurricane) Pierce was a Naval flight officer, or NFO. She had flown with Dan when they had been stationed in VAQ-132 at Naval Air Station Whidbey Island in Washington State. They flew the Navy's electronic warfare plane, the EA-18G Growler, a modified version of Boeing's F/A-18F Super Hornet fighter-bomber. They had trained together as a team when they first arrived at Whidbey, and over the three-year tour, had developed into close friends. When Dan left the squadron to attend test-pilot school, Katrina resigned her active-duty commission. She transferred into the Naval Reserve to enroll in the Antonin Scalia Law School in Arlington, Virginia.

She received orders to the Naval Support Activity in the old Washington Navy Yard, where she worked one weekend every month at a Naval Research Laboratory performing administrative tasks. It wasn't nearly as exhilarating as flying low-level routes through the Pacific Northwest's Cascade Mountain range, but the Navy Reserve job meant she could maintain her affiliation with the Navy while pursuing a legal career.

After she broke from Dan's bear hug, she said, "I just finally had a break in my school schedule and got my reserve unit to send me on temporary duty this weekend to Pax River. Give us a chance to catch up. And besides, I wanted to see for myself how you manage to fly a jet without me doing all of the hard work." Hurricane Pierce had earned her callsign when she had been in the training squadron. Her commanding officer was impressed by how often her hot temper surfaced, and she let fly with a steam of off-color insults. "Wild as a hurricane," the senior naval office had proclaimed, and the callsign had stuck. Joker Garrett was christened with his callsign back in primary flight training when he became infamous for imitating movie actors when talking on the radio to the tower. After several impromptu counseling sessions with the wing commander because of his antics, Dan's instructor dubbed him Joker, a callsign that seemed to fit his personality perfectly.

"How would you like a tour of a Lighting II? There's a bird in Hanger Three that's getting an engine swapped out. I think you'll be impressed." The two good friends descended the stairs and walked out across the flight line. "So, Hurricane, you must be almost finished with law school. Find a job yet?"

"Almost. I completed an internship with Connolly, Tacon & Meserve, and I think they're about to offer me a job as an associate. It'll be great to be earning a paycheck while I study for the bar exam. Pretty happy about it."

"Is Gene still flying for Alaska? I can't imagine you get to see him much. Do they even fly into Dulles?"

Gene Pierce and Katrina had been married for ten years, and Dan knew they still owned a house in Seattle. "Alaska has a route to Reagan, and Gene's senior enough that we get to see one another about every other week. And are you still seeing Rebecca?"

Dan had met Rebecca Clarke when stationed on the Reagan, and Katrina wasn't sure the surface warfare officer was the right match for her friend.

"Yes, in fact, we're going to the Navy gala tomorrow night, and I'm planning on introducing her to Dad. I hope he likes her. And this, Hurricane, is the Lighting II."

The two naval officers had stopped in front of a strange-looking jet. Katrina walked completely around the plane and picked up a plastic-laminated placard from a nearby table. She read aloud, "For the first time in US naval aviation history, radar-evading stealth capability comes to the carrier deck. The F-35C carrier variant sets new standards in weapon system integration, lethality, maintainability, combat radius, and payload that bring true multi-mission power projection capability from the sea. The F-35C matches fifth-generation survivability with major advances in network-enabled mission systems, reliability, and interoperability. It is a first-day-of-the-war fighter with the capability to dominate adversaries in the air or on the surface while surviving the most formidable threat environments."

Dan stepped up to the gray stealth plane and placed his hand on its smooth wing. "The Air Force bought the A variant, which is the land-based version. The Marines opted for the B variant that performs like the Vertical Take-Off and Landing Harrier and these C versions that can land on a carrier. But I want you to see the cockpit."

Dan pointed to a black box behind the single ejection seat after climbing up the plane's side. "That is the ASQ-239, the plane's electronic warfare package. In other words, that little box does what you used to do in the Growler, but without all of your unnecessary chatter. I call it R2D2, and we've become close friends. You're looking at the future!"

Katrina laughed at Dan's comments but thought he was probably right. It was only a matter of time before technology could identify and jam enemy radars and missiles better and faster than a human could. It made perfect sense, and yet it made her a little sad. Dan saw the look on Katrina's face and could tell his joking had gone too far. "Sorry, Hurricane. Hey, let's go over to Hanger Two. I have something else you might find interesting."

Inside Hanger Two sat the MQ-25A, the Stingray, the Navy's experimental aerial refueling drone. "So, this is the Stingray? It looks like something right out of the movie Stealth!"

The Navy planned to use the drone to provide airborne refueling of a carrier's planes. F/A-18 Super Hornets currently performed the mission using a refueling pod, but the Navy wanted to save the more expensive fighters for their primary mission: ground attack and air intercept. Katrina walked around the Stingray and then returned to Dan's side. Placing her hand on his shoulder, she said, "Let me get this straight. This drone can operate from a carrier and complete its mission previously performed by a navy pilot. It seems to me that R2D2 will be replacing you before long. I'm thinking you may be looking at your future!"

As Dan escorted Katrina back to the squadron's admin office, he thought, "you're probably right!"

National Military Command Center, the Pentagon

Buried deep beneath the Pentagon was the NMCC, the command post for the country's National Command Authority (the president of the United States and the United States secretary of defense). The National Command Authority could generate emergency action messages to ballistic missile submarines, launch control centers, reconnaissance aircraft, and battlefield commanders from this highly secure complex. More than 300 military and civilian personnel worked in the NMCC, monitoring global events that could be of defense significance. Watch teams comprising about twenty people were led by a one-star admiral or general assisted by an Army or Air Force colonel or a Navy captain. The facility included several war rooms, including the one portrayed in the movie, Dr. Strangelove.

The Joint Chiefs of Staff Conference Room was the most impressive of the NMCC's spaces, with a large wooden conference table surrounded by twelve upholstered chairs resting on plush wall-to-wall carpet. About twenty people, some in uniform, had gathered and were talking to one another when the door opened. Colt Garrett stepped into the room, followed by Deputy Secretary of Defense Steve Holmes and Lenny Wilson. After asking everyone in the room to be seated, Colt Garrett began the meeting.

"I'd like to thank you, General Wickett, for flying in from MacDill this morning for this briefing. I have to make a decision in the next twenty-four hours, and any information you can provide will be beneficial."

General Caleb Wickett served as commander, United States Special Operations Command. The four-star general was responsible for the Navy, Army, Air Force, and Marine Corps' special operations component commands, a worldwide responsibility. General Wickett's uniform displayed eight rows of ribbons representing his awards and service medals. Despite having just celebrated his fifty-third birthday, General Wickett appeared to be as ready to attend Green Beret training this day as he was at age twenty-two. His close-cropped haircut and his military bearing marked him for what he was: a warrior. The general nodded at the defense secretary, handed him a thick file, and said, "Happy to help, Mr. Secretary. I think you'll find what we are about to share quite interesting. Major, I think you can begin."

"Secretary Garrett, General Wickett, ladies and gentlemen, I'm Major John Spealman, and this briefing is classified top secret." The serious Marine Corps major stood at a podium and started a PowerPoint presentation projected on the screen behind him. "This briefing will cover US special operations conducted in Cambodia during 1975. But before I discuss 1975 operations, I'll provide some background on the Military Assistance Command, Vietnam, Studies and Observations Group, or MACV-SOG."

Major Spealman pressed a button, and a military patch

projected on the screen. The red patch depicted a smiling human skull wearing a green beret, superimposed over a fouled anchor. The silver wings of an Air Force command pilot were positioned directly above the skull, and the entire patch bordered in yellow. "As you may recall, MACV was the joint command responsible for conducting operations in what we now refer to as the Vietnam War. In the early sixties, the White House decided to move responsibility for all covert, paramilitary operations outside of Vietnam from the Central Intelligence Agency to MACV. The Studies and Operations Group, or SOG, was created as a subcomponent of MACV, but it reported directly to the Pentagon because SOG's activities were outside of Vietnam, MACV's area of responsibility."

Deputy Defense Secretary Holmes raised his hand, "And what were SOG's primary responsibilities, Major?"

General Wickett smiled as he recalled preparing for this briefing during the past twelve hours. He knew the major had supporting slides ready to go should he be asked any of the thirty other questions for which the team had prepared.

Major Spealman replied, "Thank you for that question, Mr. Holmes. SOG's primary mission was the interdiction of the supplies, troops, and ammunition flowing into South Vietnam from Cambodia and Laos. Essentially, to stop the traffic on the Ho Chi Minh Trail." Major Spealman advanced to the next PowerPoint slide, showing the trail's paths into Vietnam. "All the SOG teams were either disbanded or absorbed into other units by 1973, except for SOG Base PYTHON." Major Spealman displayed the next slide, highlighting the Mekong River flowing south from Laos and Cambodia.

"The communists were bringing supplies into Vietnam via a land route called the Sihanouk Trail, which originated in the Gulf of Thailand at the Cambodian port of Kampong Som. The land route continued east to the south of Phnom Penh and then northeast on the Mekong River. Over the next 200 miles of the Mekong, the communists moved supplies and reinforcements east until they intersected the Ho Chi Minh Trail and were further disseminated to support the Viet Cong insurgency in the Mekong Delta. The Sihanouk Trail's interdiction was the one crucial element of the US plan to support South Vietnam. SOG Base PYTHON, located in a dense forest between Kampong Charm and Snoul, was perfectly positioned and remained operational after all other US combat forces had left the region. The last report we received from PYTHON was on May 4, 1975, when they reported being attacked by Soviet gunships."

Major Spealman then displayed twenty-two grainy black-and-white photographs of the attack's aftermath. The conference room was silent as each image clicked on, with detailed views of buildings destroyed, vehicles and helicopters burned, and dead soldiers everywhere.

"Thirty-seven Americans and more than 100 Cambodians and Montagnards dead. The DOD listed two Americans missing: an Army Special Forces medical sergeant and a Navy SEAL. That concludes my brief, Mr. Secretary. Questions?"

The screen showed two young men in their twenties, each in the dress uniform of their service. The conference room was so quiet that the second hand on the clock on the wall above Colt's head could be heard ticking. After what seemed to be an eternity, Colt asked, "Do we have any idea of what happened to these two men?" Major Spealman was about to advance to the next slide but stopped when he saw General Wickett raise his hand, palm out.

"Let me take this, John." Turning to Colt, the general began, "Mr. Secretary, at that time, the SOG PYTHON mission, and even its existence, was off the books. With Saigon's evacuation just days earlier, nobody in this building, the White House, or even the Kremlin was interested in raising the issue. PYTHON's attack simply didn't happen, and the people we lost there were listed as killed in a training exercise in the Nevada desert. The two missing men were listed as MIA in Vietnam."

Colt slowly nodded. "Okay, I think I understand. But how did the Soviets find out about PYTHON? It must have been a closely held secret."

General Wickett closed his briefing folder and answered, "That's why I asked Mr. Hale to join us today. Mr. Hale?"

Colt followed the general's eyes to an older gentleman seated in a chair at the conference table's end. "Good afternoon, Secretary Garrett. I'm Spencer Hale, and I have a story to share with you."

Everyone in the room was captivated as Spencer Hale described his brief role in the Vietnam War's last hours. He talked about his job at the CIA station and that the deputy chief of station asked him to destroy classified files. He described boarding the Air America helicopter to escape to the waiting Seventh Fleet ships, and he shared that agency morale was devastated after he returned to the Langley headquarters.

"In 1981, during the debriefing of a defecting KGB officer, we learned that they found the PYTHON file on the Pittman apartment floor. Apparently, I left it there after falling during a power outage. Nobody outright blamed me for causing the Soviet attack, but I knew I'd never complete a career at the agency. I resigned a year later and found work in the venture capital business."

Steve Holmes passed Colt a note that read, "He's *the* Spencer Hale, as in the Hale Broadcasting System, the Hale News Network, the Hale Sports Network, and the Hale Business Network."

Colt took another look at the man who just shared his story and suddenly recognized the cable TV mogul. "Mr. Hale, thank you for taking the time today to come to this brief and for shedding some light on this tragedy. I'm certain the staff has some national security forms for you to sign. It wouldn't do for any of this to appear on your network news."

"No problem at all, Mr. Secretary. Happy to be of assistance." The distinguished businessman stood and walked to the end of the table to shake Colt's hand. He leaned in close and quietly said, "Not a day has passed since I heard about the attack that I haven't thought about those poor souls. I'd be relieved to know if you can find their remains and bring them home. I'd be eternally grateful."

As Spencer Hale turned to leave the room, Colt could see the man's eyes were red and moist. Walking back to his office with Steve and Lenny, Colt said, "I'm seriously considering going to Cambodia on Wednesday with the MIA team, and we should add the PYTHON site to the visit list. Regarding the two PYTHON Base MIA, I think I know a person who may have a few answers."

US Marine Corps Base, Quantico, Virginia

Over forty years before Captain John Smith explored the Potomac River banks in 1608, the Spaniards had visited Quantico. Early Scottish colonists later settled in the Quantico area, growing tobacco for export. The region was also home to many Revolutionary War heroes. American, British, and French armies used nearby roads to move from one battlefield to another quickly. During the Civil War, Confederate cannons blockaded Union boats on the Potomac near Quantico. By the

1880s, speculators acquired the parcel, and eventually they would sell it to the Marines in 1917. Over one hundred years later, the 59,000-acre base would employ more than 28,000 military, civilian and contractor personnel and provide training facilities for more than thirty federal agencies. Just thirty-five miles south of Washington, DC, Marine Corps Base Quantico was also the Marine Corps Officer Candidate School's home. The ten-week program turned college-educated men and women into commissioned officers of the United States Marine Corps.

Colt Garrett listened to the OCS commanding officer speak to the more than 300 Marine officer candidates as they stood in formation on Quantico's parade field. The colonel talked for ten minutes, reminding the candidates of their challenges since starting the program. He reviewed the Corps' core values and welcomed them into what would be a life as a Marine. After the colonel completed his remarks, the master of ceremonies introduced the secretary of defense.

"General Wilber, Colonel Bodnar, parents, friends, and candidates. I'm particularly pleased to be here today to participate in this ceremony because I consider the oath you're about to take perhaps the most important moment of your career. When you graduated from college, your friends were seeking jobs in the civilian world, hoping someday to become officers of corporations or non-profits. In a moment, you will become officers of the United States of America, with responsibilities far beyond the corporate board room. The oath you are about to take requires you to preserve, protect, and defend the Constitution of the United States, not the president, prime minister, king, queen, or even me!" The officers and guests laughed at Colt's last words, unexpected from a cabinet member.

He continued, "This was a new idea at the time, that military officers should swear allegiance to a concept, rather than a person. I'd like you to think about that as you take your oath today. Remember the words: honor the commitment. And now, raise your right hand and repeat after me. I, state your full name, do solemnly swear that I will support and defend the Constitution of the United States against all enemies, foreign and domestic; that I will bear true faith and allegiance to the same; that I take this obligation freely, without any mental reservation or purpose of evasion; and that I will well and faithfully discharge the duties of the office on which I am about to enter. So help me, God. Congratulations, Lieutenants!"

Colt wanted to meet with the newly commissioned officers and their families, but instead he was surrounded by senior officers and their spouses seeking to make a good impression. Lenny Wilson stepped in to save his boss. "Excuse me, Mr. Secretary. I need to get you to your next event."

"Thank you, Mr. Wilson. I'm sorry, ladies and gentlemen, it looks like I have more work today. Thank you for letting me celebrate with you!"

The Quantico training complex operated more than forty-three live-fire ranges that supported training from small arms to explosive demolitions, from artillery fire to the delivery of live aerial munitions. Officers representing the FBI, DEA, CIA, Secret Service, US Capitol police, and the State Department trained at Quantico. But this evening, Colt and Lenny wanted to join Colt's protective service detail for their weapons qualification event.

"Okay, sir. Before we get started, I want to show you our newest addition to our protection arsenal." Chief Warrant Officer and Supervisory Special Agent Glenn Carpenter opened a small black ballistic nylon backpack, reached inside, and removed a small weapon with a curved magazine and a folded stock. Carpenter, a U.S Army Protective Services Battalion officer, led Colt's security team. The plainclothes squad of highly trained officers protected the defense secretary 24/7. "This is the Sig Sauer MPX pistol, with a folded arm brace. It's gas-operated and has a closed, rotating bolt. Its controls are the same as on our M4A1s. The magazine holds thirty rounds of 9X19 Parabellum ammunition and can fire at 850 rounds per minute."

Colt picked up the MPX and unfolded the arm brace. "It's so compact! How long is it?" Special Agent Carpenter placed the small automatic pistol on the bench. "It measures twenty-four inches long, but when I fold the brace, it shrinks to seventeen inches. The team calls it our "bag gun" because we carry it in this small backpack. Would you like to fire a few rounds, sir?" Colt fired two full magazines at the target, removed the magazine, and checked to see that the bolt was locked back and the safety was in the "on" position.

"That's amazing, Glenn. Thanks for letting me try it!" The rest of the protection detail shot their service pistols for qualification, while Colt and Lenny shot their personal weapons. Lenny shot his Glock 19, a 9mm semiautomatic pistol he usually kept at home in a safe, while his boss shot the firearm he received as a gift from his old friend Admiral Kurt Shaffer, commander, US Seventh Fleet. The Combat Elite in 9mm was manufactured by Colt Defense and featured the model 1911 design invented by John Browning. Colt Garrett preferred the classic pistol with its heavy stainless-steel frame and slide to Lenny's polymer-framed Glock. And he was a fantastic shot.

"Damn," exclaimed Special Agent Carpenter after comparing his target results with Colt's. "You still know how to handle that thing, Mr. Secretary!"

Colt smiled as he set the pistol on the bench and made sure it was safe. He wiped the gunpowder residue from the pistol's slide and frame before placing it into the range bag. "I think this pistol and I understand one another. We're the two oldest things on the range today! How do you like your new service pistol?"

Glenn Carpenter handed the new Sig Sauer M18 pistol to Colt. "I have to admit I was skeptical when I heard we had to trade in our M11s for these new polymer-framed models. But the trigger is amazing, particularly for a striker-fired mechanism. The balance is great, and the interchangeable grips mean it fits a wider range of hand sizes. And when you consider the M18 carries two additional rounds, I think the Army made the right choice. Go ahead and shoot a magazine or two." Colt inserted a full magazine into the weapon, racked the slide to chamber a round, and fired seventeen rounds at his target.

"That's a fine weapon, Glenn," commented Colt as he handed the M18 back to Special Agent Carpenter. "I might have to think about picking one up!"

The Bridge, USS Robert McNamara (DDG-145)

One of the many privileges of attaining command of a Navy ship was having an upholstered chair on the ship's bridge. Commander Ron Leach sat in his perch on the bridge's starboard side and gazed out of the windows to the ship's bow and then beyond to the white-capped waves of the South China Sea. The large, guided-missile destroyer cruised within her assigned station at a comfortable twenty knots, or twenty-three miles per hour. Ron remembered that he first heard the term knot when he was a midshipman at the US Naval Academy. Meaning one nautical mile per hour, the term dated from the 1600s when seamen measured a ship's speed through the water with something called a "log." The tool consisted of a length of rope with evenly spaced knots tied to a piece of wood. The piece of wood was lowered into the water from the ship's stern and allowed to pay out freely as the chunk of wood fell behind for a period measured by an hourglass. After the time had passed, a sailor grabbed the line and counted the number of knots between the sailor's hand and the piece of wood.

The ship's speed was said to be the number of knots counted. Ron appreciated that the Navy had embraced so many ancient traditions of the sea while simultaneously incorporating and perfecting the most advanced technologies in the world. Most of the traditions he loved the most were those he learned during those four years at Annapolis. Ron wondered what the friends he made there nearly two decades earlier were going to think of him after his court-martial and likely prison sentence. And he had other problems as well.

Diane's lawyer's letter contained her divorce settlement offer, and she pretty much wanted everything he owned. The criminal investigation had further damaged their struggling marriage. Diane was embarrassed by the incident and had contacted her dad's attorney for help. She'd also get half his retirement pay, assuming the Navy allowed him to keep it, and she wanted him to sell the summer home and give her half of the equity. He owed money to his high-priced lawyer for defending him against the Navy corruption charges, and his financial woes would force him to sell his small sailboat and his gun collection to pay off some gambling debts. Thinking of his lawyer, he recalled the defense secretary's rejection of his offer to help the Navy avoid further embarrassment in exchange for dropping the charges. Ron's lawyer mentioned that Garrett had personally rejected the offer. Apparently, the secretary had been insulted and riled by Ron's attempt to, in his words, blackmail the DOD. "Well," he thought, "I wonder if Garrett would have the guts to say that to my face. Probably not!"

"Excuse me, Captain. Here's the night orders book for your signature. I added the requirement to call you if the Chinese destroyer closes within two miles." Ron nodded to Kathy Robertson. "Thanks, XO. I'll have dinner up here this evening. It looks like it's going to be a beautiful sunset." He opened the logbook, reviewed the notes that his executive officer had prepared, and signed the last page. He handed the book back to Kathy and watched her speak with the OOD before leaving for dinner in the wardroom with the other officers.

"Captain. Sounding and Security reports all secure."

"Thank you, Juan. Isn't the sky gorgeous this evening?"

The officer of the deck answered, "Yes, sir. It sure is."

The young ensign's curt reply to his captain's question reflected how most crew members felt toward their commanding officer. Most believed he would be relieved for cause when the ship returned to port in a few days, and rumors of Petty Officer Lewis' sexual harassment accusations against him had widely circulated throughout the ship's crew on top of that.

"God, what was I thinking?" Ron Leach thought. "Lewis was always flirting with me, touching me whenever she passed me in the passageway. I thought she was interested, and now this harassment complaint!" Forgetting that he asked the XO to have his dinner sent up to the bridge, he climbed down from his chair and left for his cabin. As he descended the ladder, he heard someone on the watch team shout, "Captain's off the bridge!"

Day Six

The Oval Office, the White House

The wording of the twenty-second amendment to the United States Constitution could not be more precise:

Section 1. No person shall be elected to the office of the President more than twice, and no person who has held the office of President, or acted as President, for more than two years of a term to which some other person was elected President shall be elected to the office of President more than once. But this Article shall not apply to any person holding the office of President when this Article was proposed by Congress, and shall not prevent any person who may be holding the office of President, or acting as President, during the term within which this Article becomes operative from holding the office of President or acting as President during the remainder of such term.

Harrison's team of Justice Department lawyers and political advisors had spent more than a month analyzing that single paragraph, attempting to find a glimmer of hope, some previously undiscovered loophole, that might support Bill's attempt to run for a third term. After all, Franklin D. Roosevelt had been elected president of the United States for a record four teams. Only his death caused by a cerebral hemorrhage in 1945 prevented FDR from running for a fifth, or even sixth, term. That all changed on February 27, 1951, when the states ratified an amendment that effectively limited an individual from serving more than two four-year terms as president. Ronald Reagan's administration suggested modifying the amendment in 1985, and in the following years, both Democrats and Republicans had made similar attempts. None had been successful. That was why Bill found himself in the Oval Office this Tuesday morning with Vice President Maria Hernandez discussing candidates for her administration's national security team. The meeting wouldn't have been necessary if he could run for a third term, which he thought he could easily win.

Bill's chief of staff, Eric Painter, sat next to the president on a beige sofa while Vice President Maria Hernandez and her campaign strategist, Samantha Winchell, sat on the matching couch facing the two men. The president looked down at the luxurious carpet at his feet bearing the President of the United States seal. "I'm going to miss this room," he thought as he glanced up at the dark-suited Secret Service agent standing near the office door. Bill still marveled at how the agents' expressions never changed, regardless of the topic discussed in the world's most impressive office.

"Madam Vice President, where shall we start?" asked President Harrison while he helped himself to one of the lemon cookies from a plate on the coffee table between the two sofas. Before Maria could respond, Eric Painter offered, "I think the president is asking if you are any closer to making a final decision regarding your national security team."

Maria looked to her left in time to see a smile cross Samantha's face. The two women had previously shared their opinion of Eric Painter's tendency to mansplain, regardless of a woman's competence or level of experience. Maria had experienced the phenomenon throughout her entire career in politics and knew it was better at times to ignore the behavior rather than confront it.

"Mr. President," she began, "I saw Colt's interview on 60 Minutes Sunday evening, and I've given serious consideration to your recommendation that I retain him. I understand I need to gather the right mix of advisors, particularly in areas where I have less direct experience. Samantha and I believe the campaign's success will depend upon convincing the public that a Hispanic woman can effectively govern this country, and secondly, that I am that woman. I know you're a strong supporter of me keeping Colt in the administration, but I'd like to hear what Eric has to say about the choice. He knows more about election strategy than anyone I know, and I believe he was involved in your decision to nominate Colt as secretary of defense after Pat O'Kane died. I'm particularly interested in getting Eric's take on a candidate for National Security advisor, given Secretary Unger's recent health issues."

Eric Painter had been advising Bill Harrison since their first political campaign to get Bill elected as Florida's attorney general. Many considered Painter to be the most influential of the party's strategists. He saw opportunities when others saw problems, and he prided himself on being prepared for what he considered obvious questions.

"Madam Vice President, without question, former Secretary Unger would be the best choice to serve as your National Security advisor. His long career as a diplomat and his previous experience leading the state department would provide your team with a balanced approach to foreign policy. Colt Garrett has a reputation for being a bit abrupt when dealing with foreign leaders and the press. Having both men on your team will allow you to hear from different perspectives, and better decisions will result."

"And Garrett?" asked Maria. "You championed his appointment as defense secretary. Are you having second thoughts about his performance over at the Pentagon?"

"Not at all, Madam Vice President; he's doing amazing work

across the river. It's just that sometimes his views regarding national defense can be a bit hawkish, and I think you'll need to get other perspectives before making crucial decisions."

Maria thought for a moment and then said, "Thank you, Eric. I appreciate your insight and candor. I have a meeting with Mr. Garrett later this morning. I'll let you gentlemen know my decision regarding my national security team selections later this week."

St. Francis Island, The West Indies

The charter airplane's main landing gear softly touched down on the island's sole runway as it taxied next to a single-story passenger terminal that appeared severely in need of repainting. Sean had never flown in a Cessna Conquest II before, but he enjoyed the short morning flight in the twin turboprop from Miami to the small island nation. The small charter plane felt quite roomy because he was the sole passenger in an airplane designed to carry nine.

"Mr. Thomas, sir, how long do you expect your meeting will last?"

Sean looked at his wristwatch and replied, "I should be back in two hours. Are you planning to refuel for the trip back to Miami?"

"No, sir. We've got plenty of fuel. Besides, I'd rather not put any of what they're pumping into our tanks." Sean glanced out the window and noticed the rusting fuel truck parked near the dilatated passenger terminal. "I hear you!" he said as he descended the plane's stairs. "I'll call you when I'm on my way back to the airport."

As the two pilots began preparing the small plane for its

return flight, the copilot commented, "Did you notice that guy was wearing a gun? I saw it when he got up to use the toilet." The pilot turned to his younger colleague and replied, "When we fly charters for that agency, I find it's best not to notice anything."

Sean Thomas paid the taxi driver with cash and stepped out onto the cement courtyard. He showed the guard his credentials and walked into the ancient prison. After meeting with the prison commandant and confirming his identity once more, the guard led Sean down several dark and damp hallways until stopping in front of a heavy steel door. The silent guard opened a series of locks, pushed the rusted door, and motioned Sean inside before locking it behind him.

"Good morning! It's Special Agent Thomas? Yes! Always a pleasure to see a familiar face! I don't get many visitors, but you already know that. Please have a seat. I'm afraid I cannot offer you a beverage, but I know you'll forgive me."

Sean stepped into the small cell and sat down at the wooden table across from the frail, grey-haired prisoner. Colonel Dimitri Petrov stared back at the FBI counterintelligence agent, wondering what had brought the American all this way to visit him, a former Russian military spymaster. It had been more than a year since the FBI had finished interrogating Petrov for his role in Secretary Garrett's attempted assassination while he was on an American aircraft carrier. The FBI had framed Petrov for the murder of a Russian intelligence officer and was illegally and secretly holding him prisoner in this filthy prison, keeping him alive should he be of future value. "Tell me, Special Agent Thomas, why are you here?"

"I'd like to learn what you know about a Russian assault on a US base in Cambodia following the fall of Saigon. It's not a high priority, but we're looking to confirm some information we gained from other sources."

Sean watched as the older man stood and paced the floor. "That was a long time ago, my friend. I'm getting to be an old man with a fading memory. Why should I trouble myself with this task? What would I get in return, my freedom?"

"I think we both know that's not going to happen, Colonel. I might be able to arrange for you to get some fresh air, say, once a week? It would have to be after dark."

"Of course, you're concerned that my country's surveillance resources might identify me in the light of day. That would never do." Petrov stopped pacing and sat back down at the small table. "Even in the dark, it would be pleasant to leave this cell and breathe the clean ocean air. Perhaps I do recall a few Soviet operations conducted after your country ended that terrible war. Did you bring a notepad, young man?"

The Vice President's Office, the White House

"Thank you for meeting with me this morning, Secretary Garrett. How was traffic?"

Secretary of Defense Colt Garrett wondered why the Vice President had asked for the meeting, but he was reasonably sure it wasn't to talk about Washington traffic. He suspected she wanted to discuss the defense department's recommendation for Base Realignment and Closures, or BRAC, in the upcoming budget. Annually the defense department identified military bases to be consolidated or eliminated in the interest of efficiency and cost reduction. Still, the influence of local and federal politicians often made such reductions impossible. The former governor of Texas was known to be a strong supporter of her state's fifteen military bases and the over 100 billion dollars they annually contributed to the Texas economy. Most of the installations were located near San Antonio and Corpus Christi and stabilized the local economy when times were tough.

"The traffic was fine, Madam Vice President. What can I do for you?"

"Let's make ourselves a bit more comfortable, shall we?" she asked as she motioned to the two upholstered chairs next to the fireplace. "And please call me Maria, and you go by Colt?"

Joining the vice president in a chair by the fireplace, he answered, "Colt would be fine."

Crossing her legs and smoothing her dress, Maria began. "Colt, I'd like to understand your level of interest in continuing as defense secretary in my administration, should I be elected. This isn't a formal offer, you understand. I'm just trying to create a shortlist of potential cabinet members so that the campaign can start the vetting process. I'd like to have the team at least informally identified so that they could start developing policy initiatives and getting ahead of the inevitable press questions regarding where my administration would stand on domestic and foreign policy issues."

Colt couldn't have been more surprised. The press had speculated that Maria would bring someone from outside the beltway to run the defense department. Someone like Robert McNamara, the former president of Ford Motor Corporation. McNamara had served as defense secretary in the Kennedy and Johnson administrations. His preference for using systems analysis as a basis for making critical decisions on force requirements, weapon systems, and other matters caused much debate. Several executives running major defense corporations had publicly expressed interest in "helping" the defense department acquire new weapons systems. Colt assumed that one of these company presidents would be Maria's choice to lead her defense department.

"Maria, thank you very much for considering me to be a potential member of your cabinet. I do need to tell you I have been planning on leaving government service after President Harrison's term is over." He looked down at his hands for a moment. "You see, my wife's death changed everything for me. My son is stationed at Pax River, but my daughter and her family live on the West Coast. That's where Linda and I lived. I don't see myself as a career cabinet prospect; I sort of fell into this job."

Maria was surprised by Colt's response to her offer. He appeared to thrive in the role, and most people, including President Harrison, agreed he had performed admirably. It was a rare thing in Washington that someone would turn down an offer to serve on the president's cabinet, and she found herself becoming intrigued. "He does just say what he thinks," she thought. "I get that he feels lonely after his wife died; I feel as if I'm alone as well. But the prospect of becoming the president of the United States is just too great an opportunity to pass up."

Maria stood up and offered Colt her hand. "Thank you, Colt, for stopping by this morning. I appreciate you speaking frankly with me, but I'd like you to consider my offer and set up another meeting to talk in more detail. I think we could do great things together, and I'd ask you to reconsider your position on continuing as defense secretary."

After Colt left her office, Maria Hernandez selected a folder from her desk drawer titled Colton Garrett and reviewed the background file prepared by her campaign manager. She started to make some notes on a pad of paper. "And here I thought I was the one who would decide who my defense secretary would be. Colt Garrett might have a vote as well."

Defense Secretary's Office, the Pentagon

Colt Garrett sat at his office conference table with his two most trusted confidants, Deputy Defense Secretary Steve Holmes and Special Assistant Lenny Wilson. The three men had worked together for many years and trusted one another implicitly.

"It sounds to me as if you've already decided to go on tomorrow's trip to Cambodia, sir. Perhaps instead of discussing the merits of you going or not, it might be a more efficient use of this meeting to step through how you got to the decision; then, Lenny and I can attempt to challenge the logic of you taking this personal risk." Colt Garrett wasn't offended by his deputy's direct approach; it was one of the man's best attributes. Referring to his notes, Colt began describing how he came to his decision.

"Let's start with the obvious. As you know, I have a strong personal and professional interest in the Vietnam MIA issue. I acknowledge that interest has impacted my decision, but I don't think that interest disqualifies me from dealing with the issue objectively. So, the facts? On Friday morning, Representative Michele Phan received a communication from her fraternal uncle claiming that he witnessed the execution and burial of two American servicemen by what appeared to be Russian soldiers. The execution reportedly occurred in a Phnom Penh prison in the days following Saigon's fall in 1975. We don't know if Ms. Phan's uncle witnessed the event or even if her uncle sent the communication she received. The man claims to have photographic evidence of the American servicemen in a prison cell before their execution, photos of the burial after the execution, and close-ups of the Russian soldiers. He claims he can identify the location of the buried bodies." Steve and Lenny took copious notes while Colt continued with his timeline.

"In an attempt to verify the story, yesterday we were briefed by SOCOM that indeed the US did have ground forces in Cambodia in 1975 at a covert SOG base named PYTHON located near the Vietnam border. The base reported an attack by Soviet forces on May 4, 1975. The US listed two servicemen as MIA, and Army intelligence assessed the Russians possibly captured the men. The United States government has not investigated the PYTHON site. Coincidentally, the DPAA will be heading to Cambodia tomorrow to conduct their annual Joint Field Activity to examine several previously exploited locations. I've decided to go with the team and to ask Representative Phan to accompany me, as well. The DPAA has added the PYTHON site to the team's mission package. I'd like to add a side visit to Phnom Penh to meet with Representative Phan's uncle, take his testimony, receive his evidence and, if possible, locate and exhume any MIA remains. I guess that's it. What are your questions or concerns?"

Steve Holmes looked through his notes and removed his glasses. "Sorry, Mr. Secretary. I still don't see why you need to go yourself. I can understand why you want to go, but I don't think your interest in the issue justifies the trip's high-risk profile. Have you talked with your CID protection team about the trip? I can't imagine they're happy. And have you considered the COVID-19 risks? I know you're fully vaccinated, but they seem to keep finding new strains, and I'd hate for you to pick up something on the trip that gets you sick or worse. I have no plans to succeed you as SECDEF! Lenny?"

Lenny Wilson poured himself a cup of coffee, took a sip, and turned to face Colt. "I'm not on board with this one, boss. The risk profile is too high, and the timing couldn't be worse. We're getting congressional push-back on the defense appropriation and, no offense to Mr. Holmes, but when the members call to ask questions, they want to speak with the secretary, not the deputy. And the whole story about the prisoners' execution at the S-21 prison seems unlikely. It sounds like some sort of conspiracy theory. I guess I must be the one to bring up the problem of traveling with Representative Phan? I mean, the press could make a big deal out of it, particularly with you being recently single."

"I'm widowed, Lenny, not single." Colt stood up from the table and looked out the office windows. He shook his head at the suggestion, reminding him of what his daughter had said.

Lenny was about to respond when Steve Holmes touched his arm. "I think what Lenny was trying to point out was that the optics might be bad. A slow news day can bring out the worst in the press."

Colt sat back down at the conference table and looked at Lenny. "I know what you meant. Sorry about my tone. It's not as if we'd be traveling as a couple, Lenny. Remember, this is a Joint Field Active recovery mission. There would be at least another forty people on the VC-32A; hardly fodder for a romance novel." The VC-32A was an Air Force Boeing 757-200 converted for military and government use, and some configurations included a complete office suite and a VIP cabin. Lenny wasn't sure the press couldn't create a story about the defense secretary taking a trip to exotic Cambodia with a congresswoman who happened to be a former beauty queen. Still, he felt he had made his point and decided not to press it further.

Turning to Steve, Colt said, "I hear your concern about letting personal concerns drive my decision. But my presence will signal to the entire defense department that we will never forget those left behind, and that we will do everything we can to bring the missing back home. Regarding the CID, I spoke with Glenn

Carpenter about the Cambodian trip, and he said he'd talk with his Protective Services Battalion bosses at Fort Belvoir to get their take. He said they wouldn't like it, but it wasn't their call. One other thing, gentlemen. If the Russians not only attacked that base but also executed two of our people afterward, I want to hold them accountable. I know, these things happen in war, but only if we let it."

Steve Holmes gathered his notes and stood up from the table. "Mr. Secretary, I can see you've already decided to go on this trip tomorrow. I just have two requests. First, that you agree to follow any direction the Army CID provides regarding your safety. Second, I think it would be a good idea to keep the information about Representative Phan's uncle and his story just between us. We can share the part about the PYTHON site visit; it's why we have Joint Field Activities. But the idea that the Russians might have executed two Americans, even if it were more than forty-five years ago, would be disastrous for Russia's reputation. Who's to say to what extent they might go to prevent the world from finding out what happened in a Khmer Rouge prison?"

Off The Record Bar, The Hay-Adams Hotel, Washington, DC

The Hay-Adams Hotel's website proudly proclaimed, "Steeped in rich history and surrounded by the most iconic institutions of our nation, The Hay-Adams is the downtown Washington, DC hotel for discerning guests. Enveloped by views of the White House, St. John's Church, and the scenic Lafayette Park, the 5-star accommodations at The Hay-Adams are the embodiment of refined residence. Marked by Washington, DC's most accommodating amenities and dedicated services, The Hay-Adams is the boutique hotel of choice for the modern luxury traveler." John Hay served as a personal secretary to President Abraham Lincoln and later as US ambassador to the United Kingdom and secretary of state under William McKinley and Theodore Roosevelt. Henry Adams was a historian, a Harvard professor, and the descendant of Presidents John Adams and John Quincy Adams.

This afternoon, Travis Webb sat in Off The Record, The Hay-Adams Hotel's famous basement bar. Travis loved the extensive cocktail menu, but today he chose the bar for its reputation as the city's best place to be seen and not heard. Not being overheard was a primary concern of Travis because this afternoon, he shared a table with a major in Russia's military intelligence organization, the GRU.

Becci Quinn thoroughly enjoyed leading the double life of a deep-cover Russian agent operating within the very heart of the capitalist empire. She knew she was much more intelligent and worked harder than most people she was assigned to surveil and hopefully get them to fully turn against their country. Becci found her life stimulating because she could be discovered at any moment and deported. Or something much worse. She took another sip of her Manhattan and asked, "Travis, did you do as I asked?"

He briefly glanced around at the other red-cushioned booths and replied in a hushed tone, "Yes, I offered him the chocolates, and he took several. I was surprised because of his diabetes. I mean, what could the old man have been thinking?" Becci knew the national security advisor had a sweet tooth, and the chocolates she asked Travis to offer his boss were Jonathan Unger's favorite: Rodger's Chocolates from Victoria, British Columbia. The treats had been impossible to obtain in the

United States since the Canadian border had been closed due to COVID-19. Becci used Russian diplomatic couriers to bring the chocolates over the northern border.

"Why did you want me to give him those chocolates? Are you trying to give him a diabetic reaction?"

Becci smiled. "Let's talk more about that in a moment." She took another sip from her cocktail and asked, "What was it that you needed to tell me that couldn't have waited for our usual meeting?"

Travis glanced around the room to be certain he couldn't be overheard. "It's about Garrett. I know you've been looking for an opportunity when he's out of the country. I just learned that he's planning on joining the MIA mission to Cambodia. The plane departs Joint Base Andrews tomorrow afternoon. I know it's landing at Siem Reap in northern Cambodia, but I don't have the rest of the itinerary yet."

Becci knew Moscow was keenly interested in the defense secretary's overseas travels. She would need to send a message with the information to GRU headquarters during the next transmission window. She was forming the message's elements in her mind when Travis interrupted her thoughts.

"I don't know what you're planning, but I wouldn't lose any sleep if something, you know, should happen to Colt Garrett. The president should have me as defense secretary instead of him. I don't know what he was thinking." The president was thinking he had wanted to distance himself from Travis Webb after photos surfaced of him in blackface at a college party. The GRU was less than pleased when a blogger posted the pictures because they were using their existence as leverage against Travis. But their concerns were unfounded because Travis didn't need to be blackmailed; all he needed was money. And lots of it. His gambling losses had continued to accumulate, and his only relief came from high-interest loans provided by loan sharks and their organized crime bosses. When these loans became impossible to repay, Travis became a very attractive target for foreign intelligence agents.

"I understand your negative opinion of the defense secretary, but your position and effectiveness as deputy national security advisor require you to put these personal issues aside. Your path to success in the Harrison administration does not flow through the defense department anymore. Jonathan Unger's health appears to be declining every week; one never knows what the future could bring for you, but I am imagining it as very lucrative. Keep that in mind, please. The national security advisor is the most influential policy position in American foreign policy. And it doesn't have the additional overhead of having to manage the largest department in the government."

Travis whispered, "What was in those chocolates?"

Becci crossed her legs and licked her lips. "Travis, be a dear and order me another Manhattan!"

US Army Protective Service Battalion, Fort Belvoir, Virginia

The US Army Protective Services Battalion (CID) was headquartered at Fort Belvoir, Virginia. The battalion's mission was to provide worldwide, executive-level protection to the secretary of defense, the deputy secretary of defense, the chairman and vice-chairman of the Joint Staff, the secretary of the Army, the chief of staff of the Army, the vice chief of staff of the Army, the chief of the National Guard Bureau, and their foreign counterparts on official visits to the United States.

Lieutenant Colonel Mike Castro enjoyed his twenty-year career as a military policeman and was eagerly looking forward to being selected for promotion to colonel by next month's board. Exchanging the silver oak leaf on his uniform for the silver eagle of a full-bird colonel would mean he would be assured of a thirty-year Army career and its associated retirement benefits. Mike Castro felt lucky when he received orders to assume the Protective Service Battalion command three years ago. Although most military police considered protection duty outside of traditional police investigative work, protective services officers developed close relationships with the senior Army officials they protected. Those relationships could be beneficial to those seeking career advancement.

Mike Castro had taken full advantage of his position as commander of the Protective Service Battalion to personally brief every official under the battalion's protection about the scope of services he provided and to convey his personal assurance of their safety. During his tour, there had not been a single instance of a protected "principal" becoming endangered. His goal was to maintain that perfect record until the day another officer relieved him of command. But this afternoon, Supervisory Special Agent Glenn Carpenter has just informed him of the defense secretary's plan to fly to Cambodia on an MIA investigation and recovery mission.

"Why the hell is Garrett insisting on this trip? Doesn't he understand the risks he's taking and the protection challenges the trip presents for us? God, this is a nightmare! We can't even depend on host nation support. Did you try to talk him out of it?"

Glenn Carpenter sat across the conference room table from the battalion's commander and was privately amused by the man's reaction to the news that Garrett would be heading to Cambodia. Glenn had been a protective service officer for the last twenty-five years and had seen many other men and women serve as battalion commanders. They all wore the crossed gold pistols branch insignia indicating they were members of the Military Police Corps, but none of them had ever served as protective services officers. Their tour in the battalion was just one brief stop in a long career, and few understood executive protection. Glenn wore the dark suit of a plainclothes special agent. In contrast, Lieutenant Colonel Castro wore the new Army green service uniform, a historical nod to the uniforms worn by those who served in World War II and Korea. The two men's experiences and perspectives were as different as the clothes they wore to work.

"Yes, sir. I made the secretary aware of the risks he'd be taking on the trip and that our ability to protect him would be limited. The president has already approved Garrett's travel, so I think it's a done deal. I think we should focus on selecting our team and what remote assistance headquarters will be able to provide."

"Nora, what's your take?"

Major Nora Hall was aware of Mike Castro's stress and knew he was grasping at straws in search of some way to keep Garrett off that plane.

"Sir, I have to agree with Glenn. Garrett's well aware of his exposure whenever he leaves the Pentagon, or even his residence for that matter. I was here when the GRU attempted to kill him on the Reagan. He's seen the intel suggesting they might try again. It seems to me that Secretary Garrett has accepted the risks of his job, and he's determined to make this trip to Cambodia. My advice to you, sir, is to not get in his way."

Mike Castro thought about what his second-in-command had just recommended. He slammed his fist on the conference table, causing Nora to startle and Glenn to brush his coat jacket back with his right hand instinctually. "Damn it, Nora! But you're right, I'm sure. There's nothing much I can do about this. I just hope everything goes well. Why can't the guy just stay in Washington?"

Glenn Carpenter knew he was pushing his commander, but he felt that twenty-five years as a special agent gave him a license to speak his mind. "Well, sir, unless you're planning to reduce the battalion's mission scope from worldwide to just the 202 area code, I'd say this is what we get paid to do."

Nora Hall closed her office door after Glenn Carpenter walked in. "Jesus, Glenn. Did you have to make that crack about the battalion's mission? You know Castro's just trying to make colonel. I thought the man was going to burst a vein. I'll need to deal with him later. Now, what can I do to help you get ready for the mission?"

"Sorry about that, Major," Glenn said as he took a seat. "I suppose that was the 'Bad Glenn' you're always talking about."

"Okay, he'll be fine. I've looked at your recommendation for the protection detail. You seem to have picked the best."

"I'm limited to a team of only six agents, including myself. Here's my equipment and weapons requisition. I also worked up a travel budget estimate. The Office of the Secretary of Defense will reimburse CID, but we still need the authorization to expend the funds."

Major Hall looked through the documents that Glenn handed her and added her signature where he had indicated. "Glenn, why do you need this personal weapon authorization? A 1911 pistol?" She signed the form and handed the stack of papers back to the senior agent.

"That's not for me; it's for Garrett. He wants to bring his personal sidearm on this trip." When he saw the concerned look on Major Hall's face, he said, "Look, if things go south, I could use the extra gun." As he was about to leave Nora's office, he turned and said, "At least we know he can shoot!"

River's Edge Conference Center, NAS Patuxent River, Maryland

"Dad and Jillian, allow me to present Captain DeAngelo, Pax River's CO, and Mrs. DeAngelo, Commander Holt, VX-23's skipper, and Mrs. Holt. You've previously met Lieutenant Clarke."

Colt Garrett and Jillian Murdoch walked around the table and greeted each person. It was apparent from the look on his face how pleased Captain DeAngelo was that the defense secretary had agreed to attend the Navy birthday gala. The base conference center was packed with naval officers in dinner-dress blue uniforms, featuring a short black mess jacket with three buttons on either side, worn open with a white shirt, black bow tie, and gold cummerbund. Gold embroidered stripes to indicate rank and miniature medals to display personal and service awards completed one of the Navy's most impressive uniforms. The attire was black tie for civilians, and Colt felt a bit out-of-place, not wearing his old uniform. But it would have been inappropriate for the defense secretary to wear a uniform, even if he had earned the right as a retired Navy captain. The Constitution prohibited a current member of the military from serving as defense secretary.

Jillian Murdoch turned to Colt. "So, what are you planning to say in your speech tonight? It must be nice to have a speechwriter on your staff."

Dan watched with interest as his father responded, "No speech tonight, Jillian. But Commander Holt has asked me to help with the missing-man table ceremony. Can I refill your wine glass, Rebecca?"

Mrs. DeAngelo cleared her throat and then asked Rebecca, "Tell me, dear, how did you and Dan first meet? You certainly make an attractive couple." The base commander's wife made it her business to know the details of any personal relationships at Pax River.

Rebecca glanced at Dan. "We met while I served on the Reagan, and Dan was in VAQ-132. After my tour ended, I requested duty at Pax River to continue to see each other. I'm a surface warfare officer but I'm applying to the Defense Acquisition Corps selection board. I'd like to work on major systems acquisition projects."

"A surface warfare officer, working on aircraft acquisitions? Do you think you are qualified for that type of duty, dear?"

Dan Garrett tried his best not to change the expression on his face as he looked at his date. He didn't know how she would reply to Mrs. DeAngelo's slight, but he suspected it would be memorable.

Lieutenant Rebecca Clarke smiled at Mrs. DeAngelo and said, "Oh, I don't know. You might be surprised by how capable some surface warfare officers are. Don't you agree, Secretary Garrett?"

Mrs. DeAngelo didn't understand why her table companions chuckled at Rebecca's answer because she was the only person at the table who didn't know that Colt Garrett had been a SWO while on active duty. Dan Garrett quickly changed the subject.

"Dad, Jillian mentioned you're flying out tomorrow on a trip to Cambodia? She said it's one of those MIA missions?"

"Yes. Probably be gone only a week or so." Turning to the others, he explained, "We visit Cambodia every year in an attempt to locate the remains of service people we might have left behind."

Mrs. DeAngelo looked confused. "But, Mr. Garrett, surely the defense secretary doesn't usually go on these trips. Why this one?"

"Some new information has recently come to light. The MIAs are of special concern, and I think my presence may be useful when dealing with the Cambodian government. Representative Phan from the National Defense Subcommittee will also be joining the team."

"Representative Michele Phan, from Washington's 7th District? She's stunning. Wasn't she a beauty queen?" Mrs. DeAngelo was proud that she knew something about Michele Phan, but she wished she hadn't mentioned it when she saw the look on Jillian's face. Captain DeAngelo came to his wife's rescue when he said, "Pete, I think it's time to kick things off." The commanding officer of Air Test and Evaluation Squadron Two Three, Commander Peter Holt, walked up to the podium and adjusted the microphone.

"Good evening! Our Navy traces its beginnings to the Continental Navy, established at the beginning of the American Revolution. On October 13, 1775, the Continental Congress decided to purchase two armed ships to attack British ships and keep their supplies from reaching British troops in America. Another resolution passed later that day, creating a naval committee to oversee the ships' purchase and write operations regulations. The Continental Navy was born, and October 13 remains the official birth date of the US Navy. And now, it is my high honor to introduce this evening's special guest. When the XO asked Lieutenant Commander Garrett if he'd ask his distinguished father to join us for the Navy's birthday celebration, Dan replied, 'Well, sir, what's in it for me?'"

The room erupted with laughter as Dan covered his face with his right hand. After the hoots and howls died down,

Commander Holt continued. "I don't know if a deal was made or not, but I did notice that JOKER hasn't been on the duty roster for the past two weeks. Probably just a coincidence!" The room erupted again. But of the several dinner rolls that were thrown at Dan, two hit his father. Captain DeAngelo was terrified that his career had just come to an abrupt end but then relaxed when he saw Colt smile.

Commander Holt continued, "Okay, people. Let's calm down before Mr. Garrett's security detail gets upset. Thank you. Now, I have a special treat for you. I've asked our guest to lead our missing-man ceremony. Without further ado, I present the United States secretary of defense, the Honorable Colton Garrett."

Everyone in the room stood and applauded as Colt walked to the podium and raised his hand. "Thank you, thank you very much. And please be seated ladies and gentlemen. I'd like to thank Captain DeAngelo and Commander Holt for inviting me to attend this evening's event. And if Lieutenant Commander Garrett benefited in any way from my attendance, then Commander Holt, you may consider it a direct order from me to give him double duty next week!"

Dan Garrett laughed with everyone else at his father's joke. He thought, "The old man still knows how to work a room!" He looked at Rebecca. "Damn, I'm glad she decided to dump the uniform and wear this dress!" Dan grabbed her knee under the table. Rebecca whispered, "You do realize you're exactly like him?" Dan smiled and whispered back, "I think I've finally grown up enough to understand that's a pretty good thing." Rebecca took a sip of red wine and thought, "I think I could marry this man."

Colt Garrett continued, "The National League of Families of American Prisoners and Missing in Southeast Asia's sole mission is to obtain the release of all prisoners, and the fullest possible accounting for the missing and repatriation of all remains of those who died during the Vietnam War. The league works closely with the Defense Department as we uphold our duty to ensure no one is left behind. I'd like to thank Commander and Mrs. Holt for inviting the league to set up a display at the rear of the room. Please consider donating to this amazing organization as you leave this evening."

"As you entered the room this evening, you may have noticed a special table; it's reserved to honor our missing service people. The six empty chairs represent Americans who were or are missing from each of the five services—and civilians, all with us in spirit. All Americans should never forget the brave men and women who answered our nation's call and served the cause of freedom. Let me explain the meaning of this table, and join me for a moment of silent prayer." Colt picked up a water glass and took a sip before continuing.

"The table is round—to show our everlasting concern. The cloth is white, symbolizing the purity of their motives when answering the call to serve. The single red rose reminds us of these Americans' lives and their loved ones and friends who keep the faith while seeking answers. The yellow ribbon symbolizes our continued uncertainty, hope for their return, and determination to account for them. A slice of lemon reminds us of their bitter fate, captured or missing in a foreign land. A pinch of salt symbolizes the tears of our missing and their families. The lighted candle reflects our hope for their return. The Bible represents the strength gained through faith to sustain us and those lost from our country, founded as one nation under God. The glass is inverted to symbolize their inability to share a toast. The chairs are empty. They are missing."

He looked around the now silent room and reached again for

his glass. "Let us now raise our water glasses in a toast to honor America's POW/MIAs, to the success of our efforts to account for them, and to the safety of all now serving our nation!"

After the dinner was over, Dan and Rebecca escorted Colt and Jillian to the center's door. He embraced his father and said, "Take care of yourself. Call me when you get back." On the drive back to Washington, Jillian asked Colt, "Why is Representative Phan going to Cambodia on this trip? I'm surprised an elected official would be willing to dedicate so much time on something unlikely to attract votes."

Colt decided to ignore Jillian's slight against politicians, and he answered, "Like I said earlier, she serves on the National Defense Subcommittee. Her father emigrated from Cambodia. I suspect she has personal reasons for going."

Jillian Murdoch looked out the window as the large, armored SUV sped along the highway. She thought, "Personal reasons? That's exactly what I was thinking."

Armat Drive, Bethesda, Maryland

Jonathan Unger, the national security advisor to the President of the United States, enjoyed living in the suburbs of the nation's capital. Only thirty minutes' drive to his office in the White House's West Wing, the 5,000 square-foot home of the former secretary of state sat on a two-acre lot that bordered the McCrillis Gardens. This five-acre property featured shady woodland walks and a rare collection of ornamental shrubs and trees. Jon and his wife Shelley enjoyed wandering the garden's paths while remembering the days when their children and grandchildren chased one another in what the family called their secret garden, hidden in the exclusive residential neighborhood. Jon told his friends that he had the best backyard in Bethesda and insisted on walking the garden's paths with friends and visitors to his home before sharing a meal in his beautifully furnished brick home. The Ungers no longer needed the five-bedroom house and were considering downsizing to something more manageable. The two-story building's stairs were becoming a challenge for Jon and Shelley, and they realized a rambler was more suited to people of their age. But whenever they started the process of finding a new place, they couldn't face the prospect of moving from the home where they raised their five children. Too many memories, joyful and painful, filled the house's rooms.

Today was an important day because after returning home from work, Jon told his wife he had decided to resign as national security advisor. The grandchildren had visited over the weekend, and when it came time to go to work on Monday morning, Jon realized he'd rather be spending the time with his family. He had attended Pat O'Kane's funeral at Arlington a few years earlier and remembered thinking that his friend Pat had worked until the day he died. Jon's physician had cautioned him during his annual exam to reduce his life stress before he suffered the same fate. After dinner, he joined Shelley in the living room. She was reading a novel while he worked on his latest book. Looking over at the woman he had married more than fifty years ago, he knew he was making the right decision to retire. They could make plans now to spend Christmas at their Vermont mountain cabin. Maybe the rest of the family would be willing to celebrate the season there. They could all be together, something his job had made much harder recently.

His only misgiving about retiring was the prospect that Travis Webb might succeed him. Travis was smart enough, and he had a good grasp of the issues. But the president needed to trust his national security advisor, and Jon knew there was something off with Travis. He couldn't quite pinpoint it, though. The man seemed to have an agenda of his own, and he had caught Travis on several occasions looking through his official papers. Jon decided he'd talk with the president about Travis Webb tomorrow when he submitted his resignation. A retiring federal official didn't typically have much leverage when naming his replacement, but Jon hoped he could prevent Travis from being considered.

"Jonathan, you look tired, dear. You can work on that book another time. Why don't you go to bed and read a bit? I want to finish this chapter, and I'll join you upstairs."

The bedroom was dark as Jon struggled to find the lamp switch. Finally successful, he could see the clock showed it was just after midnight. He had been asleep for only three hours. He wasn't sure what had awakened him, but he didn't feel well. He struggled getting out of bed, found his bathrobe and slippers, and made his way downstairs to the kitchen. Shelley stored his medicines on a high shelf in the pantry to keep them away from curious grandchildren. After checking his blood glucose levels and body temperature, Jon found a bottle of antacids to relieve the severe heartburn he experienced after getting up. "What did I eat for dinner? A green salad, pot roast, and mashed potatoes. Vanilla ice cream for dessert. Why is my heart racing?"

Pablo, the small tiger-striped cat that had adopted the Ungers last month, rubbed against Jon's leg and then stood in front of the sliding door leading to the deck. Jon let the cat out, filled a glass of water, and sat down at the kitchen table. He rested his head in his hands, elbows propped on the table, and started breathing deeply. He thought of waking Shelley but then decided to wait and see how he felt in a bit.

An hour later, he felt worse, and he realized the cat had not reappeared at the sliding door. He opened it, called the cat's name, and stepped outside onto the cedar deck. "I'll get the cat back in the house and then wake Shelley. God, I feel terrible!" He walked out into the large, manicured lawn and peered into the overgrown garden, trying to find his cat among the flowers and shrubs. He thought he saw something move and then yelled, "Pablo!" Jon looked back at the house and decided to make one more attempt to find the cat before going back inside. He walked into the garden and then grabbed his chest as he fell to the ground. Lying with his face in the cold and damp soil, Jon tried to call his wife's name, but no sound emitted from him. He felt something warm and soft on his cheek, and he thought, "Well, thank God I found the cat!" And then he felt nothing at all.

Day Seven

The West Wing, the White House

Deputy National Security Advisor Travis Webb spent an hour reviewing the morning intelligence summary, the president's daily brief. The PDB was a daily summary of high-level, all-source information and analyses on national security issues produced for the president and key cabinet members and advisers. The PDB is compiled and delivered by the Office of the Director of National Intelligence with contributions from the CIA and other intelligence community elements. It has been presented in some form to the American president since 1946. Travis found that the PDB gave him the best possible understanding of the threats facing America in the shortest amount of time. He felt confident that after absorbing everything included in the PDB, he wouldn't be surprised by any national security issue. What did surprise him was when the president's chief of staff knocked on his office door.

"Good morning, Travis. Do you mind if we speak for a moment? Perhaps it would be better if I close your office door." Without waiting for Travis to respond, Eric Painter stepped into the deputy national security advisor's office, closed the door, and sat in a chair facing Travis.

"Two hours ago, the Bethesda Fire Department, responding to a 911 call from Shelley Unger, found Jonathan lying unconscious in his backyard. He was pronounced dead at the scene. Shelley said he hadn't been feeling well and went to bed early. Apparently, Jonathan got up in the middle of the night, took some medicine, and went outside, perhaps after letting the cat out. Shelley is terribly upset, and the Unger family has started to gather. I just left the Oval, and the president has appointed you acting national security advisor, that is, if you're agreeable."

Travis began to sweat as it occurred to him that he just might have killed Jonathan Unger, with help from the Russians. It was only yesterday when he offered Jon a few pieces of Rodger's Chocolates from the box that Becci Quinn had handed him the day before. Of course, he had known that there must have been something harmful in the candy that Becci asked him to give to Unger. But Travis thought it would simply make the national security advisor ill or perhaps scare him into resigning. But now Jonathan Unger was dead and he was likely the person who, as an agent of Russia's GRU, just killed the national security advisor to the president. To top off the anvil-like irony, he had just been asked if he was willing to accept the president's request to succeed the man on an acting level. Aware that the chief of staff was watching him, Travis rubbed his dry eyes and did his best to appear shocked and humbled.

"Oh, my God! I spoke with Jon last night just before he left for home. He's seemed tired recently, and I know he was thinking about taking a three-day weekend. I'm just shocked . . . er, I don't know what to say."

The president's chief of staff was taken aback by Travis's response to learning about Unger's death. Just three days ago, Jonathan had been in Eric's office, practically demanding that Eric remove Travis as his deputy. Regardless, the president had sent him to determine if Travis was willing to serve as acting NSA.

"Travis, I didn't realize that you were so close to Jonathan. But I do need you to tell me if you would accept the president's appointment as acting NSA."

Travis Webb stood and announced, "Please convey to President Harrison I would be honored to serve as his national security advisor for as long as he may require."

An hour later, Acting National Security Advisor Travis Webb sat in the impressive West Wing corner office. President Harrison had made it very clear that his appointment was only temporary until Harrison could identify a permanent candidate. Still, Travis decided he would do everything he could to make the president change his mind.

Back in his new office, Travis enjoyed sitting in the expensive leather desk chair and put his feet up on the massive oak desk. He wasn't sure about what he should do next, but he was confident that the Russians would double his monthly payment, probably more! Travis looked at a stack of files on the desk and picked up the first one. The cover sheet was titled, "Colonel Dimitri Petrov interview request." Opening the file folder, Travis learned that the FBI had requested permission from the defense department for a special agent to visit the tiny nation-state, St. Francis Island. The file revealed the small country had imprisoned a Russian intelligence agent in an arrangement with the US government.

The next document that Travis examined was a defense department flight plan detailing the itinerary for an Air Force VC-32A. The aircraft's flight plan indicated the team would depart Joint Base Andrews on Thursday afternoon, with fuel stops at Joint Base Lewis-McChord near Seattle and Misawa Air Base in Japan. The itinerary listed the final destination as Siem Reap, a city in northern Cambodia. The final document in the former national security advisor's inbox requested local helicopter transportation from Siem Reap airport to a location near the Vietnam border. Listed under the heading, "Justification for Transportation," Travis read the secretary of defense would be visiting the site where Russian forces attacked an American outpost in the days following Saigon's fall at the end of the Vietnam War. This he saw as very valuable information for his handlers. He thought of the financial value of all this information.

Travis asked the receptionist to come into his new office. "Diane, please have a seat. How are you this morning? I know you and Jon were pretty close."

Diane Considine stood in the large office and carefully crafted her response to her new boss. She thought that Jonathan Unger was one of the most exemplary persons she had ever met and that Travis Webb certainly didn't deserve to sit in the man's chair. "Mr. Unger served his country for decades, and the National Security Council will miss him. Congratulations on your appointment, Mr. Webb. Is there anything I can do for you, sir?"

"Yes. Would you make a lunch reservation for two at Seasons? Let's say noon?"

"Yes, sir. And with whom will you be dining?"

Travis looked up from the papers on his desk, hesitated, but then said, "Becci Quinn."

Phnom Penh, Cambodia

Kiri Phan woke from a fitful sleep and rose from his straw-filled sleeping pad on the wooden house floor. He could feel a breeze blow up through the house's bamboo-slatted floor while he changed into a pair of cotton trousers and a white cotton short-sleeved shirt, the same clothes he wore every day. Kira had not slept in weeks because of pain caused by cancer as it progressed through his emaciated body. Sometimes dull and sometimes sharp, the pain seemed to radiate from his chest out to his limbs. The doctors gave him medication for the pain, but nothing seemed to help with the near-constant wheezing and coughing. Kiri's blood-stained pillow provided definitive evidence that his lung cancer was progressing quickly, and his life was soon coming to an end. He remembered watching his wife die, and he hoped his ending would be mercifully quick. Last week, he had visited the internet café hoping to receive a response to his email to his niece, but the man working on the computer told him that nothing was waiting for him. Kiri had told the young man about his lung cancer after he nearly collapsed in the tiny café.

The university student had asked, "Mr. Phan, would you like me to see what the internet has to say about your disease?" Kiri was amazed at how much the internet knew about lung cancer and what he should expect from the disease in the coming weeks. His prospects for recovery were nonexistent, and his death would unfortunately be painful. However, he suspected he now might know more about lung cancer than the government doctor in the local clinic.

Today, Kiri walked to the café again to check if a message from his niece was waiting for him, and he was pleased, excited, and a little afraid when the man working at the computer said, "Yes, Mr. Phan, there is a message for you. Shall I print it out?" He briefly read the email, carefully folded it, and placed it in his shirt pocket. He walked back to his wooden house, climbed the stairs to the living area, and reread the email.

"Dear Uncle Kiri. I was so surprised to receive your message. I found your note about the Americans to be very sad, and I am sorry that you had to experience such a horrific event. I realize it was a long time ago, but I can only imagine the pain you have carried all these years. I was sorry to learn that you lost your wife to cancer and now suffer from the same cruel illness. I have passed your information regarding the Americans to others who have researched what might have happened to those two young men. I am happy to tell you that a team of Americans is coming to Cambodia to investigate further. Perhaps the best part of my news is that I will be coming with the team, and I am looking forward to meeting you in person. I'll be leaving Washington tomorrow, and I'll email you again after I arrive in Siem Reap to arrange a time and place to meet you in Phnom Penh, probably later this week. Your loving niece, Michele."

Kiri walked over to the only piece of furniture he owned, an ancient and warped teak chest. Opening the trunk, Kiri removed a cardboard box containing several photographs, three rolls of developed negatives, and the small uniform patch the Russian soldier had given him decades earlier. He smiled at the thought he soon would be fulfilling the promise made to his wife. Then he could die in peace.

Russian Military Intelligence HQ, Moscow

General Igor Korobov carefully reviewed the urgent report sent by GRU Major Becci Quinn. He asked his aide to have a cup of black tea brewed and served to him in his office. His favorite tea was Russian Caravan, so named because it was initially imported from China in caravans using camels. Because the journey could take over a year to complete, the tea gained a unique smokey taste from the merchant's campfires. After his aide brought the tea on a serving tray with an assortment of shortbread cookies, General Korobov moved to an upholstered chair next to a roaring fire that eased the pain in his arthritic knees. He sipped the classic Russian tea from a podstakannick, an ornate silver holder with a handle that held a crystal tea glass.

"Sometimes," he thought, "the old ways are the best."

Major Quinn's report contained three vital pieces of intelligence. First, she had successfully executed the operation to replace Jonathan Unger as the president's national security advisor with Travis Webb. There was no indication that the authorities suspected that Unger's death had been caused by anything other than the elderly man's failing health. Unger had proven to be a worthy adversary for several years, and his removal from America's national security team was good news. Having a Russian agent serve as national security advisor was a feather in Korobov's cap and likely would bring him prodigious political gain.

Second, Quinn reported that Webb had learned Defense Secretary Colton Garrett was about to leave on an airplane destined for Siem Reap, Cambodia. The trip's itinerary and passenger manifest had revealed Garrett to be traveling with a small protective service team. Once in Cambodia, the Americans would take a helicopter to a small village near the Cambodia-Vietnam border. The report indicated the Americans planned to investigate a site they presumed was where Russian military forces attacked an American outpost in the spring of 1975.

Korobov finished his second cup of tea and the last cookie from the tray before returning to his desk. He checked the time and calculated that Garrett's plane would be taking off soon from the Maryland Air Force base headed for its first fuel stop in Washington state. General Korobov opened a thick black binder on his desk to a section titled "Current Special Operations." His chief of staff reminded him daily that the highly classified information was available to him on his computer. Still, the general insisted that his staff place important information into one of his desk binders. "The old ways are indeed the best." The binder indicated that one of his Spetsnaz teams was in Phnom

Penh, providing technical assistance to a Cambodian military exercise. Captain Nikhil Morozov and a squad of five other Russian special-purpose commandos had been in the city for more than a month and were scheduled to return to Moscow in ten days. General Korobov thought, "If they move quickly, Morozov's team could be in a position to solve the Garrett problem forever."

He then considered the third piece of information in Major Quinn's report. The Americans had imprisoned GRU Colonel Dimitri Petrov on a Caribbean island named St. Francis. The GRU staff had added the island's coordinates and a map indicating the island's location. The GRU had not heard from Colonel Petrov since the attempted assassination of Colton Garrett several years earlier. Petrov had killed another GRU agent before escaping to Canada, but the colonel had simply disappeared. He needed to immediately verify this intelligence. If it was accurate, he would need to initiate an operation before the Americans could move him to another location. General Korobov pressed a button on his desk and began making notes on a pad of paper.

"Yes, General." The tall chief of staff stood at attention as he waited for Korobov to finish making his notes.

"Colonel, first, have someone dig up any details about an attack our forces made on an American outpost in April 1975 in Cambodia, near Vietnam's border. We had very few operations in the region during that time, so it should be easy to find the required information. Next, immediately have the operations staff get in secure contact with Captain Morozov in Phnom Penh. I need to know his team's capabilities and readiness to relocate to an area near Snoul, east of Kampong Cham. And, Colonel, this is very important. I want you to personally contact our embassy in Phnom Penh and speak directly with our military attaché. Captain Morozov is going to require some special assistance from the Cambodian police. We've been providing military assistance for many years. It's time for them to return the favor."

The chief of staff listened intently to General Korobov without taking a note. His perfect recall was a useful skill.

"Colonel, I need you to direct a thorough search of this small island. There is an old prison on the island's northern coast, and I need to verify if Colonel Dimitri Petrov is being held there."

The chief of staff raised an eyebrow at the mention of Colonel Petrov. He knew Petrov and General Korobov had attended intelligence training together. General Korobov handed the Colonel the island's coordinates and the small map prepared for him.

"General, if we find that Colonel Petrov is imprisoned there, what are your orders?"

Korobov stood and walked over to the office window. He thought for a moment and replied, "Just find him, Colonel. And do it quickly!"

Joint Base Andrews, Maryland

The Boeing 757-200 was ready to board passengers as it sat on the tarmac fully fueled and provisioned for the first leg of the flight to Joint Base Lewis McChord, south of Seattle. The airplane's two Pratt & Whitney PW2000 high-bypass turbofan engines could carry the big jet more than 6,000 miles without refueling, at more than 520 miles per hour. But this 757 with tail number 75798-0002 was different from a typical Boeing jet because when the vice president was aboard, the plane used the callsign, Air Force Two. The 1st Airlift Squadron, 89th Airlift

Wing, maintained four identical VC-32A airplanes to provide safe, comfortable, and reliable transportation for America's leaders to locations worldwide. In addition to the vice president, other users included the president, the first lady, the cabinet, and Congress members. Communications were vital inside the aircraft. Senior decision-makers could conduct business worldwide using advanced telephones, satellites, television monitors, fax, and copy machines. The VC-32A's passenger cabin was dramatically different from other 757s. The first section had a communications center, galley, lavatory, and ten business class seats. The second section featured a completely enclosed VIP stateroom, including a private lavatory, entertainment systems, two first-class swivel seats, and a convertible couch that seated three and folded out to a bed. The third section included a conference room and senior staff facility with eight business-class seats. The fourth section of the cabin contained general seating with thirty-two business-class seats, a galley, two lavatories, and closets.

Colt Garrett walked up the steps leading to the blue and white colored airplane and noticed the words "UNITED STATES OF AMERICA" proudly painted on the plane's fuselage. "Welcome aboard, Secretary Garrett!" said a tall and physically fit Air Force lieutenant colonel. "I'm your pilot, sir. Steve Watkins. The crew is honored to be flying you and the Joint Field Activity team. We've been thoroughly briefed on your mission and wish we could remain in Cambodia and return with you and any remains you may find." Unfortunately, Colt was only able to use the VC-32A for the trip going to Cambodia. They had arranged for another DOD aircraft for the mission's return trip.

Colt shook the pilot's outstretched hand. "Thank you, Colonel. This will be my first flight in one of these airplanes.

A bit more comfortable than my usual ride." The defense secretary's usual ride was the massive E-4, Boeing's Advanced Airborne Command Post, a highly modified 747-200B that served as a survivable mobile command post for the National Command Authority, namely the president of the United States and the secretary of defense. The defense secretary always had one of the "Nightwatch" aircraft at his disposal. Still, Colt had requested a VC-32A for this mission because it could accommodate the entire Joint Field Activity team more comfortably.

"I'm sure you're aware that Representative Phan will be joining us. I realized that, as defense secretary, I'm the senior official onboard. But I trust that the crew will treat Representative Phan with the same degree of courtesy and deference shown me."

The senior Air Force pilot had been flying the special mission aircraft for over a year and was highly experienced in navigating delicate protocol intricacies. "Not to worry, Mr. Secretary. Representative Phan will be well treated. You have my word." As if on cue, Michele Phan walked up the stairway and entered the airplane.

"Hello, Secretary Garrett." Turning to the Air Force officer, she said, "I'm Michele Phan. I believe my office forwarded my security clearance information?"

"Yes, ma'am. Welcome aboard. You'll be assigned one of the seats in Secretary Garrett's suite for takeoff. Please let any of the crewmembers know if we can do anything to make your flight more comfortable."

As the flight crew prepared for takeoff, Colt and Michele made their way along the aisle to the VIP suite. Michele noticed a blue circular seal on the suite's cabin wall. "The defense secretary's seal. I'm impressed!" She kidded Colt and enjoyed that the seal's presence had embarrassed him. "I suppose they have a box of those things in the hanger," he muttered.

After the plane leveled off at 30,000 feet, the pilot keyed the intercom mic. "Ladies and gentlemen, this is Lieutenant Colonel Watkins, the aircraft commander. I hope you enjoy this flight to Joint Base Lewis-McChord, where we will refuel before continuing onto our next leg to Misawa, Japan. The weather looks clear to Lewis-McChord, so feel free to move about the airplane unless things get bumpy."

Michele and Colt unfastened their seatbelts and unlocked their seats so that they could face one another. "I want to thank you again, Colt, for asking me along on this trip. It means a lot to me."

Colt found himself liking this attractive woman and hoped he hadn't let that influence his decision to invite her. "Michele, I wouldn't be going on this mission myself if you hadn't shared the information from your uncle's email. I decided you deserve to find out first hand if his story is true, and you can meet the man."

Michele nodded and pulled a budget document from her briefcase. She thought, "And it will provide an opportunity for me to get to know you better."

Dan Garrett's Apartment, Lexington Park, Maryland

Dan had just finished his dinner when his laptop chimed, and his older sister, Allie, appeared on the video screen. "Hey, brother. What's up?"

Allie and Dan had been inseparable when growing up in Cedar Street's big home, constantly competing in everything from athletics to schoolwork. If there was a way to measure something, each sibling wanted to best the other. When Allie entered college, they grew apart somewhat, developing distinct personalities and forming relationships with different friends. After college, Allie went to grad school. Dan attended another university and left home when he joined the Navy. Long-distance phone calls were replaced with texts and the occasional video calls, but the brother and sister continued to lead separate lives, and Allie eventually married Kyle.

"Not much. How's Kyle?"

"He still works too much. It's good that we see each other at work and home, but sometimes it would be nice to have some time on my own. I was thinking of coming out to DC for a visit next month. It'd be nice to see you."

"Sure, Allie. That'd be great. I know Rebecca would like to see you again. I've been busy with the new F-35 testing program; maybe it would allow you to spend some time with her."

"I'd love to spend some time with her. It will allow me to share my observations of your behavior and to warn her of your more serious flaws!"

Allie knew her brother had been seeing the young Navy lieutenant for a few months, and she was beginning to think it was getting serious. Dan had never introduced Allie to someone he was dating before, so Allie wondered if Rebecca might be "the one."

"Hilarious, Allie. Just remember that I have stuff on you that I haven't shared with Kyle. What goes around—"

"I know, I know. But I called to talk with you about Dad. You know he's been seeing this Jillian woman? And he mentioned that he had lunch last weekend with Representative Phan. Don't you think it's a bit soon after Mom's death for him to be doing all this dating?"

Dan let a few moments pass and then asked his sister, "Too

soon for him, or too soon for you, Allie? I mean, it's been more than a year, and the man will be seventy in a few years. I'm glad that he's interested in seeing someone again. What would you prefer, that he mope around that big house and watch old movies? I know you're going through some stuff with Kyle right now, but maybe you should focus on your stuff instead of Dad's."

Allie didn't like her younger brother giving her marriage advice, mainly because he was single. Still, deep down, she suspected he might be correct, but she sure as hell wasn't going to let him know that. "Thanks, Dr. Phil. Maybe if this pilot gig doesn't work out, you have a future as a marriage counselor."

"Sorry. I probably shouldn't have made that comment about you and Kyle. Rebecca and I had dinner with Dad and Jillian at a squadron function last night. I think you'd like her. And I think the Representative Phan lunch has something to do with Dad's trip to Cambodia. Look, I know you're worried about him. But he's very much a grown man. Now, when are you thinking of flying out to visit?"

After her video call with Dan, Allie felt a little bit better. Perhaps he had a point about her focusing on their father's issues instead of her own. She walked into the couple's combination den and office and found Kyle at his desk, working on the company's website. "How about you take a break from that website, and I'll order us a pizza? We need to finish bingeing that British crime drama."

Kyle saved his website edits and turned off the computer. "I could go for pizza and a movie! Phone in the order, and I'll get us a couple of IPAs from the beer refrigerator and meet you in the family room."

COLT'S CROSS

Air Force VC-32A En Route to Washington State

Colt Garrett looked through the cabin's small window at the Idaho landscape 32,000 feet below. A history buff, he considered the challenges facing Meriwether Lewis and William Clark as they led the Corps of Discovery. On September 16, 1805, one of the worst days of the expedition, Captain William Clark had written in his journal, "I have been wet and as cold in every part as I ever was in my life. Indeed, I was at one time fearful my feet would freeze in the thin moccasins which I wore." The expedition was in the middle of crossing the treacherous Bitterroot Mountain Range on the Lolo Trail, with Shoshone guides' help. Despite battling hunger, dehydration, frostbite, freezing temperatures, and exhaustion, no one died. After more than a week on the trail, the exhibition met members of the Nez Pierce tribe, who took them in and nursed them back to health. Eventually, the Corps of Discovery built five dugout canoes, descended the Clearwater River to the Snake River, and into the Columbia River. Just three weeks later, Clark wrote in his journal on November 7, 1805:

> *Great joy in camp we are in*
> *View of the Ocian,*
> *this great Pacific Octean which we been*
> *So long anxious to*
> *See.*
> *and the roreing or noise made by the waves brakeing on the rockey*
> *Shores (as I Suppose) may be heard distictly.*

Colt contrasted his journey with the Corp's challenges and wondered what William Clark would say about how far the country had come. The telephone on Colt's desk rang, and he pressed a button on the wall-mounted phone. "Garrett here."

Colt heard a voice sing, "867-5309!"

"Lenny, damn you! Got me again," he laughed. "I can't get that song out of my head, you bum!"

Michele Phan sat in the first-class seat on the other side of Colt's desk, and she marveled at the man's close relationship with his special assistant. She found it interesting the two could at one moment be kidding one another as if they were attending a baseball game and then instantaneously revert to the formal defense secretary-assistant roles.

"Boss," began Lenny, "I've made your Siem Reap hotel reservations. And I've worked with the state department to arrange your visit with our ambassador in Phnom Penh. Per your instructions, we're keeping any knowledge of Representative Phan's uncle and his story to just those with a need to know. Your trip to Phnom Penh to see the ambassador will provide convenient cover for your meeting with Kiri Phan."

"Thanks, Lenny. I'll call you after we land at Lewis-McChord."

"Mr. Secretary, is this a good time?" Colt looked up from his desk to see the kind face of Karen Seymour, the JFA's Recovery Leader.

"Perfect timing, Dr. Seymour, and thank you for bringing Dr. Kaufman as well. Please have a seat. Representative Phan, may I present Karen Seymour, PhD, our forensic anthropologist, and Jacob Kaufman, MD, the team's forensic pathologist."

Michele shook the scientists' hands and said, "I'm afraid I don't completely understand the differences between your areas of expertise."

Kaufman immediately responded with a broad grin, "Just remember bones and blood! Karen knows more about the human skeleton than anybody in the country, and I have some level of knowledge of human tissue and fluids. Most people find the topic a bit ghoulish, but one gets used to it."

Colt had heard Jacob describe the scientist's roles when he met them after they boarded the plane, and he could tell that Jacob had used the line on previous occasions. "Karen is also the recovery lead for this mission. If anyone gets ill or injured on the trip, Jacob is also a board-certified emergency room doc. We're lucky to have him on this mission."

Karen handed Colt and Michele copies of the team roster and a high-level schedule of events. "Most of the team comprises forensic science technicians, trained to locate, extract, preserve, and transport human remains. When we get to the PYTHON site, I'll walk you through our plan to exploit the site and then go over some of the techniques we'll be using."

After the two scientists left the VIP suite, Colt closed the door. "Michele, as we discussed yesterday, we'll arrive in Siem Reap tomorrow morning, head to a hotel to freshen up, and get something to eat. After that, the team has chartered several helicopters to take us to the PYTHON site, where the scientists will survey the site to make certain we aren't disturbing any possible remains. After that, they'll set up camp and lay out the survey grid. I think you'll find the process interesting."

Michele looked through the event schedule and then asked Colt, "When will we go to Phnom Penh to meet my uncle?"

"Either tomorrow evening or the following day. It all depends on how things progress after we get to the PYTHON site. If Lenny can arrange the helicopter transportation, we could be on our way to see you uncle tomorrow."

After Michele left the suite to visit with her assistant, Colt pressed a button on a panel, and Glenn Carpenter knocked on his door. "Yes, sir? What can I do for you?"

The executive protection agent sat in the chair across from

the defense secretary.

"I know you have reservations regarding our visit to Phnom Penh, but this trip is important, and you'll just have to do the best you can with the protection detail."

"Yes, sir. I understand. Mr. Wilson is planning for two chartered choppers to take us from the PYTHON site to Phnom Penh. Small aircraft, Mr. Secretary, Bell 505s. I'll be riding with you and Representative Phan in one bird, while two other agents will be flying in another helo with our luggage. I have some threat profile information I'd like to share with you if you have time."

The big Boeing VC-32A refueled at Joint Base Lewis-McChord and, within two hours, was airborne again and on the way to the next stop of the journey: Misawa Air Base, Japan. One of the Air Force crewmembers asked Colt, "Sir, do you mind if I convert the sofa into a bed now?" Colt got up from his seat and found Michele sitting in the plane's conference room reading a novel.

"Michele, I have trouble sleeping on airplanes. Would you like to use the suite's bed tonight? I'll ask the crew to make up one of the business class seats for my use."

Michele's first reaction to Colt's offer was that it seemed sexist of him to think she, as a woman, should have the more comfortable accommodation. She was about to respond with a less-than-friendly remark, but she reconsidered when she saw the kind look on his face. He was being courteous, even gallant.

She gathered her belongings and stood. "Thank you, Colt. That'd be great!" She walked into the private suite to find a queen size bed waiting for her. She opened her suitcase and started to prepare for bed.

Spetsnaz Team in Phnom Penh

The 346th Independent Spetsnaz Brigade was Russia's equivalent to the US Army Rangers, the Army's premier direct-action light infantry raid force. The brigade's parent command, the Special Operations Forces Command (KSSO: Komandovanie Sil Spetsial'nykh Operatsiy), saw combat during the 2014 Crimean annexation. Although not as capable as tier-one US units (Navy SEAL Team Six, Army Delta Force, Army Regimental Recon Company, and the Air Force's 24th Special Tactics Squadron), Russia's Spetsnaz units were highly competent special operations units with very well-trained troops.

Captain Morozov, Lieutenant Kuzman, and Sergeant Gusev had been staking out a Phnom Penh hotel for three weeks, closely watching a former Cambodian army general who appeared to be working against Russian interests. The three-person team had bugged the general's mistress's hotel room and the man's Mercedes sedan to confirm he was actively forming an anti-Russian political party. If the team could verify the general's activities, they were under Moscow's orders to assassinate him. But then Morozov received the coded and urgent message from GRU Moscow to break surveillance and plan for a new mission: the assassination of US Secretary of Defense Colton Garrett. The communication from Moscow included detailed information regarding Garrett's scheduled helicopter flight from Siem Reap to a location near the Cambodia-Vietnam border. Morozov immediately realized his team would need to move fast to be in position in time to intercept Garrett's helicopter.

"Captain Morozov, what are your orders?" Lieutenant Kuzman was the team's sniper, trained to hit a target the size of an orange at a range of more than a thousand meters. If the winds were constant, the humidity within acceptable limits, and the target well illuminated, he could send a bullet through a wedding ring several hundred meters further.

Morozov reread Moscow's message and answered, "First, we need to get to our embassy to arrange for a helicopter to fly us to a position near the Vietnam border." He typed a set of coordinates into his tablet computer and showed Lieutenant Kuzman the location he intended to position the team. "We'll need to obtain some additional weapons and gear for this mission. Moscow has given this mission the highest priority and has authorized any resources we require."

"Captain, I would like to requisition a Stronskiy SV-98 for this mission. I realize it's a heavy rifle, but if I'll be shooting at long range, it's the most effective choice."

"I'll add the Stronskiy to our requisition list, Lieutenant. There may be an opportunity to test your skill, but I suspect we may need to find a way to bring down the helicopter in which Garrett is flying. I wonder if the embassy can get us a MANPAD on short notice? It would give us the best chance against a fast-moving helicopter." A MANPAD, or man-portable air defense system, was designed to protect ground troops from high-performance jet airplanes. Several countries manufactured the small, shoulder-fired missiles, combat-tested by military units and by terrorist organizations. In the decades since being first introduced, MANPADS had evolved to shoot down a wide variety of planes and even drones. Fourth generation MANPADs were able to reach aircraft at higher altitudes and greater ranges than earlier models. The Russians had one of the best MANPADs in the world, the SA-25 Verba, the Russian word for Willow.

"Yes, Captain, I would like to have a chance to fire the Verba!"

Day Eight

Sofitel Angkor Phokeethra Hotel, Siem Reap, Cambodia

After French explorer Henri Mouhot alerted the West to the discovery of Angkor Wat and its ancient Khmer civilization, the small village of Siem Reap began the transformation into a bustling city. King Suryavarman II built Angkor Wat in the first half of the 12th century as a Hindu temple. Spread across more than 400 acres, Angkor Wat was the largest religious monument in the world. Originally dedicated to the Hindu god Vishnu, Angkor Wat became a Buddhist temple by the end of the 12th century. The French School of the Far East funded an expedition into Siam to clear and restore the entire Angkor Wat site, and tourists flocked to the city. The Angkor temples became one of Asia's leading attractions until the late-1960s, when war kept tourists away. In 1975, the Siem Reap citizens, like all other Cambodian cities and towns, were forced into the countryside by the Khmer Rouge communists. Nearly 3,000,000 people visited the temple complex in 2020, but Colt suspected many didn't come just to marvel at the archeological wonder. He was sure that many tourists came to see the Ta Prohm temple, used as a movie location in Tomb Raider.

Michele and Colt shared a table in the magnificent restaurant, Mouhot's Dream, named to honor the famous explorer. The picturesque restaurant built in the French Colonial style was situated on a small peninsula in Sala Lake at the Sofitel Angkor Phokeethra Hotel. Both travelers felt surprisingly refreshed after the long flight from Washington; a quick shower and change of clothes made a world of difference.

"Have you found anything interesting, Michele?" asked Colt as he looked through the French restaurant's expansive menu.

"I think I'll have the pan-fried scallops with lobster bisque risotto. How about you?"

Colt closed the menu. "I think that sounds perfect." He turned to the waiter and announced, "That's two of the pan-fried scallops and a bottle of the Joseph Cattin Pinot Gris Alsace Grand Cru Hatschbourg. And a liter of Perrier."

The restaurant's sommelier brought the bottle of wine, poured two glasses, and then quietly disappeared into the kitchen.

Michele raised her wineglass. "Here's to a worthwhile trip!" and the two diners clinked glasses. She noticed his wristwatch and said, "Colt, tell me about your watch. It's quite unusual."

Colt set down his glass of wine and looked at the rectangular pink gold watch with a white face, black roman numbers, and a brown alligator leather band. "It's a Tank Louis Cartier. I know, it's nothing compared with a smartwatch. My son's watch even warns him if his airplane's cabin pressurization system fails. This one just tells the time."

"May I look at it?"

Colt unfastened his watch and handed it to Michele.

"It's beautiful, Colt. A bit old-fashioned, but a true classic." She turned the watch over to view the bottom and read aloud, "To Colt. With all my love, Linda."

Colt placed his wineglass on the table and said, "Uh, yes. It was a gift from my wife."

Michele could tell that something was bothering Colt; probably, the inscription brought back fond memories of his dead wife. She attempted to change the subject.

"So, please tell me, why is it called a tank?"

Colt seemed relieved to shift the topic. "That is interesting. Louis Cartier created this particular model in 1917. Cartier was inspired by the Renault tanks he saw in the Western Front during World War I." Colt strapped the watch on his wrist and continued, "Cartier even presented the prototype to General John Pershing of the American Expeditionary Force. Pretty cool."

Michele closely watched Colt as he drank from his wineglass and then looked across the restaurant at the Army CID special agents, who were detailed to protect the defense secretary. She thought, "I suppose they're a constant reminder to him that there are people who might do him harm." And then it occurred to Michele that sitting across the table from Colt made her a target as well. Her thoughts were interrupted when the waiter returned with their meals.

After the wait staff cleared the plates and served tea, Colt decided to discuss his plan to rendezvous with Michele's uncle Kiri in Phnom Penh. "You mentioned that your uncle does not have a mobile phone?"

"That's true, Colt. I can only reach him via a community email address that he can access in a local internet café."

"How about this," Colt began. "Go back to your room after we've finished our tea and send Kiri an email message. Ask him to go to the courtyard of the old S-21 prison where he works at midnight on Saturday, Sunday, and Monday. He should remain there for just one hour and then go directly home if we don't arrive that evening. We should be able to get there on one of those three nights."

Michele was taking notes on her smartphone. "Anything else you want me to tell him?"

"Yes. Tell your uncle to bring any photos or artifacts he

162

has to the rendezvous, and we'll ask him to show us where the Russians buried the two Americans."

Michele finished taking notes and put her phone into her purse. "Colt, I can't tell you how much I appreciate you coming here and showing faith in my uncle's story." She reached across the table and touched his hand.

"Michele, I'm just glad that I was in a position to help make this happen. And I'm looking forward to meeting your uncle."

"Mr. Secretary, you have a call. It's Jillian Murdoch, sir." Colt looked up to see Glenn Carpenter hand him his mobile phone as Michele waved and headed to her hotel room to change into field clothes and boots.

"This is Garrett," said Colt into the phone.

"Colt, it's Jillian! How are you? Are you in Cambodia already?"

Glenn Carpenter walked a few steps away to give the defense secretary some privacy.

"Hi, Jillian. Yes, we arrived in Siem Reap this morning and are about to head to the airport to fly out to the recovery site. How are you?"

"I'm fine, Colt. I've been thinking about you. I enjoyed dinner with you and Dan the other evening. How long before you expect to return to Washington? It would be nice to get away from the city for a few days and spend some time together."

Colt was distracted as he attempted to calculate the correct tip amount in Cambodian currency, and the cell phone reception was fading.

"Sorry, Jillian, the cell signal is cutting out. I've got to head back to my room to pack and then rush with Michele to the airport. I'll try to call you in a few days from the embassy in Phnom Penh. Bye!"

Jillian set her phone on her desk and decided she needed to

spend some time thinking about her relationship with Colt and where she wanted it to go, with him spending so much time with Michele Phan.

Siem Reap Airport, Cambodia

Colt appreciated that the Cambodian government provided the small conference room for his use while the two chartered helicopters were being prepared for departure. Michele and Colt sat at one end of a weathered oak table while Glenn Carpenter and three CID special agents spoke in low tones at the other side of the small and humid room.

"I didn't think weather could be worse than Washington in August," stated Michele as she wiped her brow and then gathered her hair in a ponytail to keep it away from the sweat on her neck.

"Representative Phan, would you like some water?" asked Glenn Carpenter as he placed a bottle on the table. Turning to Colt, Glenn asked, "Are you certain that you need to fly to Phnom Penh this afternoon, sir? CID headquarters continues to be concerned regarding that intel we discussed yesterday."

The intelligence community had reported increased indications of a Russian operation in the region. Still, no information suggested that operation had anything to do with the American recovery mission.

"I appreciate your concern, Special Agent Carpenter, but we're still going to Phnom Penh later today." Colt noticed his phone was vibrating and answered the call. "Lenny, I only have a few minutes before we board. What's up?"

"Boss, I wanted you to know that Jon Unger died last night. It probably was his heart. The president's appointed Travis Webb as acting national security advisor. Steve Holmes is meeting with him now."

"That's terrible news. Let Steve know I said he should be careful with sharing too much with Travis. I expect the president will be appointing someone else as NSA within a few days."

"Got it, boss. Have a good flight, and remember, 867-5309!"

Colt placed his phone in his jacket pocket and chuckled, "Damn that Lenny!"

The two Bell 505 Jet Ranger X helicopters gently lifted off from the hot tarmac, quickly banked left, and headed to the southeast for what was formerly the PYTHON base. The Bell 505 Jet Ranger X was an American/Canadian light helicopter developed by Bell Helicopter and produced by Bell Textron Canada. The single-engine aircraft could carry three passengers in a bench seat with two seats up front for the pilot and another passenger. Colt and Glenn sat in the rear seat, with Michele between them, while CID Special Agent Abraham Velazquez sat up front with the pilot. The second helicopter held two other special agents and the team's luggage. Before long, the two small helicopters cruised over the dense, green jungle and small villages. Michele could see farmers tending their crops, while scooters and motorcycles seemed to be everywhere. She remembered the stories her father shared about growing up in Cambodia and that he hoped to return one day. She wondered if he had lived, would he even have recognized his homeland?

Earlier that morning, the Cambodian Air Force had transported the rest of the recovery team directly from Siem Reap to the PYTHON base as soon as the VC-32A landed in Cambodia. But instead of riding in the modern Bell helicopters, the recovery team flew in three Russian-made Cambodian MI-8 transport helicopters. The large military aircraft could carry far more passengers and equipment than the smaller Bell 505s.

Still, the ride had been loud, jarring, and uncomfortable, with the ever-present leaking hydraulic fluid spraying the passengers throughout the flight.

The two Bell 505's approached the PYTHON base and landed on the end of an abandoned runway next to a small creek bed. After the rotors stopped turning, the Americans stepped out of the helicopters and were greeted by Dr. Karen Seymour.

"Mr. Secretary, Representative Phan, welcome to PYTHON!"

Executive Officer's Stateroom, USS Robert McNamara (DDG 145)

Lieutenant Commander Jason "Mask" Vilhauer rapped his knuckles on the executive officer's stateroom door, and he heard Kathy Robertson say, "Enter."

Jason Vilhauer served as the officer-in-charge of the MH-60R helicopter detachment assigned to the McNamara. The detachment was an element of Helicopter Maritime Strike (HSM) Squadron 75, based at Naval Air Station North Island, San Diego. The helicopters dramatically improved the ship's anti-surface and anti-submarine capabilities, carrying various sensors and weapons. Jason Vilhauer was responsible for the five officers and eighteen crew detachment that flew and maintained the two Seahawk helicopters on the destroyer. He was an experienced naval aviator and proudly wore the tight-fitting, olive-green flight suit typical of his profession.

"XO, I need to talk with you about the captain," he said and then pulled up a chair next to Kathy's desk. "I just spoke with one of my Sailors, Petty Officer Ramos. She told me that Commander Leach has inappropriately touched her on more than one occasion and commented rudely about her appearance.

I need to tell you, Kathy, that I've already sent an email to the squadron at North Island with the highlights of her accusation, and my skipper has forwarded it to the wing commander. This complaint isn't going to go away."

Kathy Robertson stood, closed her door, and poured herself another cup of coffee. "I don't suppose you want any, Jason?"

"Nope. The caffeine makes my hands shake, not a good thing when you're landing a bird on this boat."

"Ship, Jason. We call the McNamara a ship!" Surface Sailors were constantly reminding aviators that they were in the Navy, and the aviators seemed to take pride in not using the language of the sea. Kathy read the report Jason had handed her, and she showed him the report that she had been writing. "I don't want you to hide anything. And to be candid, I'm glad you sent that email up your chain of command. I'm in the middle of an investigation looking into a similar accusation from a member of the ship's crew. I'll need to interview Petty Officer Ramos as a part of my report. The captain asked me to slow-walk this a bit until we return to port, but if the Petty Officer Ramos accusation stands up, I won't have any choice but to forward it to 7th Fleet. And I know you think that Leach will fry us on our fitness reports. You're probably right. Who wants to be promoted to commander, anyway?"

"I guess this is one of those decisions that test our character as naval officers, Kathy. Who knows, Leach might surprise us and do the right thing."

After the handsome pilot left her stateroom, Kathy continued to make more notes regarding the sexual harassment investigation. She had hoped that doing an excellent job during her executive officer tour would set her up for the afloat command selection board, and she would eventually receive her own ship. That seemed like a pipe dream now, and she decided follow Jason's advice: do the right thing.

Operation PYTHON Recovery Site, Cambodia

Dr. Seymour led Colt Garrett and Michele Phan away from the landing zone toward a small group of tan DRASH tents that provided shelter and working spaces for the recovery team. She walked over to one of the 12' x 22' tents and open the zippered door. "This is our command tent." Colt and Michele followed the recovery team leader inside and joined her at a table in the tent's center. "I thought I'd start by describing the DPAA lab and the two phases of each recovery operation. The DPAA lab is the largest and most diverse skeletal identification laboratory in the world. We're accredited by the American Society of Crime Laboratory Directors, and we employ more than thirty archaeologists, anthropologists, and forensic odontologists." Karen Seymour motioned to the map taped to the table's top. "The process starts here in the field. We use standard field archaeology techniques in the site's excavation, and you'd be right if our work seems like what you might have seen on television crime dramas. Some of our recovery sites are limited to a single burial site, but as you can see from our site map, this mission's perimeter is roughly the size of a football field. The next step in our process is setting the search grid with string and stakes. That's what the team's been working on since we arrived earlier this morning. After the team completely stakes the search grid, we'll excavate one grid at a time, looking for potential remains or other evidence. Depending on what we find, we may even wash the soil through wire mesh with water hoses. We'll do some initial analysis here, but we'll bring back everything we find to one of the labs for further examination."

Michele found Dr. Seymour's explanation interesting and wished she could stay with the recovery team as they excavated the site, but she was on the mission to meet with her uncle. "Dr. Seymour, what happens after you return the remains and evidence to the labs?"

"That's when the tough science starts. First, the human remains, military uniforms, and personal effects are securely stored and preserved. DPAA then assigns a new forensic anthropologist to the case, someone not involved with the field phase. A new lead is appointed because we need to ensure the anthropologist has no idea of the suspected identity of the person or people under analysis. The DPAA mandates that we conduct a blind analysis to prevent bias from influencing the scientist's research. The next step is to profile the remains to determine the sex, race, stature, and age at death. Then, specialists may analyze trauma that might have occurred near the time of death. We look for pathological conditions of bone such as arthritis or previous healed injuries to help with the identification procedure."

Colt asked, "But you use DNA as well?"

"Certainly, Secretary Garrett. We'll gather mitochondrial, or mt, DNA when we can, but we also closely analyze material evidence and personal effects. The lab uses mtDNA in about three-quarters of our cases. Technicians analyze samples taken from bones and teeth at the Armed Forces DNA Identification Laboratory, where they extract and amplify the surviving mtDNA to determine the genetic sequence. The DNA lab compares this sequence with sequences from family reference samples provided by living individuals maternally related to the unidentified American. These family reference samples are collected as needed by the casualty and mortuary offices. Generally, all persons of the maternal line have the same mtDNA sequences. Since these sequences are rare but not unique within the general population, they cannot stand alone as evidence for identification. In addition to the factors previously mentioned, each separate line of evidence must be examined at the lab and correlated with all historical evidence. All reports undergo a thorough peer-review process that includes an external review by independent experts."

"I suppose the whole process is easier if the remains have a dog tag attached," speculated Colt. "In my old squadron, aircrew would attach one to their flight boot's lacing in the event of a catastrophe, and if the rescue team could only find their lower extremities. I guess finding something was better than nothing."

Michele stared at Colt and shuddered, thinking about what type of aircraft mishap would result in the only recoverable human remains would be a foot inside a leather boot. Dr. Seymour wasn't shocked by Colt's comment and replied, "Identification tags are a huge help if available, but I'd have to say our medical examiners more commonly depend upon overlapping lines of evidence to identify the remains."

Michele thought about what Dr. Seymour had shared, and she asked, "What about teeth? Do you use dental records as a part of the analysis?"

"Dental remains are vital to our identification process. A person's dental records are often the best way to identify remains as they have unique individual characteristics and may contain surviving mtDNA. Ideally, the agency's forensic odontologists will have before-death X-rays to use for comparison. Still, even handwritten charts and treatment notes can be critical to the research and identification process."

Colt noted someone had circled three areas of the site map in red ink with a number written next to each location. "Dr. Seymour," Colt asked, "what do these circled sections indicate?

170

Have you already found something?"

"Yes, Secretary Garrett, you probably saw these when you landed. Number one is an American Jeep, number two is an American observation plane, and number three is the wreckage of a Russian MI-8T helicopter."

Colt looked at the red circle on the map where the Russian attack helicopter wreckage was found. "How ironic that the same model of the helicopter that attacked the PYTHON base nearly fifty years ago carried an American recovery team here."

An hour later, Colt and Michele joined Dr. Seymour and Dr. Kaufman for lunch inside the mess tent. The recovery team hadn't yet set up the field kitchen, so the team enjoyed meals, ready to eat, or MREs. Colt opened the brown plastic package with his small pocketknife and announced, "My favorite, beef ravioli! I'm not sure anyone would confuse this MRE with real ravioli, but it's not too bad when heated. The best part is the bacon cheese spread. In the field, I know that Marines can sell the stuff and make serious money!"

Michele recalled her days in the Air Force and countered, "No, Mr. Secretary, the best MRE is chili mac. The entrée is tasty, and this one has pound cake and coffee." The two DPAA scientists opened their MRE selections. Jacob Kaufman, a medical doctor, didn't expect that the meal would have any benefit other than providing the advertised 1,250 calories, one-third of the daily recommended food for a combat soldier.

After lunch, the Garrett party boarded their two Bell helicopters and headed for Phnom Penh. Glenn Carpenter insisted Colt and Michele ride in the second chopper with him for security considerations. In the event of an attack against a VIP flight, the lead helicopter was typically targeted.

Russian Spetsnaz Team, One Kilometer East of PYTHON Base

Captain Morozov was not pleased that his team was more than a kilometer from the American base. This was the closest he could position the team and still conceal the chartered helicopter that had brought them from Phnom Penh to the eastern Cambodia jungle. Lieutenant Kuzman had insisted he could make the kill shot with his Stronskiy sniper rifle. Still, Morozov knew a successful attempt at that distance was not a sure thing, and his orders were clear: do not miss this rare opportunity to kill Colton Garrett.

Morozov was not aware of why Russia wanted Garrett killed, but long ago, he accepted his role to execute policy and not question it. There were times that the Russian officer wished he had pursued a different specialty, particularly when his two children asked him what he did during the long absences from their home near Moscow. He had learned to compartmentalize his life, effectively erecting a wall between his responsibilities to his young family and his duty to his country.

His thoughts were interrupted by Sergeant Gusev shouting from a nearby tree, "Captain, the two American helicopters are airborne and headed this way."

"Gusev, climb down from that tree and grab the other Verba!" Lieutenant Kuzman had previously unpacked and readied two of the four shoulder-fired Verba missiles and aimed one of the antiaircraft weapons in the direction of the American PYTHON base. He powered up the weapon system and pressed his right eye into the rubber infrared imaging sight.

"Captain," Kuzman shouted, "I have the lead helicopter in my sight and am tracking the target." The SA-25 Verba used three different sensors: ultraviolet, near-infrared, and mid-infrared. The multispectral optical seeker enabled fast discrimination between real targets and decoys and reduced the effectiveness of a military aircraft's defensive flare systems.

"I'm tracking the trailing helicopter, Captain!" shouted Sergeant Gusev.

"I want the leading target taken first and then the second. Wait for my command!" ordered Morozov. He was worried that if the missiles fired simultaneously, they may both target the same helicopter.

Kuzman turned to Morozov. "Both aircraft are inside 500 meters and closing, sir. We have good tone on both targets, Captain!"

Morozov closed his eyes and said, "Kuzman. Fire!"

In a fraction of a second, the first missile launched from its tube and headed for the first helicopter. The missile's 1.5-kilogram high explosive warhead detonated within one meter of the leading helicopter's engine, severing the rotor from the aircraft and then igniting the aviation fuel in the helicopter's tanks. The sound was deafening. Morozov grimly watched the wreckage fall from the sky and thought he saw men jump from the aircraft. He placed his hand on Sergeant Gusev's left shoulder and shouted, "Fire!"

Bell 505 Jet Ranger X, Registration Number: XU-7341

Aircrew flying a military aircraft typically receive indications of a missile launch. A missile warning system detecting the aircraft is being tracked or fired upon emits warning alarms and even provides the location of the threat and the missile type. A well-trained military crew would notice the missile's initial launch and exhaust trail. Both warnings trigger the crew to start missile avoidance maneuvers and launch flares in an attempt to decoy the missile's guidance seeker. The Bell 505, in which Colt was flying, was not a military helicopter, and the helicopter pilot had no military training. The first indication either helicopter had that they were in danger was when the leading helicopter exploded in the air. Pieces of the leading helicopter flew by the second, and the first person to react was former Air Force helicopter pilot Michele Phan. "Bank hard left and dive for the deck!" she shouted from the back seat into the intercom and tightened her seat harness in preparation for the anticipated high-G turn. Colt looked out the side window as the small helicopter spun to the left, wishing he was flying in his old EA-6B Prowler with its proven ejection seat system. Then, the second missile exploded, and the helicopter lost power.

"Autorotate! Autorotate now!" Michele yelled into the intercom, immediately realizing the second missile's proximity fuse had detonated early and they still had a chance to survive. She watched the civilian pilot struggle to bring the falling helicopter into a controlled descent, and she regretted her decision to sit in the helicopter's rear seat rather than in the copilot seat where she could have taken control. The pilot finally gained some control but not in time to prevent the small helicopter from violently crashing into the dense jungle below.

National Military Command Center, The Pentagon

Rear Admiral Jamie Purcell was looking forward to spending the next few days replacing the cedar split-rail fence that divided his Arlington yard from his neighbor's place. The one-star US Navy admiral usually had plenty of time to think about personal matters during his twelve-hour watch as Deputy Director of

Operations of the NMCC. The twenty-person watch team was more than capable of monitoring world events while the admiral made his weekend plans. Admiral Purcell had just finished making a list of materials and tools he would need to complete the project when his assistant, Colonel Felix Hunter, announced, "Admiral, we have a problem. The DPAA recovery team in Cambodia is reporting SECDEF's chopper may have exploded. Here's the message, sir."

Admiral Purcell pushed aside his fence plans and carefully read the message reporting the helicopter the defense secretary had been flying in may have crashed. He drafted a brief message on his pad of paper and handed it to the Army colonel. "Felix, send this as FLASH traffic, OPREP-3 PINNACLE." The admiral watched as Colonel Hunter read his message and said, "That's right, Felix. It goes to the world."

Purcell gathered his fence plans and put them in a manila-colored folder as he pressed a button on the communications console. "This is the DDO, Rear Admiral Purcell. I need to speak with the chairman immediately!" While he waited to talk to the chairman of the Joint Chiefs of Staff, Purcell realized he needed to let his wife know their fence project would have to wait until next weekend.

Crash Site, Bell Jet Ranger X, Side Number XU-7341

Colt opened his eyes and tried to remember where he was. Then he recalled the helicopter falling out of the sky after the horrific explosion and slamming into the ground. The aircraft was lying on its right side in a thick jungle valley. All five passengers remained restrained in their seat harnesses. Colt was now directly above Michele in the left rear seat, and she was above Glenn Carpenter. Looking forward, Colt could tell that both the pilot and the other CID agent had died when the helicopter crashed. A large tree had smashed through the front windscreen and severely crushed both men. Colt heard Michele make a moaning sound, and he watched her as she touched her face and neck.

"My God," she whispered, "I'm alive!"

Colt brushed the hair from her face. "Are you all right, Michele? Can you move your arms and legs?"

She quickly surveyed her condition and looked at Glenn. "I think I'm okay, but I think Mr. Carpenter's hurt pretty bad." The helicopter had fallen on a tree stump when it came to rest on the jungle floor; the stump had collapsed the right side of the aircraft. Colt could see that Glenn's body was crushed by helicopter's fuselage and that the special agent was severely bleeding.

"I'm going to see if we can get out first and determine what we can do to help him." Colt managed to open the door above him and climb out of the crippled helicopter. He reached down and helped Michele to follow him up and out of the aircraft. Colt climbed back into the helicopter, and while he checked Glenn's neck for a pulse, the CID special agent said, "I'm not dead yet, Mr. Secretary. I woke up a few minutes ago, but you and Ms. Phan were still conked out."

"How badly are you hurt? Can you move at all?" Colt asked.

"Sir, I'm completely pinned in, and I think I may have broken my back. I can see blood pooling below me. I'm pretty sure it's mine. To make things worse, I think the fuel tanks are ruptured and are leaking."

Colt smelled the aviation fuel for the first time and watched as a few sparks crackled from the instrument panel. He realized the helicopter could start to burn and explode at any moment.

Glenn grabbed Colt's arm. "Look, I don't think I'm getting out of here. You need to listen to me. Whoever shot those missiles knew our flight path. That means someone in the Pentagon or White House told them. Those same people are not far away, and they'll be coming here soon to finish the job." He began a long series of coughs, and Colt could see blood on Glenn's lips. "You two need to get away from here now and get to the embassy in Phnom Penh as quickly as you can. Head west and find the Mekong, then follow it downriver to Phnom Penh. Take the black bag. It has a sat phone, but don't use it until you get to a safe place. And don't trust anyone."

Colt looked up at Michele and saw her softly crying. He grabbed the black backpack and handed it up to her. "I think we should just use the sat phone and contact the recovery team at PYTHON. They have those Russian choppers that can get him to a hospital."

"No, sir. Bad idea," croaked the special agent. "You saw the same intel as I did. Corrupt police officials could be working with the Russians. If the GRU had anything to do with this, some of the police at the PYTHON site might be involved. You both served as military officers. Remember your training. Just keep moving. Go now!"

Colt was about to argue some more but stopped as he saw Glenn's head tilt down. He felt for a pulse and then climbed up and out of the helicopter to join Michele.

"Is he dead?" she asked.

"Yes, he is. And Glenn was probably right about getting away from here. Let's go over to that clearing and try to figure out how to get to the river before nightfall."

Michele and Colt walked over to a clearing next to a small stream and opened the black bag. Inside they found Colt's 9mm pistol, the security detail's Sig Sauer MPX machine pistol with three 30-round magazines, a satellite radio, a small first aid kit, and a green canvas wallet. Colt opened the wallet's zipper and found thirty $100 bills: three thousand dollars.

"I was hoping for a compass," he remarked as he returned the items to the small backpack. "I think I remember how to use a wristwatch to find north." Colt removed his watch and examined the watch's face.

"I'm pretty sure that technique doesn't work in the tropics, Colt. It might be easier if we used the compass application on my smartwatch."

Colt Garrett nodded, slung the backpack over his shoulder, and stepped over to watch Michele open the compass app on her watch. A small compass dial appeared with a red needle indicating north. The pair started walking up out of the valley and headed west while the crashed helicopter behind them began to burn.

Deputy Defense Secretary's Office, the Pentagon

Steve Holmes sat at his office desk, closely looking at a road map of the United States. A route was traced in red ink, starting in Astoria, Oregon, and ending in Portsmouth, New Hampshire. "3,700 miles in 50 days. That's more than 80 miles per day! Will I be ready?" Steve had been riding long-distance races for decades, but nothing that compared with the challenge of the Across America North ride. The ride started with a wheel dip in the Pacific Ocean near Astoria and ended with a wheel dip in the Atlantic at Portsmouth—in between the two, the Cascades, the Rockies, and the Appalachian Mountains. Steve was planning to leave government service after President Harrison's second term, and he was using the cross-country bicycle ride as a symbolic way to start his retirement. Steve's wife, Trixie, enjoyed an occasional Saturday bike ride but had no interest in joining Steve on his bucket-list ride across America. She offered to meet her husband for dinner in Portsmouth after the trip and share a few days in a bed-and-breakfast on the Piscataqua River. He had just started looking through the Specialized-Bike brochure when his desk phone rang. Ten minutes later, Lenny Wilson knocked on his office door.

"Come in, Lenny. Have a seat."

"What can I do for you. Is everything okay, sir?"

"Lenny, we've just been informed that Secretary Garrett's helicopter may have been shot down after it left the PYTHON base on its way to our embassy in Phnom Penh. The details are just starting to come in, and we don't know much more than that. The president has appointed me to serve as acting defense secretary, and I'd like you to remain as special assistant until we find out what happened to Colt. Representative Phan was in his helicopter when it went down. I know how close you and Colt are, and I'd like you to notify Allie and Dan before they hear it on the news. Please let them know we'll do everything we can to find Colt."

Lenny Wilson sat silently, first absorbing the news and mentally going through how to tell Colt's grown children that their father might be dead. He realized that Steve Holmes was watching him and said, "Sorry, sir. Of course. I'll get ahold of Allie and Dan right away." He stood up and walked to the door and then turned to face Steve.

"This is tough, sir. Really tough," and he headed to his own office to make two heart-breaking phone calls.

Somewhere in the Cambodian Jungle

The Tboung Khmum province borders the provinces of Kampong Cham to the west, Kratié to the north, Prey Veng to the south, and shares an international border with Vietnam to the east. The province's name consists of two words in Khmer, tboung (gem, precious jewel) and khmum (bee), which together mean "amber."

Colt Garrett and Michele Phan had been stumbling through the dense jungle for several hours and were completely exhausted as daylight began to fade. The sky turned a dark shade of maroon as the sun set to the west behind another ridge. Neither cared how the Cambodian province earned its name and hoped as they slowly climbed the next hill to finally see the broad and slow-flowing waters of the Mekong River. But that historic and majestic river was still several miles away.

"Colt, I think we should stop for the night," offered Michele as she carefully sat down on a fallen tree. "I don't think I can take another step."

Colt walked a few steps further and turned around. "You have great timing, Michele. You're sitting next to a small creek!"

Michele pivoted on the log and saw a small stream of water flowing down from the top of the ridge. "Do you think it's safe to drink, Colt?"

"It will be." He filled a one-liter plastic bottle he found in the first aid kit and filled it with water from the stream.

"I'd prefer we filter the water first, but this will have to do." Colt placed two small tablets into the bottle and set it aside. "These are chlorine dioxide tablets and should kill off giardia, bacteria, and viruses. But we need to wait for half an hour before drinking the water."

"Did you learn that in survival school?" asked Michele. "I

don't remember anything from my training."

Colt smiled and shook his head. "Nope. That was a long time ago for me, as well. I was an assistant scoutmaster in my son's Boy Scout troop, and I taught the wilderness survival class."

An hour later, they were still hungry, but they had replenished their fluids and were no longer dehydrated. Colt looked through the black backpack once more and removed his semiautomatic pistol and holster. He attached the leather holster to his belt on his right hip and inserted the stainless-steel Colt Commander Combat Elite into the holster. He wasn't sure what the next day would bring but figured the pistol would be of more use on his belt than in the backpack.

Michele had opened two of the foil space blankets they had found in the first aid kit and spread them out on the ground, one on top of the other. She motioned to Colt that he should join her on the blankets.

She looked up at Colt and said, "I suppose it's time we get some rest. Tomorrow will be another difficult day."

He lay on the foil blankets next to Michele and tried to make himself comfortable. He knew he wouldn't sleep at all.

Day Nine

Air Force C-17 En Route to the Gulf of Thailand

Master Chief Jim Farrell walked over to the pallet holding Charlie squad's gear. The near-empty C-17 Globemaster III was the most flexible cargo aircraft in the US Air Force. Able to deliver combat troops and every type of cargo to main and forward operating bases, the C-17 could also transport litters and ambulatory patients. The aircraft had four Pratt & Whitney turbofan engines, based on the commercial Pratt & Whitney engines used on the Boeing 757. Each engine provided 40,440 pounds of thrust that could be reversed to create in-flight drag for maximum rate descents, giving the C-17 the ability to operate into and out of short runways and austere airfields. This morning's mission included the airdrop of Master Chief Farrell's squad of five Navy SEALs and their gear near the USS Tripoli (LHA-7), operating in the Gulf of Thailand. The SEALs of Charlie Squad boarded the C-17 at Hickam Air Force Base in Honolulu just eight hours earlier after receiving the emergency orders from SEAL Team Three in San Diego. The 6,500-mile trip required mid-air refueling and a stop for fuel in the Philippine Islands.

Jim Farrell nudged First Class Petty Officer Doug Kim. "Hey, Charlie Two, I think it's time to get the boys up and check over our jump gear. I want to be suited up and ready to go when the Air Force tells us we're an hour from the drop zone."

Doug Kim looked up at Jim and answered, "Rodger that, Charlie One. I'm going to eat another of those box lunches and

184

then have the squad start inventorying and checking the gear. I'm really looking forward to being haze grey and underway again."

Navy SEALs were used to operating independently, away from the rest of the regular Navy with its rules and regulations. Farrell knew his Sailors weren't looking forward to the regimentation and discipline of a commissioned ship, but he also knew his young SEALs needed to be reminded from time to time that they were a small part of a much bigger team.

"Good, Doug. Let me know when you're done with the gear check. I'd like to spend some time walking through this mission. There will be lots of eyes watching us this time out, and I want everything done by the book. If the defense secretary survived that chopper crash, it would be up to us to find him and to bring him home."

Farrell walked back to his seat and buckled the safety belt. He had seen the images of the crash site, and if his team found Secretary Garrett, he doubted very much that he would be alive.

Russian Team at Helicopter Crash Sites

The Russian Spetsnaz team located the crashed helicopter in the dense jungle and searched the burned-out wreckage immediately, concerned that others might be arriving soon. Morozov climbed into the crumpled cabin and found two bodies in the forward seats and one in the rear bench seat. These weren't the first dead bodies the Russian officer had seen in his career, but these badly burned corpses didn't resemble people, and the smell of the cooked human remains was horrid and sickening. Morozov carefully examined each body, searching for anything that might identify the remains. The person in the right front seat was the pilot, his hands still grasping the collective and cyclic controls, likely dying while fighting to land the damaged helicopter. The person in the left front seat and the person in the rear seat had badges and pistols strapped to their trouser belts, so probably protection agents.

"Lieutenant Kuzman. You and Sergeant Gusev start at the aircraft's nose and search a hundred meters around the helicopter. Look for anything that might indicate that there were other passengers on board. Move quickly!" Morozov ordered. After searching the crash site for more than an hour with no result, the Russians headed down the valley, searching for the wreckage from the leading helicopter.

"Captain!" shouted Sergeant Gusev. "I found the first helicopter or at least a section of it!"

Morozov walked in the direction of the sergeant's voice and found him and Lieutenant Kuzman standing next to the crumpled cabin of a Bell 505 helicopter. The engine was gone, but the cabin's rear seat still held what appeared to be a man's severed left arm, with an Omega stainless steel dive watch still attached to the arm's wrist. The Russian team searched the area and found a small Montblanc suitcase containing women's clothing and cosmetics. Morozov asked his two teammates to come and join him at the wreckage.

"Well, men. What do you think?"

Sergeant Gusev waited to see if Lieutenant Kuzman would offer an opinion and then said, "Sir, I believe that Garrett and Representative Phan were flying in the lead aircraft which received the direct hit. The expensive watch probably belonged to Garrett, and the designer suitcase is a woman's carry-on. If we had the time, we probably would find other body parts in the jungle. But you mentioned that Americans are likely on the way here now, and we should head for our extraction point."

"What do you think, Kuzman? Do you agree with Sergeant

Gusev?"

"I agree with Gusev," began Lieutenant Kuzman. "I think the lead helicopter carried the two officials. The second helicopter appears to be the security aircraft; the weapons and badges make that case. We should take the severed arm with us, and the DNA will confirm it belonged to Garrett. And we should go immediately!"

Kuzman thought for a few moments about what his two Spetsnaz soldiers had said and finally stated, "Agreed. Gather the evidence and prepare for the climb up to our extraction point. I'll let the charter pilot know we're on the way back."

The three Spetsnaz soldiers began climbing up the steep path out of the valley. Morozov started to consider the message to transmit to Moscow after returning to the Russian embassy in Phnom Penh. It felt good to complete a mission as vital as this, and he thought how proud his wife would be when he could tell her he would be soon wearing the two red stripes and single gold star of a major.

Somewhere in the Cambodian Jungle

Colt Garrett slowly woke from a fitful sleep and took a few minutes to recall where he was. Then he remembered yesterday's helicopter crash and the near-death experience. It was terrible to watch Glenn Carpenter slowly die, and Colt worried about the families of the other CID agents. When he finally opened his eyes, he lay on his back on the thin foil blankets, and a sleeping Michele Phan's head was rested on his chest with her left arm draped across his waist. She was sleeping soundly, and he could feel her warmth against his body. He found her closeness comforting, and he would not have woken her except for one thing: his back was killing him. He thought his back pain might have been triggered by the helicopter crash or perhaps yesterday's march through the jungle. Whatever the cause, the pain was intolerable, and he needed to get off his back.

"Michele, I need to get off the ground. My back is killing me." Michele opened her eyes and rolled away from Colt, embarrassed that she had slept on his chest.

"Oh my God, Colt. I'm so sorry about that. Is your back better now?"

Colt had rolled to his side and slowly stood up. "Yes, I think, a bit better. I need to walk around to loosen it up."

Michele rubbed the sleep from her eyes and tied her hair back into a ponytail. The helicopter crash, a hike through the jungle, and a night sleeping on the ground had taken a toll on her hair and makeup. She was glad that she didn't have to look at herself in a mirror. She wished she could wash her face and brush her teeth, but their only water source was the small stream and the purification tablets. They both drank several liters of water and then started making plans for the day's journey. Michele opened the backpack and removed the satellite phone.

"Colt, do you think we should use the phone and get some help? There must be people looking for us. Maybe we should have stayed with the helicopter?"

"I don't think so, Michele. Remember what Glenn said about whoever shot those missiles at us. They had to know where we were and where we were going—somebody told them. We were right to get away from the crash site, and I think using the sat phone would be a mistake."

Colt returned the phone to the small backpack and quickly began to gather the rest of their belongings. "I wish there were some food in this backpack," said Colt. "I think that a sausage and egg breakfast would taste pretty good right now. And homemade sourdough toast on the side!"

"I know," agreed Michele. "I was dreaming of a Denver omelet. Maybe we'll get to the river today? I'm getting hungry."

Colt smiled at Michele. "Me too. And the sooner we get to the river, the sooner we can find something to eat." He slung the backpack over his shoulder and asked Michele, "Are you ready to head out?"

Allie Garrett's Home, Gig Harbor, Washington State

Allie decided to take the day off from work after learning her father's helicopter had crashed in a Cambodian jungle. The government didn't know if he had survived. She knew the defense department would do everything possible to find him, but also, she knew that there were few survivors of helicopter crashes, and she feared the worse.

"First Mom, and now Dad?" she thought as she mindlessly stirred the Americano she had just brewed. She was regretting her last conversation with her dad and wished she had behaved differently. Allie stared at her cell phone, wondering when her brother Dan would return her call when it suddenly played the song Danger Zone, and Dan's name appeared on the screen.

"Danny! Thank God! Have you heard anything else from Lenny Wilson?"

Dan Garrett could hear the stress in his sister's voice and realized he had to be the sibling who remained calm through this family crisis. It was a strange and unfamiliar reversal of roles. Allie was three years older than Dan, and for as long as he could remember, she was the one who had always been in charge. She had taught him everything, from riding a bike to navigating the college application process. The typical firstborn, older sister,

189

Allie was most comfortable when in control. Unfortunately, that was not the case this morning.

"I haven't heard anything since last night," responded Dan. "It's going to take some time to organize a search team, especially in Cambodia. First, they'll have to find the wreckage, and then look for survivors. It could be several days before we know anything. There's nothing we can do until they know more, Allie." Dan could hear his sister breathing heavily while he talked and could tell she was near tears.

"Danny, he can't die now! Not so soon after Mom, and not after how I treated him when he said he wanted to start seeing someone. I was way off base, and it seems so stupid now," and then she began softly crying.

"I'm sure that Dad wasn't hurt by what you said about him seeing Jillian. However, you should know that things aren't all that great between Dad and Jillian right now. After a few beers the other night, he told me that he found a box of letters a man wrote to Mom when she and Dad were living apart. The letters really got to him, and I think he's developed some trust issues with Jillian. Quite a mess."

Allie didn't know what to say. Could her mother really have had an affair? It was more than she could process now. "Wow, Danny. I had no idea. I feel sorry for Dad."

"He knows we're both adults now, Allie, with our own lives to live. He told me he understood why you were upset, but Dad said that he would date Jillian regardless. Remember, he usually does what he wants to do anyway, right?"

Allie thought about what Dan had said and answered, "I guess. I keep thinking about when I was a little girl, and I thought he could do anything. He taught us to drive the ski boat and then how to drive a car. It wasn't until I was in middle school that he started to become embarrassing, and I didn't want to be seen with him."

"I know," added Dan. "But then, after we finished college, he seemed to get more intelligent and that it seemed he might have known a few things. Funny how parents get smarter as we get older."

Allie found herself thinking how smart her little brother had gotten recently; he'd successfully shifted her thoughts to happier days with their dad. "Okay, mister naval aviator, how is it possible to survive a helicopter crash? Lenny said something about autorotation, but he said he didn't know if Dad's helicopter had the capability."

Dan shifted into test pilot mode and regurgitated the FAA definition of autorotation. "Allie, autorotation is the state of flight where the main rotor system is being turned by the force of the relative wind rather than engine power. As a result, a pilot can safely land a helicopter in the event of an engine failure. If whatever caused the helicopter to fall from the sky just took out the engine, then an experienced pilot can land the chopper safely. The military helicopter pilots practice it all the time."

"But what about Dad's helicopter? Lenny said it was a civilian charter flight. Can you find out if it could autorotate?"

Dan was glad the conversation had shifted to talking about how their father could have survived. "Allie, all helicopters must have that capability to be certified. The Bell 505 can autorotate. And one other thing, I recently found out some things about his military service—it turns out Dad was in some sort of special program. So I'm just saying I think he might just find a way out of this."

"That's good news, Danny. Excellent news. And thanks for helping me through this. You're a good brother. . . and a good friend."

"How's Dan handling the news?" asked Kyle after Allie

completed the call with her brother. "They're pretty close."

"Oh, God! I completely forgot to ask him how he was doing. My feelings so consumed me I wasn't even thinking about his. I'm such a shit! I need to call him right back," and she reached for her phone once more.

"Wait, Allie. I think that you two need to be together now until we know what happened to your dad. Things are okay at work. Why don't you use some of those Delta miles we've been saving and catch a flight to Dulles and stay with Dan? While you were on the phone with your brother, I found you a seat on a flight with a 1:40 pm Seattle departure; it arrives in Dulles at midnight. I'll book it."

Allie looked at her husband and felt tears swell in her eyes. "Thanks, babe. I love you!"

Kyle booked the flight and found Allie's passport in the desk drawer. He was searching for her luggage in the hall closet when he heard her say into her phone, "Guess what, Danny? I've decided to come to visit you for a few days! So, you better do a quick cleanup of that bachelor apartment and make sure you can pick me up at Dulles at midnight!"

Somewhere in the Cambodian Jungle

Colt almost stumbled again as he followed Michele along a game trail that appeared to be bringing them out of the dense jungle. They had been walking for more than five hours, and the lack of food was affecting their ability to keep moving toward the river. Colt hoped to hear sounds from what he prayed was the Mekong sometime that afternoon, but each time they stopped to rest, the only noises they heard were those made by birds and other creatures to warn that humans were in the area.

Colt was more concerned about the animals that didn't make a sound. The Indochinese leopard, the Siamese crocodile, and the Thai tarantula were all native to the region, but what worried Colt most were the king cobra and the blue Malayan krait. Not only were the snakes deadly, but Colt also just hated snakes. He remembered when Allie and Dan were in elementary school, and a local naturalist called the Reptile Man made his annual school visit. The Reptile Man even allowed the kids to hold a massive Burmese python. Colt still shivered when he thought of that yellow snake wrapped around Allie's shoulders, and he knew each time he placed a foot on the jungle path that he would step on something dreadful. The weather wasn't making things any better. The air temperature climbed with the humidity, and Colt's hair streamed sweat onto his face; he wished he hadn't left his ball cap back at the PYTHON base camp when they ate their MRE lunch.

Looking ahead on the trail, he noticed that Michele seemed to be handling the heat and humidity better. Her khaki shirt was soaked with her perspiration, but she kept up a steady pace, only occasionally checking the compass on her watch. Michele had voiced her concern that her watch battery was nearly spent, and they desperately wanted to reach the river while they still could tell which way was west. He didn't mention that if they didn't get to the river soon and find water and food, it might not matter if the watch stopped working. With their energy levels depleted, they would have to stop traveling and hope help arrived.

Colt decided that if they didn't reach the Mekong within the next two hours, he would turn on the satellite phone, regardless of what Glenn Carpenter had said about not giving away their position. He was running out of options, and they needed help. Colt found himself thinking about Allie and Dan and how they would go on with their lives if he didn't make it back. Both were well-established in their careers, and he didn't have to worry about their financial futures. Still, he hoped that Dan would settle down with someone in a more permanent relationship, and he was concerned about Allie and Kyle's marriage. He found it odd that he was still worried about his grown children and then remembered his friends warning him that his job as a father would never end. Unless he didn't return home.

Colt was very impressed with how Michele had not once complained about their situation. Instead, she seemed to accept their predicament, and she remained focused on solving the problem. Colt thought Michele showed a great deal of character in how she dealt with their ordeal, and he found himself admiring her. She certainly had accomplished much, and he wondered where her political fortunes would lead. Colt decided to speak with Vice President Hernandez if they were lucky enough to find their way out of the jungle and back to Washington. Perhaps there might be a place for Michele in the new administration? He wondered if he had any influence with the vice president or if his support of Michele could backfire.

An exhausted Colt continued to follow Michele as she pressed further west, and he wondered about the person or people who might have fired the missile that killed Glenn Carpenter and the others. Glenn had shown him intelligence reports suggesting the Russian GRU was targeting him once again; at least he could be sure that Colonel Petrov couldn't be responsible for the attack. The Russian intelligence agent remained confined in a dank prison on a small Caribbean island that occasionally performed services in exchange for the opportunity to sell locally distilled spirits to North American markets. Petrov would die in that decaying prison. Colt hoped his death would help him forget about what had happened in Gibraltar so many years ago.

An hour later, Colt and Michele were relieved to notice the trees were thinning as they descended another game trail that ended next to a stream that emptied into a terrible smelling swamp. The stream was not the Mekong River, but it did make the weary travelers exhale sighs of relief because as they walked further, they saw the stream flowed next to some sort of gravel field, and in the clearing rested a late model Lexus luxury sedan. Not seeing another person near the car, Colt walked over to it and then heard Michele scream, "Colt!" He began to turn to his left when something hit him on the back of his head, and he collapsed to the ground.

US Marine UH-1Y Venom Helicopter En Route to PYTHON Base

Master Chief Jim Farrell saw the irony in flying into a former secret base in Cambodia in what would appear to the casual observer as a Vietnam War-era helicopter. Dubbed the "Huey" after the phonetic sound of its original designation, HU-1, the UH-1 Iroquois helicopter had been the Army's workhorse during the Vietnam War. Even though the new helicopters were still affectionally referred to as Hueys, the outward appearance of the UH-1Y Venom was perhaps the only thing it had in common with the decades older UH-1 single-engine chopper. The Venom could fly faster, farther, higher, and lift more than its Vietnam War cousin. In addition, its flat panel, multifunctional display provided the pilots with the information they needed to operate the highly capable aircraft. The Venom's pilot and copilot were Marines attached to the 31st Marine Expeditionary Unit embarked in the USS Tripoli (LHA-7), patrolling the Gulf of Thailand. The Tripoli, a landing helicopter assault ship, was more than 840 feet long and used its Marine forces with their airplanes and helicopters to conduct amphibious operations to respond to crises worldwide. Farrell and his Charlie squad of four Navy SEALS had parachuted into the sea near the Tripoli, and the Marines were providing the Navy special warfare team a lift to the former SOG PYTHON base near the Vietnam border.

Farrell glanced at the other members of his squad. The three SEALS were all dressed like the master chief: green digital camouflage fatigues with tactical vests, HK-416 rifles, and Glock-19 pistols. But Deacon, the youngest squad member, was dressed quite differently. Deacon was a three-year-old Belgian Malinois and a fully qualified multi-purpose canine, or MPC. MPCs could track, search, patrol, detect narcotics and explosives, rappel out of helicopters, ride in SEAL boats, and even skydive. The dogs started the training program soon after birth so that they could immediately bond with humans. The Navy had invested more than $50,000 to train Deacon, and he was worth every penny. Deacon loved his job with the SEALs and was particularly fond of his handler, Petty Officer First Class Nick Vlahos, a 28-year-old Navy SEAL from Baltimore. Nick's family owned the Calypso Restaurant in the Greektown neighborhood, located on a street surrounded by other restaurants, authentic coffee shops, and bakeries.

Nick's parents assumed their oldest son would take on more responsibilities in the restaurant after graduating from high school and weren't initially supportive when Nick first announced he had enlisted in the Navy. Nick's mother refused to write letters to her son while he endured basic training at Great Lakes. She only occasionally spoke with him on the phone during his training to be a SEAL at Coronado, California. But the day Nick graduated from Basic Underwater Demolition School, his parents swelled with pride as their son stood with his

BUDS classmates in the bright California sun. The Vlahos family even added a new item to the restaurant's menu to celebrate their son's accomplishment. The Nikolas Special was a fresh take on the classic Greek dish of squid rings and tentacles, seasoned, dredged in flour, and fried until crispy and golden brown. Nick reached over and scratched Deacon behind his ears. "Sorry, my little fur missile. No fast-roping today. This Marine bird is about to land us right in the middle of the camp!"

Farrell and his squad met with Dr. Seymour to learn what the scientists saw after the two helicopters departed with Secretary Garrett's party.

"We didn't see very much," said Dr. Seymour as she walked with the SEALs across an open field. "They took off from here and then flew toward that ridge over there," and she pointed to the west. "Dr. Kauffman and I were walking back to the mess tent when we heard the explosion. When we looked back, a cloud of black smoke, and what appeared to be pieces of the helicopter fell out of the sky."

Jacob Kauffman nodded. "I couldn't swear to it, but I think I may have seen a body falling. Horrific. I can't seem to get that image out of my mind."

Master Chief Farrell was writing on a small notepad. "So, you were both looking in that direction when the second helicopter was hit?"

Dr. Seymour nodded. "Yes. We both saw what looked like a missile shoot up and detonate near the second helicopter. However, it didn't explode like the first one. Instead, smoke poured out of it, and the helicopter descended pretty quickly like the pilot still had control."

The SEALS interviewed the other witnesses and then made their way back to the Marine helicopter and were about to board when Dr. Kauffman ran over to them.

Out of breath from his sprint, the physician said, "Here, take this! Secretary Garrett left it in the mess tent. I saw you have a working dog; perhaps this might help you find Mr. Garrett if he managed to survive."

Farrell examined the cap Dr. Kauffman handed him. It was a dark blue baseball cap with the words SECDEF embroidered in yellow thread on the cap's crown. Farrell gave the hat to Nick, who said, "There's a fair amount of sweat on the inside of the hat. If Secretary Garrett made it out of the chopper, Deacon can find him!"

Somewhere in the Cambodian Jungle

Colt Garrett was having his recurring nightmare of the Gibraltar mission, and it ended the same way, with him firing a pistol and then screaming until he waked. Except this time, instead of finding himself in his bed in a quiet and darkened room, he opened his eyes and realized he was laying on the ground, and the screaming continued, but he wasn't the one yelling. He wiped the blood from his eyes to see a man struggling with Michele as she fought to keep him from raping her. The man had trapped Michele against the car and was behind her, trying to remove her pants as she fought to escape his brutal attack. He had already unbuckled his belt, letting his pants fall to the ground around his ankles.

Colt shook his head and experienced intense pain worse than any migraine headache. He carefully moved to his hands and knees and slowly stood upright, facing Michele and her attacker. His shock at seeing Michele sexually assaulted grew to anger and then rage as his head cleared. He knew he was in no condition to attack the man, so instead shouted, "Stop it, you pig! Stop it, now!"

The man immediately released Michele, allowing her to squeeze between him and the car and stumble away. The man slowly turned around to see Colt standing twenty feet away with blood flowing down his head and the left side of his face. He could see that he had injured the American and that he was slightly shaking. The man also noticed Colt held a stainless-steel pistol, pointing directly at his chest. He thought through his options and then calmly said in English, "I surprised you stand on your feet. Perhaps you sit down for a moment. And please lower your gun. You not look well."

Colt remained silent and closely watched the Asian man slowly raise his hands above his head. The man was well-dressed in expensive-looking clothes, and the Lexus LX behind him looked new.

"Who are you?" asked Colt, thinking the man and his car were utterly out of place in the middle of a Cambodian jungle.

"I happy to introduce myself, but first, I would like to pull up my pants." He bent his knees and slowly lowered his hands to his pants. Then, he smoothly reached for the Makarov 9mm pistol on his belt when Colt quickly fired three rounds into his chest, slamming the man back against his car. Michele watched Colt continue to point his gun at the fallen attacker as he calmly stepped forward and momentarily placed his index and middle fingers on the side of the man's neck. Then, Colt removed the Makarov from the man's right hand, removed the magazine, and ejected a chambered round. He wiped some blood from his face and then joined Michele, who lay shaking on the ground.

"Is he dead?" asked Michele while she adjusted her bra and buttoned her torn blouse. She was relieved that the attack was over and the danger had passed.

"Yes, he's dead. He won't be hurting anybody anymore." Colt

looked over at the lifeless body. "I think he's Chinese. I wonder what he was doing here?" Michele didn't care why the man was there, but she was glad that Colt had been there to stop him. She reached over to examine Colt's head wound and stopped when she heard something banging from the car's trunk. Colt placed his index finger against his lips and stepped over to the dead man's body. He found a car key fob and positioned himself to the side of the car's trunk. He drew his pistol once more and pointed it at the truck with his right hand as he pressed the trunk release button with his left hand. The trunk popped open, and Colt was surprised to see a teenaged boy bound and gagged inside. He holstered his pistol and removed a green rag from the boy's mouth and then untied the twine that bound the boy's hands and feet. Michele and Colt helped the boy out of the car's trunk and onto the ground. They watched as he rubbed his wrists and ankles where the twine had cut into his skin.

Finally, Michele asked him, "Who are you? Why were you in the trunk? Who is this man?"

The young teenager looked at the two strangers and answered in perfect English, "My name Leap Nang. I was walking home from school, and this man got out of his car and said my grandfather had sent him to pick me up. He said that grandfather had been in a car accident. An ambulance had taken grandfather to the hospital, and I needed to get into the man's car. I was about to get in when I realized I had never seen this car before, and the man wasn't one of grandfather's workers. He only hired Cambodians. I asked that man how he knew my grandfather, and he got angry and pointed a gun at me. He tied me up, put me in the trunk, and started the car. We drove for a while, and the car finally stopped. I heard noises and people talking; then I heard the shots. That's when I banged my feet on the trunk lid."

Colt thought about what Leap had said and asked, "Why

do you think the man grabbed you off of the street? And you mentioned your grandfather's workers, Leap. What's his business?"

Leap Nang was quiet for a few moments and then responded, "Grandfather is in the shipping business. I think this man may have worked for a rival company. It's a dangerous business."

Colt looked at Michele and then back at Leap. "The shipping business?" he asked. And then, "Where is your grandfather's business? Do you know where we are now?"

Leap nodded his head. "Yes, I know where we are. I've been here before. My grandfather works at his house. It's about thirty kilometers from here on the river."

"The Mekong River?" asked Michele.

"Yes," the young boy responded.

Colt thought for a few moments and then announced, "We'll go there now."

Leap looked relieved to be finally going home and announced, "I think we should place the body in the truck and take it to grandfather. He'll know what to do."

Russian Military Intelligence HQ, Moscow

General Igor Korobov was pleased when the Spetsnaz team in Cambodia reported they had successfully downed the Garrett party's helicopters as they headed to Phnom Penh. The lead helicopter carrying Secretary Garrett and Representative Phan had been destroyed in the air while a second helicopter with the remainder of the executive protection team had crashed and burned. The Spetsnaz team had already flown back to Phnom Penh after ensuring nothing remained at the crash site that might tie the incident to the Russian government. The special operations soldiers were making flight arrangements to leave Cambodia immediately. The GRU general closed the file and placed it in his desk drawer, satisfied that the mission to remove Colton Garrett was successful. He could now focus on putting the next steps into play to get Travis Webb nominated to be the next defense secretary and finally end the anti-Russian O'Kane Doctrine.

There was another reason why General Korobov was in such a good mood. Just an hour earlier, he had read that the operation to free Colonel Dimitri Petrov from his prison cell on St. Francis Island had been a success. Once he learned from Travis Webb that the Americans held the colonel on the tiny Caribbean island, it only took a few days to confirm the intelligence and execute a rescue mission. The GRU prided itself on its reputation to bring its agents home, and specialists were debriefing the colonel while the general drank his tea. He didn't expect to learn anything of value from the interrogation, but regulations mandated the process whenever an agent had been captured and held by the enemy. There was always the risk the agent might have been turned against the motherland by the capitalists; that's how the game was played, after all. General Korobov stood and walked over to his bookshelf and looked at a photo of Petrov and him after graduation from basic intelligence school. Arm in arm, the two friends smiled and posed, with no way to know that one day, Korobov would be in a position to save Dimitri Petrov from languishing in a crumbling prison. They also could not have imagined that the same Korobov would probably be ordering the execution of Petrov for allowing the Americans to arrest him.

The general walked over to the large, bullet-proof windows and gazed out to the fields below the headquarters building. It would have been more satisfying if the Spetsnaz team could have found Garrett's body and been able to confirm his death. Then

Korobov suddenly remembered that Garrett had been part of a unique program many years ago, and a thought occurred to the GRU general. "What if Garrett somehow escaped death in the helicopter? What if he found a way to get out of that jungle and resume his duties as defense secretary? And what was that particular program that Garrett was a part of when he was a naval officer?" General Korobov pressed a button on his desk phone and ordered, "Bring me the file on the American project they called Broadsword!"

Nang Shipping Company, Cambodia

Colt slowed the black Lexus as he approached the main entrance of Nang Shipping and stopped next to a gatehouse. A serious-looking man dressed in a linen sport coat motioned to lower the car's window.

"My name's Garrett, and we're here to see Mr. Nang. His grandson Leap is in the back seat." Colt was glad that he followed Leap's suggestion to call ahead using the dead man's mobile phone. The guard peered into the car, slung his automatic rifle over his shoulder, and pressed a button to open the iron gate. Colt could see several security cameras aimed at the car as he slowly drove through the highly secure entrance. Finally, he brought the car to a stop in front of a two-story building where an older man and two armed guards waited for them. Leap opened his door and raced into his grandfather's arms as Colt and Michele exited the vehicle. Leap began speaking with his grandfather in the Mon-Khmer language, gesturing with his hands, and eventually started crying, now that his terrifying ordeal had ended. One of the guards escorted the boy into the building, and Mr. Nang turned to Colt and Michele.

"I am Sovann Nang. Thank you for bringing my grandson home to me," said the man as he offered Colt his right hand.

"I am Colton Garrett, and this is Michele Phan, Mr. Nang. Our helicopter crashed in the jungle, and we have been walking since yesterday."

Sovann smiled and responded, "I know precisely who you are, Secretary Garrett and Representative Phan. Please follow me out of this unbearable sun, and we'll provide you with food and water."

Michele and Colt felt surprisingly refreshed after getting something to eat and drink in a conference room inside the house, but both knew they were in serious need of a shower.

"I hope you're feeling better," said Sovann when he joined them in the room. "I suppose I should explain why Leap was taken and how I know your identities."

Colt set down a bottle of water and patiently waited for Sovann to begin.

"My shipping company is a member of a collective or consortium of other similar businesses in this region that cooperate to ensure we do not compete in our geographical zones. The arrangement had worked well for decades, until recently when a competitor from China expanded operations into Cambodia."

"You are part of the Sino-Khmer mafia, Mr. Nang? And your business is heroin?" asked Colt, who had been briefed on the drug trade in Cambodia before the recovery mission.

Mr. Nang slowly nodded. "Yes, well, we do trade in a variety of products, but heroin is certainly the most profitable. One kilogram purchased in Cambodia for 20,000 dollars can be sold for several times that amount . . . in your country. The man who attacked you was a member of the Chinese Triad that has been attempting to break up our consortium and assume our business and the resulting profits. As a result, the Triad has resorted to kidnapping our children and killing them to force us to bend to their will." He walked over to a small table and picked up a long knife. "This is a watermelon chopper," he said as he waved the heavy ten-inch blade through the air. The Triad prefers this weapon for assassinations because it leaves no forensic evidence, simply a mutilated corpse. My men found this weapon in the car under the front seat, and I'm confident the man intended to use it on Leap when he was interrupted by you two, thank Buddha!"

"How do you know who we are?" asked Colt, thinking about the horrific death that Leap would have suffered.

"Quite simple. I have close relations with the local police officers. They are overworked and underpaid. It's my business to know what they know. For example, the local police captain told me that your helicopter had crashed. If the police found you, they were to radio their regional headquarters and then hand you over to representatives of the Russian embassy. The police work very closely with the Russians, you see."

Colt looked over at Michele, who had placed her head in her hands. It was all too much. "Mr. Nang, I would like to drive the car to Phnom Penh and reach the safety of our embassy. Can you provide fuel for the car and directions?"

"I owe you both a great deal, more than I can repay. But you cannot drive to Phnom Penh in that vehicle or any other. The police will have several roadblocks along the way, and the Triad will be looking for that particular car. However, if you do not mind taking advice from an old smuggler, I have another way for you to reach your destination."

Day Ten

On the Mekong River, Cambodia

Colt Garrett woke from a deep sleep and remembered that he always slept soundly in a boat's bunk. It didn't seem to make a difference if the bunk was in a 21-foot sloop or a 1,106-foot nuclear-powered aircraft carrier. The term "barge" didn't adequately describe the luxurious yacht in which Colt and Michele found themselves as passengers. More than 120 feet long, Mr. Nang's ship was constructed in teak and mahogany and had the exterior appearance of a modest Chinese junk. Mr. Nang used his barge to travel the Mekong River and its delta. The local authorities commonly saw the beautiful vessel whenever they conducted river patrols to interdict drug smuggling, but generous payments from Mr. Nang guaranteed the police would not search it.

The crew included the captain, a chef, engineer, and deckhand. Inside, the boat was expensively constructed and furnished with only the best workmanship and materials that money could buy, money from the transportation and distribution of illegal drugs. The pair of Volvo marine diesel engines could drive the barge at speeds of more than twenty knots, and the pilothouse included a wide array of navigation and communications equipment that would be the envy of any commercial fishing boat captain. Mr. Nang had insisted Colt and Michele take his company boat to Phnom Penh to avoid the roadblocks he suspected the police had established on the main highway to the capital.

Michele and Colt boarded the barge the night before, and,

after perhaps the best showers they had ever experienced, the Americans consumed a sumptuous four-course dinner. The chef set two glasses of Hardy VSOP cognac on the table and magically disappeared into the barge's galley, allowing them a degree of privacy. Colt found he was becoming attracted to the congresswoman from Seattle and thoroughly enjoyed the romantic dinner. He was sorry the evening ended so early, but he and Michele were exhausted from their time in the jungle and needed to rest before arriving in Phnom Penh.

That morning, Colt threw back the covers and swung his legs over the bed's edge, and set his bare feet on the thick carpet. After another long shower, Colt found fresh clothes hanging from a hanger in his closet; he wondered how the crew had determined his exact size in every apparel. He quickly dressed and made his way down the passageway to find Michele waiting for him in the small dining room.

"Good morning!" said Michele as she put down her cup. "Can I pour you a cup of coffee?" Colt pulled out a chair and sat across from her at the small table.

"Good morning. How did you sleep?" Colt asked.

"It was amazing! And I'm still hungry!"

The chef walked into the dining room, pushing a cart full of breakfast meats, fruit, toast, and scrambled eggs. He placed fine linen napkins on Colt's and Michele's laps and then filled their plates with food.

"Can I provide anything else? Fruit juice? Perhaps an omelet?" Mr. Nang had apparently decided that these guests would receive the best service,

Michele nodded at Colt. "Thank you, but I think Mr. Garrett and I have everything we need at the moment. We'll let you know when we need more coffee."

After the chef left them to enjoy their breakfast, Michele

asked, "Colt, are you sure that we should still meet my uncle tonight after we arrive at Phnom Penh instead of heading directly to the US embassy? Getting to the protection of the embassy as soon as possible seems to be more important than getting information on something that might have happened decades ago."

Colt considered what Michele said and put his fork on the table. "You're right, of course. That would probably be the smart move. Yet, I still think that meeting with your uncle gives us a rare chance to discover what happened to those Americans in that prison, and I don't think we should waste this opportunity. The embassy will still be there after we meet with Kiri."

Michele wasn't sure that Colt was right but admired his focus on finding what happened to those two boys. "You seem intent on proving to the world that the Russians attacked the PYTHON base and then tortured and killed those men. Could it be that you're still fighting the Cold War? Our country is facing asymmetric enemies now, organizations that can bring harm and destruction without declaring war."

"New strategies and technologies no doubt challenge us, but I think our defense is evolving to meet those threats. When I was in school, I thought it was simple to know right from wrong. The movies and television cast the heroes and villains very distinctly; the bad guys even wore different clothing. When I got older and a bit more educated, I understood the world was a much more complex place. Issues and conflicts didn't always cleanly separate into black and white, good and bad, right and wrong. Problems and their solutions shift over time, and it requires attention and flexibility of thought to see things as they truly are. The most challenging part is to understand that those holding a different opinion are not stupid or necessarily evil."

"So, if what you're saying is true, then you don't seem to be the right person leading our defense department, Colt."

He could see that Michele had skillfully maneuvered him into a corner and that she was enjoying his discomfort. "That's where you're wrong," he said as he poured himself another cup of coffee. "I run the defense department, not the state department. I don't need to concern myself with a nation's motivation or rationale for acting against our country. My job is to focus on the threat, wherever it may come from, and immediately counter it with overwhelming and devastating force."

"How do you resolve what you said earlier about heroes and villains with your role as defense secretary."

"It's the difference between action and motivation, Michele. When facing a threat that appears to be evil, I'm not an avenging angel seeking to restore justice; I am the sword."

Michele considered what Colt had shared with her, and she wasn't entirely convinced he could so easily separate his feelings from his duty. She was about to ask him another question when the barge's captain rushed into the dining room.

"Forgive me, but the police patrol boat is approaching, and it will board us shortly. Quickly, follow me!"

Dan Garrett's Apartment, Maryland

"Good morning, Allie! I was starting to wonder if you were going to sleep all day!"

Allie Garrett still looked sleepy when she sat at the kitchen table and stretched, wearing her brother's grey hooded sweatshirt over her pajamas. "It's only eight-thirty Pacific time. How about a cup of coffee?"

Dan placed a steaming mug of black coffee in front of his sister. "I hope you don't mind it black. Not as fancy as your expensive espresso machine."

"It's fine. And thanks again for picking me up from the airport. I didn't want to deal with finding a cab at Dulles. Have you heard any more news about dad?"

"Not much. I know the DOD has a team in-country looking for the wreckage; it might take some time because of the dense jungle and difficult terrain. I was planning on calling Lenny Wilson after you got up to see if he has an update. I spoke with the housekeeping staff at dad's residence to see if I can stop by and pick up Drake to bring him over to my apartment. They offered to have one of the protection agents drive him here. I guess the detail is pretty upset about Dad's chopper going down."

Allie was completely absorbed with her anxiety over her father's fate, but now she paused to consider the effect the accident was having on the people with whom her dad worked.

"Have you talked with Jillian yet? I know she's not family, but I think we should reach out to her. The accident must be very hard on her, and the news has been sparse."

"Yep," replied Dan. "I spoke with her an hour ago. I mentioned you'd flown out, and she asked if she could come over and wait with us. I said that she'd be welcome to join us. Rebecca will be coming over after she gets off watch."

"Good, Danny. I want to meet both of them."

"One thing, Allie. Would you try not to call me Danny when they're here? You're the only one that calls me that anymore."

Allie got up from the table and hugged her younger brother. "Okay, but no way am I going to call you Joker!"

On the Mekong River

Colt and Michele followed the captain as he walked forward
to the barge's cramped crew compartment with old-fashioned
pipe berths attached to the outside bulkheads and suspended by
iron chains from the compartment overhead. The confined space
smelled of fish and working men and was in stark contrast to the
opulent accommodations in which Michele and Colt had slept
the night before. Michele slipped on a grease spot on the deck
and slammed her right arm into one of the pipe berths. "Ouch!"
she exclaimed, cradling her right arm.

"Quiet!" whispered the captain, and he pointed to the deck
above their heads. The barge's engines had stopped, and Colt
could tell that another boat had pulled aside. They could hear
footsteps and then voices through the wooden deck, but Colt
couldn't understand the language.

"It's the Cambodian police, and they're looking for a couple
that matches our descriptions!" whispered Michele. Colt forgot
that her father was born in Cambodia; he must have taught his
daughter the language.

The captain removed a sizeable rectangular panel from the
side of a clothing locker and motioned to the space inside. Colt
peered inside and saw a hidden compartment behind the locker,
approximately six feet tall, two feet wide, and two feet deep. The
captain whispered, "You hide in here now!"

"Me? Where will you hide Michele?"

"You both hide in there now! Hurry, silent!"

Without an alternative and hearing the police start searching
the barge, Colt climbed into the small space, turned around, and
helped Michel climb in through the opening. The two Americans
stood facing one another with their bodies pressed together in
the coffin-like enclosure while the captain replaced the panel

and tightened the screws. Colt could hear and feel Michele's breathing quicken when the captain closed the panel, and the small space went completely dark. He considered asking if she was claustrophobic and then realized it was too late for that. They would have to endure being trapped in the dark space until the captain could convince the police the barge didn't hold the people for whom they were searching. He assumed the crew used the hidden area to smuggle Mr. Nang's heroin into Phnom Penh or perhaps even into Vietnam and then to a ship in the harbor. Regardless, he was glad Mr. Nang had built the hiding space, and Colt prayed that the police would be fooled. He knew the police were notoriously corrupt, and he hoped that the captain would convince whoever was searching the barge they should look elsewhere.

Michele slowly moved her arms above her head, hoping to ease the pain from her fall. As they stood pressed together in the metal enclosure, Colt and Michele could hear the police enter the crew compartment and begin their search. Although Colt couldn't understand the language, he could imagine the activity just inches from where they remained hidden. Doors and lockers opened and slammed shut. Deck sections raised and then tossed aside in frustration. Eventually, the police left the crew compartment and searched other areas of the barge. Colt felt relieved when he heard the crew compartment close, and he felt something else—Michele softly kissing the side of his neck and then his right ear. He felt her hands reach behind his neck and pull his head down as she pressed her lips against his. Colt knew this was stupid for countless reasons, but he didn't care. Instead, he moved his hands around her tiny waist and tried to press her body even closer while their kiss became more passionate. He was thinking of what to do next when he heard the panel screws removed, Colt and Michele were blinded by the light when the captain opened the panel.

"The police are gone, and you can finally get out of there." The captain carefully eased Michele out of the hiding place, and Colt managed to squeeze through the opening after several attempts. Colt avoided eye contact with Michele while making their way aft and into the barge's main lounge. The chef had already set a tray with water and fruit, and the captain watched Colt and Michele rehydrate from their stressful experience.

"I'm so very sorry for placing you into that terrible place. I don't think the police officials will board us again; they appeared to be satisfied that you're not on the barge. We're underway once more and should arrive in Phnom Penn later this afternoon. Mr. Nang will meet us there. Again, please accept my sincere apology for forcing you together in such a small space. It must have been horrible."

Colt's eyes met Michele's for the first time since emerging from the smuggler's hole. "Please, no apologies are necessary. It wasn't that bad."

After lunch in the dining room, the captain told Colt and Michele the barge would dock within the hour at a commercial pier in the Port of Phnom Penh. Colt reached for the black backpack he had carried since the helicopter crash. "I think it's time to call the Pentagon." He pressed several buttons on the small satellite phone and heard a voice respond, "Watch floor, Major Kaiser speaking. This is a secure line. Who is this, please?"

Colt responded, "Major Kaiser, this is PATRIOT. I need to speak with the watch commander, immediately!"

Major Kaiser reached for a red binder, flipped to a green tab, and found the call sign and its associated authentication code. He paused for a moment when he saw who was assigned the call sign and said, "Roger, PATRIOT. Request you authenticate, sir."

Colt closed his eyes and replied, "I authenticate: Hotel,

Alpha, Lima, Sierra, Echo, Yankee."

Major Kaiser verified the authentication and responded, "Roger, PATRIOT, I mean, sir. Wait one." He turned to face the watch commander and said, "Admiral McGee, the Secretary of Defense wants to speak with you!"

In less than two minutes, Steve Holmes pressed a button on his Pentagon desk console and shouted, "Colt! It's great to hear from you!" Colt spoke with the deputy defense secretary for over an hour, covering the series of events that had occurred since the helicopter crash. He shared what had happened during the encounter with the Chinese hitman, and he explained how he met Mr. Nang and the close call with the police on the river. Then, after Colt mentioned he planned to meet Michele's uncle at the old S-21 prison at midnight before heading to the embassy, Steve Holmes pushed back hard.

"No way, Mr. Secretary. Terrible idea. You need to head to the embassy as soon as you can; I have a special ops squad there right now, sir."

Colt explained to his friend his reasoning for wanting to meet with Kiri Phan before seeking safety at the embassy. He also shared his increasing concern that there may be an intelligence leak at the Pentagon.

"I don't like it, Colt, but I can see your mind's made up. I'll personally brief the president and the national security advisor after I let Allie and Dan know you're safe."

"Thanks, Steve. I'll call you when we get to the embassy."

Becci Quinn's Condominium, Washington DC

Becci Quinn pressed a button on the mobile phone to end the call with Travis Webb. She stepped into her bedroom to change her clothes. She typically reserved Saturdays for working in her small garden plot, but the urgent call from Travis on the burner phone immediately changed all that. Travis has just learned that Garrett had survived the Spetsnaz attack on his helicopter and somehow had made his way to Phnom Penh with Representative Michele Phan. The Americans investigating the crash site had found small pieces of the missiles that brought the two helicopters down, and they believed the weapons were Russian-made. Garrett was headed to the American embassy in Phnom Penh, but not before meeting with someone at a former prison downtown at midnight, local time. She glanced at her watch. "This is going to be close!" Becci stripped off her underwear and stepped into the shower to rinse the garden's dirt from her body while she worked through her next steps. First, she needed to contact her GRU controller immediately and quickly arrange for an emergency face-to-face meeting so that she could pass on Travis Webb's crucial information.

Of course, the procedure was to be used only in the direst circumstance. But Becci knew the standard reporting mechanisms would be too slow to enable Moscow to act on her crucial and timely information. Next, she would need to make her way to the prearranged rendezvous location without being detected and followed by American counterintelligence assets. She was confident she wasn't under surveillance, but one could never be entirely sure. She toweled off and selected the clothes to wear to the rendezvous from her closet: a white top, red and blue Washington Nationals baseball jacket, and faded blue jeans. Becci dressed and ran out of her condominium on her way to Nationals Park on the Anacostia River. She considered it mildly ironic that her secret rendezvous with the Russian GRU controller would occur across the street from the Washington Navy Yard.

USS Blue Ridge (LCC-19), Berth 2, Busan Naval Base, Republic of Korea

Vice Admiral Kurt Shaffer, commander of the US Seventh Fleet, silently read through the stack of files on his desk while wishing he was doing something else. The papers were legal documents associated with the upcoming court-martial of Commander Ronald Leach, the commanding officer of USS McNamara (DDG-145). The commander had been charged with receiving money from a Singapore shipyard contractor in exchange for confidential DOD information. The three-star admiral had convened the court-martial, and he had set aside a few hours this afternoon to review the case and his responsibilities regarding the upcoming trial. The proceedings would follow the Uniformed Code of Military Justice, or UCMJ, a federal law enacted by Congress that defined the military justice system and listed criminal offenses under military law. All military officers received training on the UCMJ when first commissioned, but most were unfamiliar with their specific responsibilities unless they became involved with a court-martial. For that reason, Commander Steve Lingenbrink, the Seventh Fleet staff judge advocate, sat in a chair facing Admiral Shaffer, waiting for him to finish reading the legal documents he had prepared earlier that day.

"Steve," began the admiral, "let's start with my duties as the convening authority for the court-martial. Just the highlights, if you don't mind."

"Aye aye, Admiral. The basic premise is that the military justice system requires you to exercise your independent discretion at each phase of the proceedings, with no undue command influence. You have the authority to refer charges to trial, you'll select members to hear the case, and you'll take appropriate action after the sentencing."

"Will I appoint a military judge?"

"No, Admiral. Navy Judge Advocate General Vice Admiral Willis has that responsibility; he's already appointed Captain Jerome Sanchez as the trial judge. I've served with Sanchez before at Third Fleet, and he's a fair man."

"So, I need to select the jury, Steve?"

"Yes, Admiral, but I'll do the heavy lifting there, and the jury is called a panel in the military system. Because this is not a capital case, we'll need to select eight members, all senior in rank to Commander Leach, to serve on the panel. One interesting aspect of the military justice system: a court-martial with eight members will require six to convict, but only three votes to acquit."

"That is interesting, Steve. When you said that the members need to be senior to Commander Leach, do you mean they all need to be captains or above?"

"No, sir. Members could hold the rank of commander, as long as they have a date of rank that is earlier than Commander Leach's date of rank."

"How does sentencing work?"

"If Leach is convicted, the military judge will conduct all sentencing. Leach will have the option to request sentencing by members, but that's usually a bad idea because judges tend to be more lenient. After sentencing, the convening authority needs to act on the sentencing. You may set aside findings of guilt, and you can reduce the sentence. It's during this phase when you will consider written submissions from the defense before taking sentencing actions. In some situations, you can grant limited clemency."

Admiral Shaffer continued taking notes as Lingenbrink provided more detail regarding the convening authority's responsibilities. Steve was gathering his notes and was about to leave the flag cabin when Shaffer asked, "Do you have another moment, Steve?" Schaffer reached into his desk drawer and pulled out a small cardboard box. "A friend of mine called this morning to let me know that you've been deep-selected for early promotion to captain. You'll see the message sometime tomorrow, but I wanted you to have these as a gift from me."

Steve opened the small box to find two silver eagles, the collar insignia for a US Navy captain. "Thank you, sir! These mean a lot to me!"

After the beaming Captain-select Lingenbrink closed the cabin door, Shaffer opened another small cardboard box on his desk. This one contained a different set of silver collar insignia and a hand-written note that read, "Kurt, let me be the first to let you know President Harrison has approved your nomination to be the next commander of the Pacific Fleet! You can tell Marie to start packing now because you'll need to be in Pearl by the end of next month. I'm proud of you, Kurt, and thrilled that you'll be sitting at Chester Nimitz's old desk. Best of luck, Colt. P.S. I've also enclosed a pair of the four-star insignia that goes with the promotion!"

Kurt Shaffer reread the note and looked at the four-star insignia before placing them back into the small box. It was just a day ago that he learned Colt's helicopter had crashed in the Cambodian jungle, likely shot down. The two men had been friends ever since they served together decades ago, and it was

Colt who christened Kurt with the callsign Teddy after Shaffer had mistakenly landed his jet on the USS Theodore Roosevelt. Kurt had helped Colt in the days after Linda died, even flying back to Washington to lend the Garrett family support during the memorial service. Now, he worried about Dan and Allie Garrett and the pain they must be experiencing while waiting to hear what happened to their father. Shaffer stood up from his desk and crossed the cabin to the bookshelf that held several personal photos. He picked up a framed picture of a young Colt in khakis with his arm around an even younger Kurt in flight gear on the deck of the USS Dwight Eisenhower, somewhere in the Mediterranean Sea. Who could have guessed that Kurt would wear four stars and Colt would be the defense secretary one day? He placed the photograph back on the bookshelf and returned to his desk. He would miss his old friend, and he decided to call Dan Garrett to see if he and Allie needed anything.

"Admiral, you just received this message from the Pentagon."

Shaffer reached for the single piece of paper his aide had handed him. A broad smile crossed his face as he slammed his fist on the desk and exclaimed, "God damn! He's alive!"

Executive Officer's Stateroom, USS Robert McNamara (DDG-145)

Lieutenant Commander Kathy Robertson waited in her stateroom until the helicopter detachment's officer-in-charge appeared at her door. "You wanted to see me, XO?" Lieutenant Commander Jason Vilhauer sat down at the chair next to Kathy's desk and removed his squadron ball cap.

"Jason, I wanted you to know that I spoke with Petty Officer Ramos and have taken her statement. Her story seems credible, and she provided me with some concrete examples of where and when the captain touched her. On one occasion, she stated there were two witnesses to the incident, Petty Officer Davenport and Chief Rowe. I've interviewed both of those women, and they provided statements that closely align with what Petty Officer Ramos described in her statement. I don't have any other choice than to let the captain know what I've learned, and that Navy regulations require me to report Petty Officer Ramos' complaint to 7th Fleet and provide an information copy to the chain of command."

Jason looked at the deck and shook his head. "Jesus, Kathy. How do you think he'll react? What will you do if he orders you not to forward your report?"

"I've been thinking about that. He knows I'm investigating the earlier complaint. You'd have to think he's been worried that other Sailors would come forward. If he does order me to bury the complaints, that would be an unlawful order, and I'd have no obligation to follow it. The regs are clear that I must report the incident. I've decided to send an email version of the report up the chain of command before meeting with him. Even if he prevents me from sending a message from radio, the email will already be in the commodore's in-box."

"When are you planning to talk with him?" Jason asked. "I'd like to make sure I let my chain of command know right after you send your email. And I'd like to keep Petty Officer Ramos away from him until we get back into port."

"It looks like the Chinese exercise will be wrapping up on Monday morning, and we'll receive orders to return to port then. I plan to talk with him after we start back. The best-case scenario is that he retreats to his cabin for the transit and then leaves the ship as soon as we moor. What do you think?"

"I think, my dear executive officer, that you and I will be

needing a drink or two after we pull into Singapore. How about joining me at the Jade in the Fullerton Hotel after we get back? I'll even spring for dinner?" The pilot smiled, smoothed his hair back from his forehead, and put his ball cap on his head.

"Did you just ask me out on a date, Lieutenant Commander Vilhauer?"

Jason "Mask" Vilhauer opened the door and replied, "That's what it sounded like to me, Lieutenant Commander Robertson!" He stepped out of the executive officer's stateroom and headed to the helicopter hanger to speak with Petty Officer Ramos about keeping clear of the captain until the ship pulled into port.

Tuol Sleng Genocide Museum, Phnom Penh, Cambodia

Colt Garrett handed two twenty-dollar bills to the teenager standing next to his tuk-tuk, the three-wheeled motorcycle taxi that had brought Colt and Michele from Mr. Nang's barge on the Mekong. Tourists commonly used tuk-tuks throughout southeast Asia as an economical and efficient way to travel in large cities. Colt knew he was drastically overpaying for the taxi fare in a country where the average annual income was less than $2,000. Still, he wanted to guarantee the teenager would wait until their meeting with Kiri Phan concluded and then take them to the US embassy. "Please wait here until we return," Colt said. "I'll pay you another forty dollars to take us to the American embassy." The young Cambodian boy readily agreed to wait for the second trip because the streets were deserted at midnight, and the promised fare would feed his family for more than a week.

Michele and Colt crossed the street and walked to the museum's entrance, where a short, grey-haired man stood waiting. First, he greeted the couple in the Cambodian tradition with his palms together. Then, he lifted his hands to his chest and bowed slightly, and Michele returned the gesture while Colt stood back a step.

"Uncle Kiri, I am very honored and humbled to meet you! You look very much like my father! May I introduce Colton Garrett? He's an important man in the American government, and the person who made it possible for me to come to Phnom Penh and meet you."

The two men eyed one another, and before Colt could speak, Kiri Phan said, "Welcome to my city, Mr. Garrett, and thank you for bringing my niece on such a long journey to meet her father's brother. I'll unlock this gate, and we can enter the museum where I will tell you my story."

Michele held her uncle's frail arm as he led the two Americans into the former prison courtyard. He began to share what had happened to him when he was just a teenager. He described his personal experience in the killing fields of the Choeung Ek grove and his intense guilt at participating in the genocide. With a wavering voice and tear-filled eyes, Kiri Phan told them about the babies he saw crushed against the killing tree and how his hate for the Pol Pot regime had not diminished through the decades. He paused next to the ancient water well and whispered, "This is where the Russian soldiers killed and buried your soldiers." He handed Michele a canvas bag containing photographs, negatives, a Russian military patch, and Kiri's journal. "I promised my wife I would find a way to share this story. I hope that you can bring these young men home to their families." He bowed once more to Colt, slowly lowered to his knees, and began digging in the soft earth with a short wooden trowel.

Within a few minutes, Kiri Phan uncovered something buried next to the well, and Colt could see it looked like a piece of leather. He got on his knees and carefully removed the soil around the item, and he slowly uncovered what appeared to be pieces of a leather boot. Colt lifted the boot and was horrified to discover it had human bones inside and a small piece of rusted metal attached. Looking closely, he saw that the piece of metal was a military identification or "dog" tag.

"Michele, please hand me that plastic bag from my backpack." Colt placed the boot, bones, and dog tag into one of the backpack's zippered pouches. "We need to come back tomorrow when there's more light to do this correctly. And we need to bring someone from the embassy who knows what they're doing."

Colt and Michele were on their knees examining the shallow grave when Kiri said, "What is that?" and he pointed with his wooden trowel across the courtyard. Kiri's body flew back as two bullets slammed into his chest and through his heart, killing him instantly. Colt saw three men walking toward them. He pulled his 9mm from his belt and fired three rounds at the closest man before pushing Michele to the ground. They crawled behind a low concrete wall to gain some cover. Colt peered around the wall's end and saw one man down and two others crouched behind a metal courtyard bench.

"Michele, take this and watch the bench!" Colt handed her his pistol, unzipped the black backpack, and pulled out the Sig Sauer MPX. He extended the stock, inserted a thirty-round magazine, and cycled the bolt to cock the hammer and chamber a round. "I think I hit one, but there are two others. Take the bag and go to the end of the wall. Fire two rounds at the bench and then get down immediately. When they return fire, I'll open up and cover you as you run to the exit. Get to the tuk-tuk, and I'll be right behind you. Now, go!"

When the two remaining Spetsnaz soldiers saw Michele

fire at them from the end of the wall, they fired several rounds in return. They were surprised when Colt fired the automatic weapon. Thirty rounds of 9mm bullets riddled the bench at 850 rounds per minute, killing Lieutenant Kuzman and hitting Captain Morozov in his calf. The Spetsnaz officer helplessly watched Colt run out of the courtyard as he grasped at his badly bleeding leg wound. With Gusev and Kuzman dead, Morozov feared his mission had failed.

The Barge

The tuk-tuk came to a screeching stop next to the barge moored on Phnom Penh's fuel pier. Michele and Colt climbed out of the improvised taxi and ran down the gangway and into the darkened boat. The captain found them sitting in the dining room and ordered refreshments for the two exhausted Americans.

"I am surprised to see you again," he said. "I thought you were going to the American embassy. Mr. Nang arrived an hour ago and will be joining us here shortly."

Sovann Nang, dressed in an ornate black silk robe, walked into the dining room and sat at the table. He asked, "Is everything all right? Why are you back here?"

Colt finished his second glass of water. "We were attacked at the genocide museum tonight, probably by the same people who shot down the helicopters. I need to make a phone call immediately."

The experienced drug smuggler nodded. "I understand. Captain, please join me in my cabin. We need to give Mr. Garrett and Ms. Phan some privacy." The two Cambodian men walked out of the dining room, quietly closing the door behind them.

Colt reached for the black backpack and removed the satellite phone. Within a few moments, he spoke with Steve Holmes, this time via Steve's mobile phone.

"Steve? Colt. We just got back from meeting with Representative Phan's uncle at the old S-21 prison and were attacked by three well-trained men. I have to assume they were the same people who downed the helicopters. They killed Michele's uncle. I hit two of the attackers before we escaped and returned to the barge. They knew we were going to be at the prison, Steve. And that means we have a leak somewhere, very high up, possibly at the NMCC."

Steve Holmes made furious notes on a yellow pad as Colt continued. "We have to assume the Russians know I was heading to the embassy. I suspect they have a team waiting there to intercept us before we can get through the gate. So we need another plan."

Steve Holmes offered, "Perhaps our consulate at Ho Chi Minh City? It's your closest US sovereign territory option, and the opposition wouldn't be expecting that. Do you want me to contact the special ops team in Phnom Penh and arrange a rendezvous?"

Colt thought for a moment. "That's a no on the team, Steve. I just don't know how the Russians found out where we were going. Going forward, keep my location and plans to just the president and the national security council. Steve, I have proof that the Russians attacked the PYTHON base and that they executed those two MIA servicemen. Michele and I will find a way to get the proof to our Ho Chi Minh City consulate by mid-day tomorrow. I'll call you when we get there."

Colt set the satellite phone on the table and plugged it into its battery charger. He joined Michele on the sofa and said, "I think we're lucky to be alive. How are you doing?"

"How am I doing? How do you think I'm doing? I just watched my only living relative get violently killed, and we almost lost our own lives! And all you can think about is getting some proof back to Washington! Is there something wrong with you?"

Colt didn't know what to say. He had focused his thoughts and actions on solving the immediate problem of getting them to safety rather than worrying about how Michele might be reacting to seeing her uncle killed. He knew his task-focused leadership style wasn't always the most humane or sensitive, but he rationalized that it provided the most efficient way to manage through a crisis.

"I'm sorry, Michele. I guess I got caught up in working the problem. Forgive me?"

Michele shook her head and walked toward the door. "I'm exhausted. I'm heading to my cabin and going to bed."

After Michele left the dining room, the chef walked in and asked, "Mr. Garrett, can I make up a bunk for you in the crew's quarters? Mr. Nang is sleeping in the master cabin."

Colt thought back to the last time he was in the dark crew's quarters and nodded his head. "Yes, please."

Russian Military Intelligence HQ, Moscow

General Korobov read the detailed interrogation report with a surprising degree of detachment, given he knew the subject, Colonel Petrov, quite well. The interrogation report revealed the colonel shared details of his capture and imprisonment, including his interrogation by the American security services. The general was intrigued to learn that Secretary Garrett had personally directed Petrov's arrest and detention; perhaps Garrett had let his personal feelings get the better of him? Korobov made a note of that. It was unfortunate that Colonel Petrov didn't survive his interrogation. Korobov would have liked to learn more about Garrett's conversation with the colonel.

Opening another file on his desk, General Korobov read with interest that his Spetsnaz team failed for a second time to eliminate Garrett, this time at the old Khmer Rouge prison. Captain Morozov reported from the Russian embassy in Phnom Penh that his two soldiers were dead, and Morozov himself wounded but still operational. Although the Spetsnaz team had killed a Cambodian national at the prison, Morozov could not identify the body.

Korobov opened the third file on his desk, which his aide had delivered a moment earlier with the tea. Travis Webb reported Garrett had met with someone at the prison who gave the defense secretary evidence of Russian involvement in executions at the prison decades earlier. General Korobov thought through the implications for Russia's influence if the information was made public. He made a note to have his staff research Russian activities at the Khmer Rouge prison to determine if the American accusation was valid. Webb indicated Garrett and Representative Phan planned to travel to the American consulate at Ho Chi Minh City. The general looked at a map of southeast Asia and decided to prevent Garrett from reaching the safety of the consulate. He pressed a button on his desk console.

"Major, I need a secure line to our embassy in Phnom Penh!"

Day Eleven

The Barge

"The captain tells me you'll be leaving us this morning, Mr. Garrett, and that your destination is Ho Chi Minh City," stated Mr. Nang as he spread jam on his croissant. "How do you plan to travel?"

Colt was about to answer the question when Michele asked, "Mr. Nang, perhaps you could suggest? Your experience with these types of things must be extensive."

Mr. Nang slightly bowed his head to acknowledge the compliment. "Thank you, Representative Phan, most kind. Shall I assume you suspect the Russian security forces may also know your destination?"

Colt nodded his head. "I think that's a safe assumption. It would seem there's a leak within our government, and I've no idea where it might be. What are your thoughts about us traveling to Vietnam?"

Mr. Nang wiped his mouth with a linen napkin and pushed his chair back from the table. "I think that commercial transportation would be dangerous. Airports, trains, and bus stations are all relatively easy to watch. Hiring a private car might work, but it's impossible to know which companies are working with the police or other security organizations." He poured himself a cup of tea and stroked his sparse gray beard. "And there is the obvious problem with any means of travel."

Colt leaned forward and asked, "Obvious problem?"

Sovann Nang smiled. "You must forgive me, but a Caucasian

man traveling with a Cambodian woman, particularly one as stunning as Ms. Phan, would attract unwanted attention regardless of the mode of travel. A difficult problem to solve."

Colt agreed with the experienced drug smuggler's concern. In his brief time in Southeast Asia, he'd seen few Caucasians wandering the streets, other than the occasional tourist. The dining room was quiet, and the captain whispered into Mr. Nang's ear. He thought for a bit and then looked at the two Americans. "Tell me. Does either of you have any experience riding a motorcycle? Our captain here has one onboard."

Michele shook her head and looked at Colt. He finished his cup of tea and stood up from the table, and said, "Let's have a look at the bike!"

The captain led the way to an area on the barge's stern that the crew used for cargo storage. He untied two ropes wrapped around an object under a dark green tarp and revealed a 2010 Triumph motorcycle in pristine condition. "It's a Bonneville!" exclaimed Colt while he examined the classic two-wheeler. "I had one of these when I was in college, but it was one of the older carbureted models with a manual choke. This version's fuel injected with a more powerful engine."

The captain beamed as he watched Colt admire his treasured possession. "Yes, Mr. Garrett. The motorcycle has electronic fuel injection and displaces 865cc, with a top speed of more than 110 miles per hour. I bought it last year from my cousin." Colt had been riding motorcycles since he was sixteen and still enjoyed cruising on sunny Sunday afternoons whenever he got the chance. His current ride was a 2016 BMW R1200 sport tourer, a much more powerful machine than the Bonneville. Still, there was something slightly romantic about the classic, British Triumph, the favorite motorcycle of Steve McQueen.

"Would this machine suit your requirements, Mr. Garrett?"

asked Mr. Nang.

"Absolutely, but I can't pay you for this now. I can send you funds when we get home."

"That will not be necessary. Accept this as a token of my appreciation for rescuing my grandson and bringing him back to my family."

Colt noticed the captain's face drop as his employer magnanimously gave away his prized possession. He didn't know how to proceed until he saw the captain looking at his wristwatch. "Thank you, Mr. Nang. That's a generous offer. But the bike belongs to the captain. Perhaps he would be interested in a trade?" Colt removed the watch from his wrist and handed it to the motorcycle's owner. He strapped it to his arm and broadly smiled.

Sovann Nang nodded. "Mr. Garrett, it appears that you have a deal. I will send my men into the city to procure protective equipment for your motorcycle journey to Ho Chi Minh City. That will allow enough time for you and Ms. Phan to finish your breakfast and to prepare for your trip."

"I was surprised that you traded your watch for the motorcycle, Colt. Surely, we could have found another way to pay for the bike. I mean, it was a gift from your wife, right?"

Colt finished his meal and emptied his water glass. "I suppose I used the trade as an opportunity to part with that watch, Michele. You see, after Linda died, I discovered that she had been seeing someone during the time we were living apart. I've been trying to get my head straight about it, and I think I've come to grips with it now. Still, that watch with its inscription was a daily reminder of Linda and her affair. So I think that trading the watch away is just the next step in the healing process. Weird, huh?"

Michele saw that Colt was uncomfortable sharing his feelings with her about his wife's infidelity, but strangely, it made her feel good that he trusted her enough to share this pain with her. They walked outside to the main deck to find that the crew had lifted the motorcycle to the pier. Helmets, jackets, and gloves were resting on the ground.

"These should fit," commented Sovann Nang. "It was difficult to find a helmet large enough to fit Mr. Garrett's head."

Colt and Michele put on leather motorcycle jackets and full-face helmets. "I thought it best to conceal your faces, and you should wear your sunglasses as well." Nang handed the couple leather gloves and then said to Colt, "You may require further assistance after you arrive in the city." He passed Colt a small card with a name and address. "I have a colleague who has a shop in the old Saigon market in the central part of the city. He knows you're coming, and he will be useful should you encounter difficulties. Good luck!"

Colt and Sovann Nang shook hands, and Colt turned the ignition key. The motorcycle started with a deep rumble and warmed while Colt and Michele put on their gloves. Colt engaged the clutch and pressed down with his left foot to select first gear. He slowly eased the clutch out while rolling the throttle open and smoothly accelerated the motorcycle down the pier and out onto the busy street.

En Route to Ho Chi Minh City

Sovann Nang had told Colt the best way to avoid police and border authorities on the journey was to stay off the main highways and, instead, follow the less-traveled back roads he used to smuggle drugs into Vietnam. These were that same routes that the Viet Cong used decades ago to move weapons and supplies during the war. Using Nang's hand drawn map, Colt skillfully guided the motorcycle along winding jungle paths and mountain streams until the couple finally emerged from the dense forest and up onto a small rural road. After consulting Nang's map, Colt switched off the ignition. "I think we're finally in Vietnam. Let's stretch our legs and take a water break."

Michele got off the bike and removed her helmet. She watched as Colt removed the bike's Cambodian license plate and replaced it with a Vietnam plate Nang that had provided. She drank from the water bottle while Colt threw the Cambodian plate into the undergrowth. She passed the water bottle to Colt.

"Nang really does think of everything, doesn't he?"

Colt smiled. "I suppose it's how he's survived all these years. If you're ready, we better be on our way. Should be much easier now that we're back on pavement. Just a weekend ride on a country road."

Like most experienced motorcycle enthusiasts, Colt preferred the slower and more scenic routes because the odds of being killed by a driver distracted by responding to a text was much less likely on a country road than a major highway. He knew too many fellow riders had died because an SUV driver was doing something other than paying attention to the road.

The couple had been riding for more than an hour, and Michele seemed to have relaxed after they left Phnom Penh and Cambodia behind. She learned to lean into the turns and had wrapped her arms around Colt's waist as they maneuvered through the mid-day traffic, watching small shops and colorful signs flash by. Colt found himself remembering his high school days when Linda would ride on the back of his Yamaha 175 through the rainy Seattle streets. There was something special about going on a first date on a motorcycle. Your date had no option but to hug you tightly.

The traffic finally thinned out, and Colt could see the road was straight for several miles ahead. He downshifted twice into second gear and rolled the throttle wide open, hearing the big twin engine's throaty growl as the bike rocketed forward. Colt could feel Michele press closer to his back and tighten her arms around his waist. The old trick still worked. He upshifted to third, fourth, and fifth gear, listening to the engine revs rather than watching the tachometer for the best time to shift. He felt as though he was a part of the motorcycle as it instantly converted air and fuel into acceleration through space. The experience could make you forget your problems, and, for a short while, Colt forgot his. When the bike reached 80 miles per hour, Colt rolled the bike's throttle forward, and he downshifted into fourth gear. It would be stupid to get pulled over by the local police for speeding. He let the bike slow to a legal 35 miles per hour and could feel Michele's grip relax.

Before long, the motorcycle approached the outskirts of Ho Chi Minh City, and the fuel gauge indicated the tank was near empty. Colt noticed a gas station ahead on the right and slowed to enter the small lot. He brought the bike to stop next to the pump furthest from the small convenience store, lowered the kickstand, and let the motorcycle lean to the left. He turned off the ignition switch and waited for Michele to dismount first.

"We made good time," offered Michele. She removed the helmet and let her brown hair fall to her shoulders. "I'll use the restroom and buy us some gas and water, Colt. Wait here for me."

Colt watched Michele walk across the pavement to the convenience store and then looked beyond the lot. He noticed that a tall concertina wire-topped cyclone fence bordered the property. Just beyond the security fence stood several military helicopters parked on the tarmac. So this was some sort of military airfield. He removed his helmet and walked over to the fence to take a closer look. He could see two different models of helicopters: Mi-17s and Ka-21s. But beyond the Russian-made helicopters was a more familiar airframe, the American-made Huey. Colt saw Michele exit the convenience store accompanied by two uniformed men, and he was immediately concerned that Michele had somehow drawn their suspicion. He watched her talk with the two officers, gesture to him, and to the helicopters over his shoulder. They spoke for a few minutes longer, and the officers drove off in a dark sedan. She walked toward Colt carrying two bottles of water and placed them into the backpack.

"What did the police have to say, Michele? And why did they let you go?"

"They're not policemen; they're helicopter pilots stationed at that base. It's a helicopter training facility, and the pilots are assigned to an aggressor squadron as instructors, training the student pilots to avoid air attacks. And here's the interesting part. Do you see those Hueys over there? That's what they fly. Those were left behind by the Air Force's 20th Special Operations Squadron after Saigon fell. You can still see the old Green Hornet logo on the fuselage."

"Is that the same Air Force squadron that's flying the CV-22 Ospreys out of Hurlburt Field in Florida? I visited that squadron last year."

"The very same. The pilots told me they'd kept the helicopters operational; everything is current. They said they use contractors to perform maintenance and replace parts."

"You sure got a lot of information from those pilots. I wonder why they were so talkative?"

Michele tossed her hair back and forth as if she was in a shampoo commercial and smiled. "I don't know, Colt. Why do you think they talked to me?"

"Oh. Right." Colt finished adding fuel to the tank, then he placed his helmet back on his head and opened the visor. "Let's get back on the road. I'd like to get to the consulate as soon as possible."

Michele climbed onto the motorcycle, and Colt started the bike's engine. He steered the Triumph back onto the street and didn't notice the man at the convenience store counter as he placed a call on his mobile phone.

Ho Chi Minh City

Today, Spencer Hale couldn't visit the US embassy where he used to work during the war because the American government demolished the structure in 1998 after establishing diplomatic relations between the United States and the Socialist Republic of Vietnam. Because the United States had constructed a new US embassy in Hanoi, a consulate-general was built in Ho Chi Minh City to provide service in the southern part of the country. This diplomatic post was erected on the consular compound near the old embassy site. Today, consular staff used the former embassy site as a soccer practice field. Children of career foreign-service officers practiced kicking drills and corner kicks on the lush green turf, the site of America's withdrawal from Vietnam.

Colt turned left onto Le Duan Boulevard and slowly pulled the motorcycle next to the curb, two blocks from the consulate. He turned off the ignition and rested the bike on its kickstand. He raised his helmet visor, watching the noisy groups of tourists stream down both sides of the busy street. It seemed that most of the tourists were in groups of twenty or so, following a tour guide holding a sign indicating the tour company name. Most guides spoke into headsets that transmitted the guide's comments to the visitors via small receivers suspended on brightly colored lanyards hanging around their necks. Colt wondered how often competing tour companies spied on one another to expand their guide scripts.

Years earlier, Colt and Linda were touring a former communist-bloc country in eastern Europe when a fellow traveler asked a politically charged question. Colt was amused when the nervous tour guide looked to his left and then his right before answering to ensure an official was not within earshot. Colt thought most Americans took for granted their right to free speech and didn't consider that most other countries didn't offer their citizens similar protections. Colt decided to move the motorcycle closer to the consulate's entrance and parked in the middle of the next block.

"What do you think?" asked Michele. "Do you see any surveillance teams?"

Colt pretended to be looking at a tourist map as he studied each vehicle parked near the consulate's entrance. Several small sedans lined the street, and a small green telephone utility van sat twenty feet from the consulate's main door.

"It's probably nothing, but I don't like the looks of that small van. I can see two men talking on their mobile phones inside; there could be more of them. That black Honda to the van's right has three men inside, and the engine is running. Not good."

"Are you saying that they know we were coming? How?"

Colt replied, "I still don't know. It could be nothing. I think we should get back on the bike and do a slow pass by the entrance. If nothing happens, I'll stop right out front, and you can just climb off and walk inside the building. I'll be right behind you. Ready?"

Colt started the motorcycle again and pulled into the traffic. He slowed the bike as he approached the consulate and had just come to a stop when the green van's doors opened, and two men stepped out. Colt rolled the throttle open and released the clutch lever. Michele was caught off guard as Colt jumped the motorcycle over the curb and headed down the crowded sidewalk, scattering tourists who screamed obscenities in their native language. He heard three gunshots as he accelerated the bike down the sidewalk while a fourth round hit the pavement, spraying bits of concrete into the air. Looking ahead, Colt saw that an older woman in a motorized wheelchair had trapped one wheel next to a concrete planter. An older man was frantically trying to lift the heavy wheelchair and then fell to the ground when he lost his footing. Michele nearly lost her grip on Colt's waist when he sharply counter-steered the motorcycle to the left. They sailed over the curb and back into the crowded street, accelerating between the cars and scooters and then turning right at the next corner. Colt didn't know if the shooters were following, but he didn't want to take any chances. He reached down with his left hand and squeezed Michele's gloved hand. Colt prayed the gunfire hadn't hit her, but he didn't dare stop to find out. He changed directions four more times before getting on the highway and rocketing out of town as fast as the motorcycle could take them.

An hour later, they were sitting inside a small bar well off the main road, trying to calm their badly shattered nerves with the local beer.

"My god! That last shot almost hit my leg! They could have killed us!"

"I'm glad I was sitting in the front!"

Michele stared at Colt and then laughed. "Right, what a gentleman! It does feel good to laugh about something. What should we do next?"

Colt ordered two more beers and waited to answer until the

server returned to her station behind the bar. "I think we need to wait here a bit longer and then find some different colored coats to replace these leather jackets in case those Russians are still looking for us. Then, after dark, we should find a place to stay; we need to get off the streets and decide what to do next. Why don't you ask the server to recommend a hotel that's near the city center? I think we need to be relatively close to the consulate if it appears the surveillance has dropped off."

Michele nodded. "Okay, sounds good. But I'm worried about checking into a hotel; they'll require our passports."

"Maybe. I think if we offer the cash from Glenn's backpack, that will be all we require to get a room without showing identification. I know this is a communist country, but I think it's more communist 'light,' a society where cash can still buy a thing or two."

The Hotel Majestic, Ho Chi Minh City, Vietnam

Built in 1925 on the western bank of the Saigon River, the Hotel Majestic incorporated French Colonial and French Riviera architectural styles. The iconic six-story hotel had survived war and government changes over its ninety-year history and now offered the finest accommodations to adventurous travelers and weary businesspeople. Colt admired the hotel's architecture as he sat on the Triumph motorcycle on Dong Khoi Street near the Majestic's entrance. Colt watched ships and barges of every size and shape cruise by on the river across the street while thousands of scooters, motorcycles, and bicycles raced along the road. Michele had suggested he wait on the motorcycle with his helmet hiding his Caucasian features while she arranged for a hotel room. Colt felt exposed on the busy street, despite his helmet, and he nervously waited for Michele to exit. He didn't know if the Russians could access the country's hotel guest registration database, but it was a risk they decided to take.

"We have a room for two nights," announced Michele as she walked up to the parked motorcycle.

"But I thought we only needed a room for one night."

"I know, Colt. But a two-night stay is much less suspicious; I didn't want the desk clerk to think I was a working girl!" she kidded. "Besides, if someone does find our hotel registration, it's better to let them think that we'll be staying for a second night. Keeps them a step behind."

"How did you avoid giving them passports?"

"Like you said, you'd be surprised what rules one can break when one pays the desk clerk in cash."

Colt momentarily wondered about the legality of using the cash in Glenn Carpenter's backpack to bribe a hotel desk clerk but realized they had much more pressing issues than DOD regulations. The Russians somehow knew Colt and Michele were trying to get into the consulate and seemed determined to prevent them. After Michele climbed on the motorcycle, Colt started the engine and steered the bike into the hotel's underground parking garage.

The fourth-floor corner suite offered a panoramic view of the city. Michele was out on the wrought-iron balcony when she heard a knock on the room's door. She opened the door to see Colt standing there with his helmet on, and the backpack slung over his right shoulder. "People looked at me on the elevator, but I think they eventually assumed I was a courier of some kind." He stepped into the suite and removed the helmet, his head wet from sweat.

"Finally! I've wanted to take that thing off for over two hours!"

Michele poured two glasses of mineral water and handed Colt one. "Here, drink this. You look terrible!"

Colt emptied the glass of water and drank another before speaking. "That tasted great," he commented, and sat down on a leather couch.

"Colt, have you given any thought to how we're going to get into the consulate? I don't think the main entrance is an option any longer."

"Well, I do have an idea, but I don't think you're going to like it."

Colt Garrett waited until dark before he walked down the hallway and opened the door to the stairway leading to the hotel's roof. Satisfied that he was alone, he extended the satellite phone's antenna and placed a call to Steve Holmes' mobile phone.

"Holmes."

"Steve, it's Colt. I don't have much time." He explained his plan to reach the safety of the consulate the following day, and it turned out that Steve didn't like his idea any better than Michele had.

"Jesus, Colt. That's insane! Do you realize how crazy that sounds? And you say that Michele thinks it's possible?"

"I think the phrase she used was technically feasible. Regardless, it's what we're going to have to do if I can arrange a few things later this evening. One other thing, Steve. It's pretty clear that we're compromised. I have a backup plan to reach sovereign territory if something goes wrong tomorrow. But you need to keep this to yourself. Not another soul!"

Steve Holmes pressed a button on his desk console. "Please set up an immediate call with the president's chief of staff. And after the call, I'll need to speak with the national security advisor."

Ben Thanh Market, Ho Chi Minh City

Ben Thanh Market was one of the oldest surviving structures
in the city. People had been trading there since the seventeenth
century. Under French rule, the market opened under the
name Les Halles Centrales. After a fire in the early twentieth
century, the owners renamed the market Ben Thanh, or "Wharf
Citadel." The main entrance featured an enormous white clock
tower that had remained unchanged for more than a century.
Covering more than 140,000 square feet, the market opened at
sunrise after shop owners prayed at a small temple for wealth
and success in the day's trading. In the evening, thriving night
markets opened at the market's northern, eastern, and western
gates. Inside, its vaulted buildings housed nearly a thousand stalls,
with shop owners selling everything from maternity clothing
and luggage to herbal tea and transmission fluid. Tonight, Colt
Garrett wasn't interested in purchasing any product. Instead, he
wanted to contract for a particular type of professional service.

Tuan Sheng-wu examined the small card Colt handed him
after the clothing shop owner escorted the two Americans into
a small storage room located in the rear of the ancient building.
Shelves packed with designer clothing and sports apparel covered
the room's walls, and hundreds of name-brand shoeboxes were
precariously stacked up to the dusty room's ceiling. Tuan noticed
that Michele appeared interested in a green silk blouse hanging
from a clothing rack. "You have impeccable taste, Ms. Phan. I'm
sure we have one in your size."

Michele faced the merchant and replied, "Thank you, but
we're not here to shop for clothes. Perhaps another time?"
Michele didn't like the slightly built man wearing a navy blue
running suit that was a knock-off of a famous sportswear brand.
She thought it was wrong that the entire market was selling

245

imitation clothing, luggage, and watches, essentially stealing from the legitimate manufacturers of those products. She wondered how often when she saw name-brand items in America that she was looking at such counterfeit goods.

Tuan nodded his head and smiled. "Yes. Perhaps." Turning to Colt, he returned the card. "Mr. Garrett, how might I be of service? Our mutual friend Nang called me this morning and said that you might be contacting me. I will do what I can."

Colt knew Vietnam's black market was a significant industry within the communist country, trafficking everything from counterfeit sportswear to illegal drugs. Anything could be had for the right price, if one could pay the going rate. And that included people. Human trafficking was on the rise in Asian countries, and the obscenely high profit margins were attractive to black market thugs.

"I need two things," Colt began. "First, Ms. Phan and I need to get onto the airbase outside of Dong Thanh early tomorrow morning. Do you know that base?"

Tuan looked to the pair of armed men standing behind the Americans, blocking their path to the room's only door. The tallest man had an AK-47 rifle slung over his shoulder while his shorter companion stood with crossed arms and a large black revolver tucked into his waistband. "Yes, we know the airbase very well. I provide a variety of refreshments to the troops there. And the base has been a convenient source of a surprising variety of valuable goods." The man with the rifle unslung the automatic weapon and cradled it in his arms and nodded at his employer.

Pushing back his chair, Tuan stood and looked out a small dirty window on the rear wall. He then turned to face Colt. "The Air Force sends a truck every morning to the city jail to collect flight students who over-celebrated the night before. The truck driver happens to be on my payroll. So, it would be possible for you two to be on that truck in the morning. The security is superficial at best, only a training base. And the truck is rarely searched when it enters the fenced area. I believe it's because of the smell."

Colt could well imagine the smell of a truckful of intoxicated students. No wonder an underpaid and unmotivated gate guard would let it pass unsearched. "I think that'll work, Mr. Tuan."

"Excellent! And your second need?"

"About an hour after we get onto the base, I'd like you to arrange for some sort of diversion. It would need to be significant enough to draw the attention of the base security forces for about thirty minutes."

Colt watched Tuan's face as it broke into a broad smile. "Oh, yes. I believe that also could be arranged. But I would need to start planning that immediately. And both of your requests will require significant payment first."

"Most of our cash is gone," Colt answered. "Perhaps you could agree to delay your collection until I return to the United States?" He removed a business card and passed it to the black-market merchant.

"You honor me with your presence, Mr. Garrett, but I'm sure that you can see that would place me in a difficult position." He walked over to where Michele was sitting and said, "These are spectacular diamond earrings, Ms. Phan. A carat each?"

Michele removed her earrings and handed them to Tuan. "One point two five carats, and worth $20,000."

Colt hated that Michele had to lose her earrings over his plan, but there didn't appear to be an alternative. "Okay, Tuan. One last thing. I need some 9mm rounds for my Sig." He removed the MPX from his backpack and placed it on the table.

Tuan picked it up and said, "That ammunition is very scarce.

If you are willing to part with this fine weapon, I will provide a replacement with suitable ammunition."

Colt knew the MPX was an expensive and rare weapon, but it was useless to him without ammunition. He nodded. "Deal."

The Hotel Majestic, Ho Chi Minh City

The Majestic's room service menu featured a superb selection of steaks, and Colt decided to order a ribeye. He believed that the steak's balanced amount of marbling gave it the best taste and flavor, typically lacking in other cuts of meat. Michele had ordered the guay teow, a type of noodle soup with chicken and wontons. An hour later, a short man with cropped gray hair delivered the meals and silently departed after Michele handed him a generous tip. Moments later, Colt emerged from the suite's bathroom.

"I decided it would be better to remain out-of-sight when the room service arrived rather than keep my face covered by the motorcycle helmet." Michele uncovered the dinner plates and set them on a small table next to the window overlooking the city below. Colt opened an expensive bottle of sauvignon blanc and set it aside to breathe as they began eating their salads. The two quickly ate their late-night meal, knowing they had an important and stressful day ahead.

"I know you're nervous about tomorrow, but I'm sure you'll do fine, Michele. In just a few hours, we'll be inside the consulate arranging a flight home."

Michele was very concerned about Colt's plan to get inside the consulate because everything depended on her. She finished her glass of wine and said, "Going home sounds heavenly. I think I'll take a shower and then head to bed."

Colt watched the city lights while he finished off the last of the wine. He gathered the dishes, glasses, and the empty wine bottle and placed them outside the door. He found an extra pillow and blanket on the shelf in the closet and was in the process of making up the couch as a bed when Michele walked into the room dressed in a white hotel bathrobe.

"I don't think either of us wants you to sleep there tonight," purred Michele as she turned out the room light and crossed the floor to the suite's sole bed. The suite was dimly lit from the lights of the city, and Colt quietly watched as Michele pulled back the blanket and sheets, removed her bathrobe, and got into the bed. Their eyes met, and Colt finally said, "I couldn't agree more."

"Wake up, Colt! Wake up!" pleaded Michele as Colt cried out in the darkened room. Finally, he opened his eyes and realized where he was and who was in bed with him. He sat up and used an extra pillow to wipe the sweat from his forehead.

"Are you all right? That was frightening. You must've been dreaming." Michele watched with concern as Colt rose from the bed and stepped into the bathroom. She heard the water run from the bathroom sink and watched Colt as he quietly returned to the bed and rested his head on a pillow.

"I'm sorry I scared you. I have these nightmares from time to time, although I usually can go back to sleep after I experience one."

"How long have you been having these dreams?"

His back was to her, and he was facing the far wall when he answered. "For longer than I can remember." Linda had begged him to share the contents of dream with her. When he had refused, she pleaded with him to talk with a counselor. Each time, Colt had refused, convinced the problem was his alone and that one day the dreams would go away. Sadly, they hadn't.

Michele reached over and rubbed his neck, and she could feel him relax as she moved her hand to his scalp. "Why don't you tell me about the dream? I mean, it can't hurt, right?"

Colt rolled onto his back and thought back to his reasons for not sharing the dream before. The government had declassified much of the information, and most of the people involved in the dream were either retired or dead. After decades of keeping what had happened in Gibraltar locked away in his mind, he finally decided he had nothing to lose but to share his burden and shame with another. He got out of bed, put on a robe he found hanging from the bathroom door. Colt moved a chair next to the bed and sat down.

"I'll tell you about the dreams. They started after something that happened in Gibraltar a very long time ago."

Michele sat up in bed and rested her arms on the pillow in her lap. "Okay, I'm listening."

"Several weeks after reporting to naval intelligence school in Denver, I was selected for something called the BROADSWORD program. In the late 1970s and early 1980s, senior intelligence community leaders had drastically reduced the community's ability to gather intelligence using human assets, or human intelligence. Instead, they preferred to rely on advanced technology to provide critical national security information to decision-makers and their policy advisors. When that direction eventually proved flawed, most agencies immediately began to rebuild their human intelligence capabilities. One of the Navy's programs, codenamed BROADSWORD or Task Group 165.2, involved the selection and training of junior naval intelligence officers to form a small cadre of specially trained human intelligence collection specialists. We received a wide variety of training from most of the three-letter agencies in the intelligence

TOM CARROLL

community. Typically, we'd receive orders to a conference or other mundane multi-day event as cover for our actual training."

"So, what happened after you received the special training?" asked Michele. "Did you receive special assignments?"

"No, not at all," replied Colt. "The whole idea of BROADSWORD was to locate the cadre in regular fleet billets should we be needed. I was sent to Rota, Spain, to work in an intelligence fusion center and didn't have any BROADSWORD tasking until the PIVOT BLUE program material went missing."

"PIVOT BLUE?" Michele said as she slipped out of bed and got a drink of water.

"You remember the stealth program? Using special shapes and coatings, stealth technology reduces an object's radar cross-section to a size smaller than can be detected by RADAR. But the problem is that as stealth technology improved, RADAR technology also improved its ability to detect smaller and smaller targets."

"I don't understand, Colt. If stealth makes everything appear as bugs, doesn't that solve the problem? I mean, how can an operator differentiate between thousands of bugs in the sky?"

Colt leaned forward and smiled. "It's simple. Birds and bugs don't fly at hundreds of miles per hour. RADAR algorithms could remove the slow-moving targets leaving everything else as legitimate targets."

Michele thought through what Colt had just said and then asked, "Okay, so what's PIVOT BLUE?"

"PIVOT BLUE was a classified program that solved the problem by reducing an object's RADAR cross-section to zero. You can't track a bug, even a speedy bug, if you can't see it. The program developed a suite of software that, when energized, made an object completely invisible to RADAR. And because the technology was software-based, it could be back-fitted into all of

251

our tactical aircraft. Perhaps the system's most important feature was that it incorporated a wartime mode that commanders could remotely energize at a future date. The Navy and Air Force were performing prototype testing on some of Rota's P-3s and C-130s when the design specification documents went missing. Navy NIS special agents suspected that Major Russ Cassidy, an Air Force project officer, was likely guilty of stealing the documents, and they determined he was driving to Gibraltar to meet with Russian GRU operatives. Russ and I had been close friends, and NIS needed someone to identify him. So I flew to Gibraltar with the NIS agents to find and arrest Russ before he could meet with the Russians to give them the PIVOT BLUE documents."

"You and Russ were good friends? That must have been terrible!"

"Yes, we both worked on PIVOT BLUE, and our wives spent lots of time together, too. Our families went on trips throughout Spain and Portugal, and we lived next door to one another in base housing."

"Why do you think he took the documents? Money?"

"I don't know, Michele. Russ was a pretty heavy drinker, and he's received two DUIs from the base police. He knew he'd be losing his security clearance, and that would mean the end of his Air Force career. So I suppose he rationalized the government owed him something, and he still had access to the PIVOT BLUE material."

"What happened when you got to Gibraltar? Did you get there before Russ arrived?"

"We did. The station C-12 landed at Gibraltar, and the Brits provided us with a sedan to drive the Gibraltar streets to search for Russ and his white Volvo. Later that afternoon, I spotted Russ with two other men in his car at a gas station on Winston Churchill Boulevard. We pulled into the gas station, and the NIS agents approached the Volvo. The Russians got out of the car and opened fire, immediately hitting one of the NIS agents. One of the Russians was also hit, and Russ wounded the remaining NIS agent. I saw the two wounded NIS agents and knew I had to do something, so I ran back to the car and drove it forward to cover the wounded agents. One was dead, but the other was still breathing. I exchanged fire with the two Russians with my service pistol, hitting them both before pulling the wounded NIS agent behind our sedan. I saw the agent's rifle on the ground and charged the Volvo. One of the Russians was already dead, but I hit the other one, who managed to crawl back into the Volvo and leave the scene. Russ was left standing in the open with a black briefcase handcuffed to his left wrist and a pistol in his right hand."

Michele couldn't believe what she was hearing. She noticed that Colt was breathing heavily and slowly rubbing his forehead. She whispered, "What happened next?"

Colt stood up and started to pace the floor. "I asked him to drop the gun and get on his knees, but he just stood there staring at me. Russ said that he wasn't going back with me and that I'd have to shoot him. He asked me to tell his wife that he was sorry for everything, that he didn't have any other choice. I watched Russ raise his pistol, and I fired two rounds from the rifle, hitting him in the chest. Russ died in my arms." Colt sat back down in the chair and then continued. "It turned out that the pistol was empty. I guess Russ wanted me to kill him. I recovered the stolen documents and returned them to Rota. The Navy released a cover story about the shooting at the Gibraltar gas station, something about Red Brigade terrorists and an attempted bombing of a Brit government building. The Navy promoted me to lieutenant commander, and an admiral pinned a Navy Cross on my chest. The whole thing was highly classified, and the award citation has been locked away in a safe in Virginia."

Michele poured a glass of water and handed it to Colt. He drank the water and set the glass down on the bedside table. "Two months later, I learned the government discontinued PIVOT BLUE because the enabling technology wasn't practicable—something to do with power and excessive heat generation. Russ died for nothing. I killed him, and they gave me a medal for it. Finally, I just couldn't do it anymore. I resigned my active-duty commission and transferred to the Navy Reserve."

Colt and Michele got back into bed and turned out the lights. Michele noticed that Colt went to sleep almost immediately. "No wonder he has nightmares," she thought as she watched him sleep. "Maybe telling someone the story will help."

Day Twelve

The Airbase Drunk Truck

Colt and Michele rode the Triumph motorcycle to a city parking lot and waited for the military truck to arrive. Dressed in green military fatigues, they could pass as members of the Vietnam People's Air Force, at least from a distance. But, of course, Colt bore no resemblance to a typical 20-year-old Vietnamese conscript, even with the authentic uniform. Still, Mr. Tuan was certain the ruse would be successful. "When people see someone in uniform, all they see is the uniform," he had stated when he gave them the clothing last night. "We do this all of the time." "Sure," thought Colt. "But I don't look anything like you!"

Nevertheless, Tuan's plan seemed feasible, and if the airbase security was as lax as Tuan said, Colt and Michele would be inside the security perimeter within an hour. While they waited for the base truck, Colt glanced at the Triumph motorcycle parked nearby. It was a good ride that had brought them safely to Ho Chi Minh City. Colt left the key in the ignition and the two helmets on the pavement with no other choice than to abandon the prized bike. He didn't doubt that some enterprising soul would discover the bike and ride off. Colt looked back at the classic motorcycle once more, thinking perhaps he should try to find a used Bonneville if he managed to get home. Linda had insisted that he only keep one motorcycle in the garage, but there was nothing stopping him now from adding another.

"Colt, I'm glad you were able to get back to sleep last night. Do you think that talking about Gibraltar helped?"

"Perhaps," Colt replied. "I slept pretty soundly, and the nightmare didn't return. And it did feel good to finally tell the story and how everything went wrong that day. I can't begin to tell you how many times friends have asked me about the Navy Cross and why it was awarded. People don't understand why I resigned my commission, either. If we get out of this mess, I think I'll have to sit down with several people to tell the story. I just hope they don't think less of me after they hear what I did."

Michele shook her head. "I don't think you did anything wrong. The Navy didn't award that medal to make you keep quiet. You received it for extraordinary bravery against an enemy in the line of duty. I understand that you feel guilty about killing Russ, but you had no other choice."

Colt leaned down, embraced Michele, and passionately kissed her lips until a large military truck turned into the parking lot. They picked up their rifles and backpacks and climbed into the canvas-covered back of the dark green, Russian-made Ural truck. More than twenty semi-conscious airmen were seated on the truck's wooden benches, obviously hungover or still drunk from the previous night's festivities. Most of the airmen were sleeping, but a small group near the truck's front attempted to sing a song from their school days. They were doing fairly well until one of the airmen stopped in mid-verse and vomited all over himself. His companions didn't notice and continued to sing as the old diesel truck bounced through downtown Ho Chi Minh City on its way to the airbase.

Michele started to gag when the diesel exhaust fumes filled the back of the truck, and she started coughing. Colt covered her face with his jacket to filter the toxic fumes. The short ride to the airbase seemed to take forever, but finally, it ended abruptly at the main gate. Colt could hear the driver joke with one of the gate sentries and he considered that a good sign. But when another sentry opened the truck's canvas curtain to inspect the rear compartment, Colt thought that things might be about to take a turn for the worse. He pulled his uniform hat down as far as possible and leaned down as if he was going to be sick. Thankfully, the guard pointed, laughed at him, and closed the canvas curtain. Michele breathed a sigh of relief when the truck's engine started, and the old air force vehicle lurched forward. "I thought for a moment that you were actually going to be sick," admitted Michele. The combined smells of the drunken airmen and the diesel exhaust was overpowering. Colt glanced around the truck to make sure that no one could hear him. "It seemed to be the best way to hide my face from the guard," he replied. "And besides, I do feel sick!"

The truck slowly drove down the installation's roads and, after turning several times, stopped across the street from what appeared to be a dilapidated maintenance hangar. Broken windows and rusted corrugated steel were everywhere, and an old, rusted fuel truck sat off to one side. "You get out here, please!" ordered the driver at the two Americans, and he pointed to his right toward a small truck parked near a line of helicopters. "Mr. Tuan said you are to wait in the truck until it's time. He said to tell you that the diversion will provide twenty minutes for your needs." Then, without waiting for a response, the driver climbed back into the truck and drove away.

The Flight Line, Vietnam People's Air Force Airbase, Ho Chi Minh City

Michele looked to her left at the line of Vietnamese Air Force UH-1 helicopters parked at the end of the runway. The experienced former US Air Force pilot saw the helicopters were the twin-engine model, similar to the Huey helicopters she flew while on active duty. The aircraft appeared to be surprisingly well-maintained from her brief inspection, easing her mind somewhat about what Colt had asked her to do. They continued walking past the row of olive-green choppers with their AK-47s slung over their shoulders and climbed into the truck per Mr. Tuan's instructions.

"So far, so good," commented Colt while he carefully watched for possible security forces. "I'm surprised we haven't run into a security patrol by now."

"I know. Tuan said security was lax, but I didn't expect the tarmac to be deserted at mid-morning on a weekday. Maybe they're all at some kind of training event?"

"Could be." Colt turned to face Michele. "What do you think about flying one of these choppers into the consulate compound? I know you haven't flown in a while, so what are your concerns?"

Michele had a long list of concerns about Colt's plan to steal a Huey and fly into the soccer field inside the consulate's gates, but the thing that most bothered her was the Vietnam war era helicopter's condition. "Your entire plan hinges on me being able to get one of those birds to start immediately before anybody stops us. I flew the N version when I was in the Air Force, but we had well-trained mechanics who meticulously maintained those airframes. Even then, there were many times when a flight was canceled because of some problem that surfaced during the start, post-start, or pre-takeoff checklists. Countless things need to be working perfectly for a helicopter to fly safely, and a failure of any one of them could mean we couldn't take off. So I'm planning on completing just the most crucial items on each checklist; those are mandatory. That should make things go faster. But I'm going to need at least five minutes to get the helicopter airborne, and that's if everything goes well."

Colt nodded his head. "I understand. But you've seen the aircraft now. What do you think about their condition?"

"From what I can tell from just walking by, they look like they've been well cared for. No rust, no pools of hydraulic fluid under the skids, and those pilots I spoke with yesterday said they fly daily. My major concern is with the condition of the batteries. I noticed the AC starting equipment locked up near the flight line, which means the Vietnamese probably use them to start the helicopters. I'll have to use chopper's DC battery power to start the engines; we'll need them charged to at least 85 percent, or we won't be going flying today. And I hope the Vietnamese refuel the helicopters after each flight, rather than before. No gas, no go."

Colt hadn't realized the number of problems they might encounter to get the helicopter airborne. He had focused on getting them on the airbase and to the flight line undetected. Colt was about to ask Michele another question when a red flash filled the sky, and a loud explosion rocked the truck. Colt and Michele watched as emergency vehicles emerged from buildings lining the runway and raced toward the control tower, now fully engulfed in flames. Black smoke billowed up in the sky as sirens screamed and people ran in all directions. Colt touched Michele's arm. "I'm pretty sure that's our diversion, and it looks like we're getting two earrings worth!" They leaped from the truck and briskly walked to the nearest helicopter. Michele opened the right front door while Colt remained on the tarmac, appearing to be an armed sentry to anyone who might spot him.

Michele, using muscle memory ingrained from her thousands of hours flying the same model aircraft, strapped herself into the seat's safety harness and slid open the plastic side window so that she could talk with Colt. She noticed the American manufactured helicopter's instrument panel gauges were in English, but the laminated checklists she found on the copilot's seat were written in Vietnamese. She smiled when she remembered having to memorize the lists as a student pilot. Nobody ever suggested that it was because one day, she might be stealing an aircraft with the checklists written in a foreign language. She rotated the battery switch to the ON position, providing direct power to the main 28-volt bus.

"Colt, we have enough battery power for about twelve minutes, plenty to start the engines."

"I hope we're long gone by then," answered Colt, who continued to watch as the airbase fire department fought the flames, heat, and smoke generated by the growing fire. More fire personnel arrived on the scene, probably from the city's fire brigade. Sirens continued to wail while guards evacuated nearby buildings and medical teams treated the injured.

"We have full fuel tanks, Colt," announced Michele as she quickly worked her way through the memorized start checklist. She flipped several more switches and turned knobs before stating, "Okay, Colt. I'm ready to start the first engine. Watch out for the rotors!"

She flipped one more switch, and the DC panel sent power to the first engine. It fired immediately, and the main and tail rotors began to rotate slowly. Colt watched the rotors spin faster and faster, and Michele smiled at him. She gave Colt a thumbs up, indicating the instruments were all reading within the required parameters. Next, Michele began the starting sequence for the second engine and was pleased when it started as well. After she completed the post-start checklist, she waved to Colt and motioned him to board. He opened the left front door, climbed into the copilot seat, and strapped into the harness. Michele finished the last checklist item and tightened her seat harness.

Finally, she pointed to the headset sitting on the glare shield, and Colt put it on and adjusted the mic in front of his mouth.

"Okay, Colt. I'm ready to go," Michele spoke into the intercom. "What the hell?"

Colt was shocked to see a uniformed airman standing in front of the helicopter, waving his arms up and down in what appeared to be an attempt to get their attention. "What do you think he wants?" asked Colt into the intercom.

Michele paused and then replied, "I think he wants us to take off. I bet they're trying to sortie any aircraft they can to keep them away from the fire." She gave the airman a thumbs-up signal, rotated the throttle to full, and smoothly raised the collective pitch control. Michele held the helicopter in a five-foot hover, turned the aircraft to the left, and it climbed away to the east. Colt looked down and back as they continued to rise and accelerate away. He didn't see any other aircraft launch and hoped that the confusion caused by the fire would allow them to escape without notice.

Airbus H130 Helicopter above Ho Chi Minh City

From major tourist destinations to the busy airspace over cities, the single-engine H130 was in widespread use by sightseeing services, shuttle and charter operations, emergency medical providers, and law enforcement agencies. As a result, the pilot-in-command position was moved from the right- to the left-hand side with all associated flight controls and instruments. This configuration facilitated cargo sling operations and allowed an extra passenger to sit up front without incurring the danger of mistakenly interfering with the helicopter's controls. For this reason, pilot Yuri Turgenev sat in the helicopter's left front seat while GRU Captain Morozov occupied the chopper's right-hand seat. Moscow assigned Turgenev to the mission after the American Colton Garrett had killed Lieutenant Kuzman and Sergeant Gusev at the old Khmer Rouge prison. Morozov's leg still throbbed from the wound he had received during the exchange of gunfire, but the pain in his leg was nothing compared to the rage he felt at losing his teammates, a rage he would soon direct at the man who killed his friends and who had shot him.

GRU Moscow had warned Morozov that Garrett and the American congresswoman would attempt to find refuge in the American consulate again today, this time using a stolen military helicopter. As luck would have it, GRU lieutenant and helicopter pilot Turgenev worked at the Phnom Penh embassy and quickly made himself available for the special assignment. The helicopter charter company was hesitant to allow the Russian pilot to fly the helicopter, but a large cash payment and a case of Russian vodka quickly solved that problem.

Morozov's tasking from Moscow was clear: prevent Garrett's helicopter from landing at the American consulate by whatever means necessary. Morozov was keenly aware he had already failed twice in his mission to kill Garrett. He was determined not to fail a third time. So, when Turgenev warned that a military helicopter was approaching from the west, Morozov ordered the pilot to hover directly above the consulate. He unstrapped his harness and moved to the rear passenger compartment. There, he found his high-powered automatic rifle in a black plastic case. Cradling the powerful rifle in his right arm, he used his free hand to open the helicopter's sliding door to the rear. He let his legs slide out into the air and rested both feet on the metal step above the skid. Then, looking through the rifle's scope, he said, "Not this time!"

Vietnam People's Air Force UH-1N Side Number 409

Michele found herself enjoying flying a helicopter again. She loved how she could make the aircraft go wherever she wanted it to and make it stay there motionless for as long as the fuel allowed. Her last Air Force assignment had been at the Francis E. Warren Air Force Base, west of Cheyenne, Wyoming. Her unit, the 37th Helicopter Squadron, supported the Air Force's 90th Missile Wing and its Minuteman II intercontinental ballistic missile (ICBM) mission. Michele primarily had flown ICBM convoy security and missile site support flights, but she preferred to fly the occasional casualty evacuation and search-and-rescue sorties. She enjoyed the immense satisfaction she got from knowing she was directly responsible for saving someone's life. Michele even considered requesting a transfer into the US Coast Guard, thinking that the mission might better suit her interests. However, when the Air Force didn't approve her transfer request, she decided to complete her obligated military service to pursue a graduate degree and possibly a career in politics. Looking back, she realized that a different decision by an officer in her chain of command would have meant she probably would be a senior Coast Guard officer now rather than a member of Congress.

Colt was closely studying a tourist map in his lap and comparing it with the landscape below. He realized the map wasn't drawn to scale and not intended for navigation, but the chopper didn't have a working navigation system. The tourist map and the small aircraft compass were the best tools available. Colt had drawn a series of red lines and magnetic course headings earlier that morning to guide them to the American consulate. But as they flew the first leg of his planned route, it became clear that the tourist map was mostly useless. He decided to look for significant landmarks on the map that correlated to buildings and land features that he could see from the sky. He was about to recommend a course change to Michele when she spoke into the intercom, "Okay, Colt. I think I see the consulate building. It's at about eleven o'clock, just to the left and a bit beyond that twin-spire cathedral."

Michele banked the helicopter slightly to the left to point the chopper's nose directly at the American consulate. Colt found a pair of binoculars in a leather pocket attached to his seat and raised it to his eyes. "Michele, there's a civilian helicopter hovering directly over the consulate building!" He passed her the binoculars, and she replied, "That's an H130, probably just a sightseeing flight. The pilot should know better than to get so close to the consulate. It's probably protected airspace." She handed the binoculars back to Colt. Then, his windshield shattered as dozens of rounds from an automatic weapon slammed into their helicopter and stitched up the fuselage as Michele instinctively pushed the cyclic forward, lowered the collective, and increased the right rudder. The chopper sharply banked right and down, away from the H130.

"Master caution light!" screamed Michele and then, "Losing oil pressure and hydraulics in engine two! Shutting it down!" Michele fought to regain control as she completed the engine emergency shutdown procedure. She had just finished the final step when several rounds hit the helicopter's right side near her pilot seat. Colt saw the H130 had positioned itself on the military chopper's right side, and a man was firing a rifle from the helicopter's open left rear door. Colt moved to the rear of his helicopter, found one of the AK-47s, and slid open the right rear door. Immediately, automatic weapon fire poured into Colt's chopper, and he returned fire at the man, emptying the 30-round magazine. He found the other AK-47 and was about to fire at the man again, and he reconsidered. Colt remembered something an Army Apache helicopter pilot had once told him. "The best way to bring down a helicopter is to kill the pilot." Colt shifted his aim forward, sighted the helicopter's forward side window, and pressed the rifle's trigger until the weapon stopped firing. He watched with detached interest as the H130's window imploded, and the pilot's skull shattered into pieces. The now pilotless helicopter fell from the sky and crashed into the Saigon River. The last thing that Colt saw was the look of terror on the gunman's face. He didn't regret causing either man's death; it was something that needed doing. It occurred to him the same thing had happened in Gibraltar when Russ raised his pistol and made him fire. He wondered why he found himself in situations like these and then decided there was no logical answer.

Colt slid the cabin door closed and moved back to his seat next to Michele. The wind noise was deafening with the front windscreen destroyed, and he placed the headset back on. "Okay. Thank god that's over."

Michele turned her head and replied, "Not quite. My leg's been hit, and I'm losing a lot of blood." Colt now saw the damage to her right leg and quickly moved to place a makeshift tourniquet above the bleeding wound. She winced as Colt tightened the web strap.

"That's too tight. I still need to fly this thing."

Colt loosened the tourniquet a bit and then shouted, "Michele, switch the radio to UHF guard, 243 megahertz, and head 090!" It was time to use his backup plan while Michele could still fly. He picked up the satellite phone and called the NMCC. A woman answered the call, and Colt shouted over the helicopter's engine noise, "This is PATRIOT. Get me, Mr. Holmes!"

The Bridge, USS Robert McNamara (DDG-145), the South China Sea

Lieutenant Commander Kathy Robertson was not looking forward to her next conversation with Commander Leach. She particularly didn't want to have it on the ship's bridge where the entire watch team could overhear their discussion. Still, the captain had rejected her request for a private meeting, and the bridge was the only alternative. She waited until he finished signing some forms, and she stepped up to stand beside him in his bridge chair. He had the chair's back partially reclined and had propped his feet up next to the window.

"Captain, with the exercise completed, I've plotted a course back to port, and the quartermaster-of-the-watch is loading the data into the nav system. We're ready to head home whenever you say the word, sir."

Commander Leach picked up his heavy binoculars and scanned the horizon from port to starboard. Without lowering the binoculars, he replied, "Thanks, XO. Anything else?"

Kathy paused and glanced around the bridge. Lieutenant Fry and Ensign Barnes were leaning over the chart table and looking at the navigation chart. The other members of the bridge watch were looking forward through the bridge windows. In a low voice, Kathy said, "Yes, sir. One other thing. I've completed my investigation of the allegations against you made by Petty Officers Lewis and Ramos. I've interviewed both Sailors, and their versions of the events seem credible. Additionally, I've taken statements from several witnesses, and each witness corroborates what Lewis and Ramos have alleged. Therefore, I've determined that I have no other choice but to report their accusations up the chain of command via message traffic. You should know that Lieutenant Commander Vilhauer has already informed his chain of command of the allegations earlier this morning."

Commander Ron Leach slowly lowered the binoculars from his eyes and looked directly at Kathy Robertson. "You do realize that if you send that message, I'll be finished? I'd consider not letting that message leave this ship, but you're smart enough to have already thought about that before coming up here, right?"

Kathy nodded her head. "Yes, sir. An email is already waiting in the commodore's inbox."

Ron Leach was about to say something in response when the bridge intercom blared, "Bridge, Combat. We just picked up a Mayday call on military air defense from a UH-1 requesting immediate assistance. We think we have them bearing 315 at about ten miles. One other thing. The pilot says she's a former Air Force helo driver and that she's got SECDEF onboard. Shall I give them a vector?"

Commander Leach got down from his bridge chair and walked over to the intercom. But before he could press the transmit switch, the command circuit speaker blared, "McNamara, this is Com Seventh Fleet, over."

Leach grabbed the handset. "Com Seventh Fleet, this is McNamara. Roger, over."

"McNamara, wait one for the chief of staff."

Leach looked at Kathy and waited for Captain Gary Winters to come on the circuit.

"McNamara, this is Captain Winters. I need to speak with the commanding officer, over."

"Yes, sir. This is Commander Leach, over."

"Leach, you have an inbound UH-1 with a wounded pilot and only one engine. A US congresswoman is flying the chopper, and the defense secretary is onboard. You're going to have to find a way to get them safely on board. Do you copy, over?"

Jason Vilhauer was sitting in the wardroom drinking coffee at a table with two pilots and his maintenance chief. They were discussing a problem both MH-60Rs were experiencing with their fuel systems. "You mean both birds are hard-down, Chief?"

"Yes, sir, Mr. Vilhauer. It must have been that last fuel transfer from the tanker. There's water in the fuel systems, and both aircraft will be down until we can purge the tanks and the fuel lines. And the ship will also need to refuel before we can fly again, sir."

Jason looked at the two other pilots and shook his head. "The captain's going to blow his stack when I tell him this." He looked at the maintenance report again. "At least we'll be heading back to port today." He refilled his coffee cup when the overhead speaker blared, "Lieutenant Commander Vilhauer, bridge!" Jason grabbed his ball cap and headed for the ship's bridge while thinking about breaking the bad news to Commander Leach. He raced up the ladder and opened the bridge door in time to hear Leach say into a handset, "But sir, this must be some sort of trick. I mean, SECDEF inbound on a chopper being flown by a congresswoman? Are you sure?"

Jason leaned over and whispered into Kathy's ear. "Who's he talking to?"

"Captain Winters, Seventh Fleet's chief of staff. We have a UH-1 inbound on just one engine and a wounded pilot at the controls. And there's more!"

"McNamara, I have the NMCC on another circuit, and they confirm Secretary Garrett is onboard that chopper. We are running out of time, over."

Ron Leach found it ironic that the one person who could have made his court-martial problems disappear was on a crippled helicopter about to make an emergency landing on his ship. He thought about the court-martial and the new allegations against him, and he decided he'd simply had enough. Leach pressed the handset's transmit button and calmly said, "This is McNamara, actual. That helicopter will not be landing on my ship, out."

"McNamara, this is Com Seventh Fleet, actual, Vice Admiral Shaffer. Commander Leach, I am ordering you to land that helicopter immediately! Acknowledge, over!"

Leach set the handset back into its cradle and left the bridge. Everyone remaining could hear his footsteps as he descended the ladder on the way to his cabin below decks.

"McNamara, acknowledge, over!"

Kathy Robertson picked up the handset. "Com Seventh Fleet, this is McNamara. Admiral Shaffer, Commander Leach has left the bridge. This is the executive officer, Lieutenant Commander Kathleen Robertson. What are your orders, sir?"

"McNamara, this is Com Seventh Fleet, actual. Bring that chopper aboard!"

Kathy looked at Jason and then pressed the transmit button. "Com Seventh Fleet, this is McNamara. Roger, out." She set down the handset and grabbed Jason's arm. "I already heard both birds are down, so having them ditch is out. I need you to get down to the helo control tower to take over from Ensign Alverez. I don't think our assistant supply officer is up to talking that Air Force pilot in."

Jason turned to go and then stopped, turned back to face Kathy, and said, "Aye-aye, ma'am," before he raced down the ladder.

Vietnam People's Air Force UH-1N, Side Number 409

"Helo 409, this is the USS Robert McNamara, over."

Michele was relieved when she heard the radio transmission and replied, "McNamara, this is 409. Roger, over."

"409, we are an American Navy warship bearing approximately 140 degrees from you, at nine miles. We acknowledge your emergency. Contact helo control station on three one zero for vectors, over."

"This is 409. Roger, out."

Michele pointed to the UHF radio panel, and Colt selected the new frequency. He gave Michele a thumbs up, and she pressed the transmit button. "McNamara helo control station, this is helo 409 with you on three one zero, over."

Jason Vilhauer opened the door and had just stepped into the small control station in time to answer the radio call from the crippled helicopter. "409, this is McNamara helo control. What is the state of your emergency, fuel level, and how many souls are on board?"

"This is 409. We are a UH-1 November with one good engine. Fuel cells are half full. We have two souls on board, over."

"Roger, 409. What is the pilot's flight experience, over?"

"McNamara, I'm a combat-qualified Air Force UH-1 November pilot with seven hundred hours. Last flight was eight years ago."

"Roger, 409. Understand you're wounded, over?"

"Affirmative. Rifle wound to my right thigh. We've applied a tourniquet, but I have to keep loosening it so that I can feel the pedals. Lost a lot of blood."

Jason thought about a rusty and badly wounded pilot bringing an underpowered helicopter to land on a heaving deck.

He knew that a few non-Navy pilots had qualified to land on Navy ships, but the skill was not common.

"409, have you ever landed on a boat before, over?"

"That's a negative, McNamara."

"No problem, 409. My name's Jason. What's your name, 409?"

An experienced flight instructor, Jason had learned that gaining a student's trust was crucial to their ability to master challenging skills. And this was going to be beyond challenging.

"My name's Michele. Michele Phan, over."

"Okay, Michele. I'm going to walk you through the approach, step-by-step. Just do exactly what I tell you, and you'll be safely down in a few minutes. Piece of cake, over."

Michele looked at Colt and keyed the intercom. "Bullshit!"

"Okay, 409. I'm going to bring you straight-in. We'll do this just once; we don't want to take a chance that your remaining engine is also damaged. Maintain current heading and descend to 300 feet and reduce your airspeed to 70 knots."

Colt watched as Michele lowered the collective and adjusted the cyclic to fly the directed profile.

"409, you have a green deck, relative wind is blowing left to right at five knots, the ship's pitch and roll are moderate." A green deck meant the ship had cleared 409 to land. Jason had proffered the wind direction and the ship's motion to help the pilot anticipate the landing conditions.

"409, start descending to 200 feet AGL. Reduce your speed to 60 knots, over."

"Roger, McNamara. Two hundred feet AGL at 60 knots, over."

Michele continued to make minute and simultaneous corrections to the collective, cyclic, and rudder pedals as the helicopter neared the destroyer's stern. The helicopter was responding to control inputs, but the loss of one engine delayed the response, and Michele soon found herself overcorrecting to stay in the landing profile.

"Easy, 409. You're doing fine. Now start descending to 140 feet AGL and reduce to 50 knots. You'll intercept the line-up line within about 800 feet of the ship. You should be able to see our glideslope indicator now."

Michele noticed a green light shining from the destroyer's landing area. "Got a green light now, McNamara."

"Roger, 409. You're doing great. You're a little high, though. The light shows your position on the glideslope. Green means you're above the glideslope. Amber means you're on glideslope, and red means you're below glideslope. I need you to fly the amber-red interface, 409. It will give you the best reference for getting aboard."

Michele concentrated on the glideslope indicator as she flew the helicopter toward the pitching destroyer. The colored lights started to dance, and she realized the blood loss had begun to affect her vision and her ability to fly. But she needed to feel the control pedals if she had any hope of landing the chopper.

"Colt, I need you to remove the tourniquet. I have to control this bird."

Looking at the growing pool of blood at Michele's feet, he knew that loosening the tourniquet would threaten her life, but it was the only way to get them aboard. He gently untied the tourniquet and Michele regained feeling in her foot while blood flowed from her thigh.

"409, you might be fixating on the movement of water from the ship's waterline to the wake. Don't do that! And there is a wind burble caused by the ship's superstructure. So, you'll need a touch of power and just a bit of attitude adjustment to fly through that."

Michele knew she was barely hanging on to consciousness as she struggled to follow Jason's coaching. Then, she started to see multi-colored lights flicker across the destroyer's landing deck, but she concentrated on keeping the damaged helicopter flying.

"409, continue flying the glideslope to cross the deck at about ten feet. Then, you'll hover-taxi to a five-foot hover until the landing officer signals you to land. Watch his eyes, Michele."

She focused her eyes on a person wearing yellow and holding two lighted batons in outstretched arms. When he signaled her, Michele quickly lowered the collective, and the helicopter crashed down onto the landing deck. She heard alarms sound, and she felt Colt remove her headset and then embrace her as everything went dark.

Sick Bay, USS McNamara (DDG-145)

An exhausted Colt Garrett looked at his reflection in the mirror mounted on the sick bay's bulkhead. The impact of Michele's death just hours earlier was just starting to hit him now that he was alone for the first time since they landed on the destroyer. Colt rubbed his bloodshot eyes and thought about their brief time together and how close they had grown over the past few days. She seemed to understand him better than anyone else, and he wondered if he would meet someone else as unique as Michele. Colt didn't know if she had any living relatives; she hadn't mentioned any to him. There was an ex-husband somewhere. He'd need to be notified of Michele's death. And Colt would need to arrange her transport home. He preferred to think about logistics rather than the effect that Michele's loss was having on him.

The ship's independent duty corpsman had given him a

perfunctory medical exam and had pronounced him reasonably healthy for a man in his late sixties and not wounded from his recent travails. After taking a short shower, he toweled off and dressed in the underwear and dark blue coveralls the corpsman had placed on the chair. The new coveralls and the pair of leather boots fit reasonably well, and Colt was more than eager to dispose of the Vietnamese fatigues stained with Michele's blood. He was combing his thinning hair when he heard two knocks on the sick bay door.

"Good evening, Secretary Garrett. I'm Lieutenant Commander Robertson, McNamara's executive officer. I understand you're feeling better."

"Yes. The shower was amazing. And thanks for the change of clothes. I assume the captain is busy on the bridge?"

"Well, Mr. Secretary, the captain is in his cabin right now. There's a court-martial waiting for him when we return to port. He's probably focused on that."

When Colt heard Kathy mention a court-martial, he remembered that the commanding officer of the McNamara had requested that Colt drop the charges in exchange for the man not further damaging the Navy's reputation. No wonder he hadn't stopped by to see him.

"That's fine, XO. I didn't really want to speak with him, either." Then, another knock on the door, and a tall officer in a green flight suit entered the sickbay carrying a flight helmet and an inflatable life vest.

"Good evening, Secretary Garrett. I'm Lieutenant Commander Vilhauer, the helicopter detachment OIC. You probably heard my voice on the radio during the approach."

"Yes, Commander. And thank you for getting Representative Phan and me aboard. That was quite a feat, talking down a pilot who'd never landed on a ship before. I'll be speaking with

SECNAV about what you and the ship have done today. Will you be flying us out to the Lincoln?"

"No, sir. Both our birds are down for maintenance. Abraham Lincoln is sending one of their helicopters over to transport you back to the carrier. We needed to push the Huey over the side to make room on the flight deck for their chopper to land."

Colt appreciated he wouldn't have to be hoisted up to a helicopter from the destroyer by a cable.

"And speaking of the inbound helicopter, I need to get you back to the flight deck right away. It's due overhead in about ten minutes, and I'd like to give you your safety brief so you can board right after they touch down. Here's a vest and helmet for the ride. You'll be able to communicate with the aircrew during the flight."

A weary Colt shook both officers' hands. "Thank you for everything."

The Knighthawk lifted into the air and headed to the USS Abraham Lincoln (CVN-72), operating more than ninety miles away from the McNamara.

"Welcome aboard, Secretary Garrett. I'm the aircraft commander, Lieutenant Hanley, and Lieutenant JG Myer is flying as the copilot. O'Connell is our crew chief, and Reeves does everything else. We should be landing on the Lincoln in under an hour. Let me know if you need anything!"

"Thank you, Lieutenant. I appreciate that!" Colt looked down at the rescue basket holding a black rubber bag with Michele Phan's corpse inside. Just a few hours earlier, he watched her fight to land the damaged helicopter. She saved his life but had died in the process. He stared out the helicopter's door window and watched the sun touch the horizon. It reminded him of using a sextant to measure the angle of a celestial object and bringing the image down to touch the horizon. In the age of electronic navigation, he wondered if naval officers were still required to learn the skill. Probably not. Colt's thoughts wandered back to when he shared the Gibraltar story with Michele. It had felt as if a heavy weight had been lifted from his soul. Strange that such a simple act could have that effect. He didn't know if he had loved Michele, but Colt knew that he would miss her. He looked back into the helicopter's cabin and noticed the young Sailor was closely watching him.

"Petty Officer Reeves, the lieutenant said that you do everything else. What does that entail?"

Austin Reeves pointed at the red patch on his jacket that read, "So that others may live."

He removed the Velcro patch and handed it to Colt. "I'm a SAR swimmer, sir. That's my primary duty. The lieutenant meant that I do all the usual aircrew stuff, too. The pilots give me shit because, deep down inside, they know their only function in life is to fly me around in this airborne truck to save people. I think they have low self-esteem!"

"Okay, Reeves," said the pilot. "Give it a rest."

Reeves just waved at the two pilots and chuckled. Colt enjoyed meeting with young service people and hearing their stories. The young aircrewman was proud of his job and the lives he had saved. Talking with him made Colt feel a little bit better about Michele. He handed the patch back to the Sailor, and he felt the helicopter start to descend.

"Sir, we're on the downwind leg; we should be landing soon." The pilot pointed out the helicopter's left side, and Colt could see the Nimitz-class aircraft carrier below with its flight deck full of Super Hornets. He tightened his seat harness and prepared for landing.

Secure Communications Room, USS Abraham Lincoln (CVN-72)

"Colt, glad you made it to the Lincoln. We're working on getting an Osprey to pick you up and fly you to Clark Air Base in the Philippines. I have a C-17 waiting there with your CID protection detail to bring you home the rest of the way to Andrews. A few stops for fuel along the way. How're you feeling?"

Colt massaged his temples and let out a grown. "Older than I am, Steve. Much older." He let his hand touch the black backpack he had carried since Glenn Carpenter handed it to him before he died. "Steve, I have the evidence with me. There should be enough physical evidence and DNA to confirm the servicemembers' identity and that Soviet soldiers murdered them. People died so that we could do something with this information. You need to start working with State to get Cambodia's permission to get the remains recovered before anyone else does."

"We're already on that, Mr. Secretary. I have a recovery team heading to Phnom Penh as we speak, and the American embassy security team has already secured the site. The Marines jumped at the chance to protect those remains. Speaking of remains, I understand Representative Phan died while landing the Huey?"

"Yes, Steve. I brought her back with me to the Lincoln. I assume we can escort her back home on the C-17?"

"Yes, sir. I'll let the Air Force know so that they can be prepared with the appropriate honors when you arrive at Clark. And I'll contact the speaker of the House regarding any notification or other protocol stuff. This is a first for me, a member of Congress dying while on a DOD mission."

"For me as well. Tell me, what have you discovered regarding

278

the helicopter shoot-down and what happened at the Phnom Penh prison and in the air over Ho Chi Minh City?"

Steve Holmes had anticipated the question. "As we suspected, this was a GRU operation from start to finish, including the rescue of Colonel Petrov from his island prison. Unfortunately, General Korobov seems intent on preventing us from implementing our policy objectives." He waited for the defense secretary to respond to the information.

Colt sighed. "Interesting. I can't imagine the Kremlin is pleased with his performance, and we know others in Moscow would like to have his job."

"Good point, sir. And we're working on the likelihood of a security compromise within the intelligence community. I've spoken with NSA Webb, and he's determined to lead an interagency investigation into the matter. I have concerns about his involvement, but we can talk more about that after you return. By the way, I've just received word that an Osprey will be overhead Lincoln in under two hours. It'll be good to see you again, Colt. I just called Dan to let him know you're safe. Allie's been staying at his apartment throughout this ordeal."

"Thanks for doing that, Steve. I've been thinking about the security leak and have some ideas of my own. I'll let you go now. I need to try to find some aspirin for this headache." He pressed a button on the console to disconnect the phone call.

The Flight Deck, USS Robert McNamara (DDG-145), the South China Sea

Boatswain's Mate Third Class Hector Santiago heard the ship's bell ring four times, indicating he was halfway through his four-hour watch and would be in his rack by midnight. There may be watches more boring than standing aft lookout, but BM3 Santiago couldn't think of a single one. He wore a headset that connected him with the boatswain's mate of the watch, a senior Sailor on the ship's bridge within arm's reach of the officer of the deck. If Santiago saw anything out of the ordinary, he was to notify the bridge immediately. Nothing had happened in the previous two hours, and Santiago had every reason to believe the remaining two hours would be equally as uneventful. So he was surprised when someone tapped his arm, and he was shocked to see that it was McNamara's commanding officer, Commander Ron Leach.

"Evening, Captain." Santiago had heard rumors of the captain leaving the bridge in the middle of a conversation with the admiral. Nobody had seen him since he went into his cabin; he didn't even show up at the wardroom for dinner. What was he doing on the flight deck?

"What can I do for you, sir?"

"Good evening, BM3. Beautiful night, isn't it?"

Santiago looked up at the moonless sky. "Uh, yes, sir, I guess. Do you need anything, Captain?"

Ron Leach thought about all the things that he needed. He was sure that Petty Officer Santiago couldn't help with any of them. Except for one. "BM3, I need you to help me with something over by the gear locker."

Santiago pressed s button on his mic. "Bridge, aft lookout. Going offline for a minute."

He removed the headset and followed the ship's captain over to a gray steel cabinet.

"Here," said the captain. "Take these over to the port side." Leach handed him two sets of steel tie-down chains used to secure helicopters to the flight deck. He grabbed two more chain sets and joined Santiago near the flight deck's edge. Santiago watched as Leach wrap all four tie-down chains around his upper body. Before the young Sailor could say anything, Leach climbed over the safety line and threw himself into the sea. A shocked Santiago watched his commanding officer disappear beneath the waves as the destroyer drove forward. He threw a lighted life ring into the water, fumbled with his headset, and screamed into the mic, "MAN OVERBOARD, PORT SIDE!" He immediately felt the ship turn sharply to port and then heard the ship's loudspeaker blare, "MAN OVERBOARD, PORT SIDE!"

"Aft lookout, bridge. Who went overboard?"

Boatswain's Mate Third Class Hector Santiago pressed the transmit button. "It was the captain. I saw him go."

Gelendzhik, Russia

The Russian tourist resort on the shores of the Black Sea was known for its sand beaches and waterparks. General Korobov enjoyed the time at his dacha, away from Moscow and his responsibility as chief of Russia's military intelligence service, but he particularly enjoyed time with his mistress and away from his wife of forty-five years. He sat propped up on pillows in a bed with a goose-down comforter keeping him warm. The bedroom featured a stone-lined fireplace, but most of the heat went up the chimney, and the roaring fireplace only served to fill the room with a smoky haze. Korobov got up from the warm bed to place another log on the fire and then quickly returned to his bed and pulled the comforter up to his chin. He reached over to the nightstand and emptied the vodka bottle before throwing it across the room.

It was clear that the Americans now had proof that Russian troops had executed American soldiers at the end of the Vietnam War. It was only a matter of time until the American government leaked the information to the press. Senators and representatives would demand public hearings to investigate the extent of the war crimes, and, as a result, Russia's reputation and influence throughout the world would suffer. Unfortunately, the O'Kane Doctrine would not only continue but perhaps be expanded, and there was nothing Korobov could do to stop it. And what about Garrett? Korobov decided to head to the dacha with his mistress, Ulyana, after being briefed about the operation to prevent Colton Garrett from leaving southeast Asia alive. Despite several attempts by Korobov to end his life, the man had somehow survived. If intelligence reports proved accurate, Garrett would continue to serve as defense secretary in the new administration. Another eight more years of that man and his anti-Russia policies!

"Yevgeni!" he bellowed at the door. "Bring more vodka! Immediately!" Korobov suspected his bodyguard was asleep in a chair outside his door. Yevgeni had been his constant companion for more than twenty years, but the soldier was getting too old for the duty and should have retired a while ago. "Yevgeni! Wake up, you old fool! Bring the vodka!"

Instead, the bathroom door opened, and a stunning young woman wearing a seaman's woolen coat, canvas trousers, and black rubber boots walked out and toward Korobov's bed. "Ulyana, my darling. Why are you dressed? Come back to bed! And what is the purpose of putting on this costume? Perhaps more role-playing?"

"No, general. No more role-playing for you." She stepped forward as she swiftly raised a suppressed pistol and pointed it at the man's chest.

General Korobov knew that his superiors were angry with his inability to eliminate Colton Garrett, and it wasn't uncommon in his profession for retirement to come with a bullet. He started to move his left arm toward the nightstand when the pistol coughed once, and a shot slammed into his left shoulder, spraying blood onto the expensive bedding.

"I removed that pistol hours ago, you fat pig!"

Korobov looked at his mistress of three years and was struck by how she had fooled him for so long. He heard the pistol cough again as two bullets tore into his heart, and a third smashed into his forehead. Ulyana checked for a pulse to confirm the man was dead before leaving the dacha. She walked down the cobblestone street toward a moonlit harbor where a fishing boat waited to take her to a small village on the Black Sea.

Epilogue

St. Patrick Catholic Church, Washington DC

Colt loved to attend mass at St. Patrick's whenever he was
in town. The parish was established in 1794 to meet the needs
of Irish immigrants at work erecting the White House and
the Capitol building. Bishop John Carroll appointed an Irish
Dominican, Fr. Anthony Caffrey, as its first pastor. The initial
structure on the present property was a simple frame chapel and
residence, one of the first church buildings in the new federal city
and completed six years before the federal government moved
to the capital in 1800. The present Gothic church was begun
in 1872 and dedicated in 1884, quickly becoming the venue for
national and international events. Colt was particularly fond of
the church's Great Rose Window. The window measured fifteen
feet in diameter with 225 square feet of stained glass, installed in
the church's west wall in 1964. Because the installation took place
shortly after the assassination of President John F. Kennedy on
November 22, 1963, and because President Kennedy was the first
Irish-Catholic president of the United States, the window was
dedicated to him.

On this day, Colt quietly sat with his family in a wooden pew
near the front of the church, waiting patiently for the funeral
service to begin. Allie sat next to her father while her husband
Kyle sat to her right. Next was Dan Garrett and his girlfriend
Rebecca Clarke, both in their naval uniforms. Colt looked to
his left and watched as members of Petty Officer Luke Gallo's
family whispered among themselves. Gallo's sister, Leslie, had

gathered the family from all over the country to honor her older brother. The Gothic church was surprisingly full of mourners, probably due to all of the publicity regarding the return of the two servicemen's bodies two weeks earlier. Spencer Hale's broadcasting empire was the first to break the story, and his competitors quickly followed with details of how the men had died and the events leading to the recovery of their remains. International human rights organizations publicly denounced Russia's involvement in the tragedy, and there was talk of censure by the United Nations. Colt wasn't sure that any of that mattered. The two men were still dead.

The pastor asked everyone to stand as eight uniformed pallbearers slowly escorted a flag-wrapped coffin up the center aisle. Special Operations Command had selected two Soldiers, Sailors, Airmen, and Marines, from each branch, to honor Petty Officer Gallo during the funeral. They formally removed the American flag, folded it, and presented it to a somber Colt Garrett. He walked over to where Leslie was sitting and kneeled on one knee. "This flag is presented on behalf of a grateful nation and the Department of Defense as a token of appreciation for your loved one's honorable and faithful service." He presented the folded flag to Leslie and returned to his seat next to Allie. She squeezed her father's hand and whispered, "Thanks for inviting us, Dad. This is very special."

When the service was over, the pastor announced there would be one final ceremony, and he motioned to the rear of the church. A single line of Sailors of all ranks in service-dress blue uniforms solemnly walked up the center aisle and stopped at the side of Luke Gallo's casket. One by one, each man pressed a gold Navy SEAL insignia into the polished wood. More than one hundred SEALS pressed their tridents in the wood, turning Gallo's coffin into a gold-plated memorial to a brother they would never forget. When it was over, Colt watched Leslie break down and softly cry.

Later, a small group of family and friends gathered in the church's fellowship hall, sharing personal stories of Luke's childhood and high school years. Colt and his family were looking at an easel covered with photos of Luke's brief life. "It's heartbreaking, Dad," observed Dan Garrett. "He was just a kid, really, with his entire life ahead of him. I'm glad you were able to bring him and Sergeant Blake home."

Staff Sergeant Austyn Blake's remains were buried the previous week at a formal Green Beret ceremony at Arlington National Cemetery. His mahogany casket was put onto a caisson and wheeled out by six horses to his gravesite near an ancient Port Orford Cedar tree. There, a solemn US Army ceremony with military precision took place with the playing of Taps, a gun salute and a folded US flag presented to Sergeant Blake's nephew. Blake's engraved headstone would be placed at the gravesite later. Several of Sergeant Blake's family and a large group of Special Forces Soldiers and DOD officials attended the ceremony to pay their final respects to the memory of Staff Sergeant Austyn Blake.

The two Garrett men warmly embraced, and Dan went to find another beer. Colt was still looking at Luke's photo board when he felt a tap on his right shoulder.

"Secretary Garrett, I'd like to thank you for allowing me to join you here today. I was touched by your thoughtfulness when you called last week."

"Mr. Hale! I'm glad you could make it. I hope the ceremony gave you a measure of closure?"

"Yes, thank you. It did. Very moving. And I wanted to personally thank you for everything you did to bring these young men back to their families. If there's anything I can ever do to repay you, I hope you won't hesitate to ask."

"You don't owe me anything, Mr. Hale. But thank you for your kind offer."

Colt was about to leave to go back to his Pentagon office when Leslie Gallo walked up. "Mr. Garrett, thank you again for finding my brother and bringing him home. I was just a kid when I made him promise to return home to me. You helped him keep that promise."

"Thank you, but I considered it an honor. Will you be returning to San Diego soon?"

"Yes. The arrangements have been made, and the burial will be on Friday at the Fort Rosecrans National Cemetery on Point Loma. I think Luke would have liked that spot. By the way, I wonder if you might be able to shed some light on something? I started a foundation to honor Luke's memory, and last week I received a huge check from an anonymous donor. Do you have any idea of who that might have been?"

Colt glanced at Spencer Hale as the man left the room. He smiled. "No. No idea at all."

Colt Garrett's Residence, Washington DC

Colt, Steve Holmes, and Lenny Wilson sat in Colt's den, enjoying a cup of coffee before the brunch was served. Allie and Kyle were helping the staff in the kitchen with last-minute preparations while Dan and Rebecca played with Drake in the living room. The large but gentle golden retriever had been diagnosed with liver cancer after Colt returned from Vietnam, and the medication was taking a toll.

Lenny Wilson glanced at Steve and then turned to his boss. "I saw you talking with Spencer Hale after the funeral. What was that all about?"

Colt Garrett nodded. "He wanted to thank me for helping to bring those boys back home. I think he still feels guilty about his part in the attack on PYTHON and how many people died there. He's been carrying that around for a long time. I hope he can finally put it behind him."

Lenny looked at Steve once more before continuing. "You should know that Hale has been making noises around town about you running for elected office, potentially the seat left vacant by Representative Phan? He's been quite vocal about it, intimating you'd have his full support. Steve and I were wondering if Hale mentioned that when you were talking earlier."

Colt glanced at his two close friends and sipped his coffee. "Come on, Colt," began Steve Holmes. "Are you seriously considering running for office? The president told me you had accepted Maria Hernandez's offer to help with her national defense strategy for the campaign. It would be very challenging to do both."

Colt got up from his desk and opened the den's door. "I think it's time to eat!"

The staff served brunch in the formal dining room and had done a magnificent job of decorating for Colt's welcome home party. Allie sat next to her father and whispered to him, "I assumed Jillian was coming. Is everything okay between you two?"

Colt passed the plate of breakfast meats to his left. "We've decided to let things cool off for a bit. Taking a break will be good, I suppose."

Dan heard the exchange between his sister and their father and kicked Allie under the table while he reached for the plate of potatoes.

"Dad, I hope I didn't have anything to do with that. Things have been difficult lately, and I probably said some things I shouldn't have."

"You may be surprised to hear me say this, but I tend to disregard my children's opinion of my social life." He grinned at Allie and Dan and announced, "I believe I heard that we're going to have dessert! I'm ready!"

Steve Holmes stood and tapped his water glass with a fork. "Ladies and gentlemen, before the dessert course is served, I'd like to thank you for coming today to celebrate the safe return of Colton Garrett. He's beginning to develop a reputation for emergency landings on Navy ships!"

The table erupted in laughter, and Steve continued. "For as long as I've known Colt Garrett, the topic of his mysterious Navy Cross has continued to surface. Nobody seems to know why he received the award, and the man himself won't share any details, claiming that the citation is highly classified or another such excuse. But during my brief, albeit brilliant, term as acting defense secretary, I solved the mystery. I used, or should I say, abused my temporary authority to convince certain powers that the citation in question should be declassified after all these years. Commander Garrett, if you would be so kind as to open that box behind your chair and read the citation enclosed therein?"

Dan beamed with anticipation and pride as he carefully untied a red ribbon and opened the box to reveal a framed letter on faded stationery bearing the seal of the Secretary of the Navy. Dan cleared his throat and read the citation:

"The President of the United States takes pleasure in presenting the Navy Cross to Lieutenant Colton S. Garrett, United States Navy, for service as set forth in the following citation: For extraordinary heroism as Senior Multi-disciplinary Counterintelligence Officer, Fleet Ocean Surveillance Information Facility, Rota, Spain, in support of Task Force Broadsword on March 6, 1988. While attempting to prevent the theft of highly classified national security information by Soviet intelligence officers in the British Overseas Territory Gibraltar, Lieutenant Garrett's team moved to block the target vehicle from leaving a service station and exchanged fire with the vehicle's inhabitants. After the Soviet officers brought the Task Force Broadsword team under sustained automatic weapons fire, Lieutenant Garrett realized his team was caught in a kill zone. Under heavy fire and without cover, he ran to his vehicle and drove it forward to provide cover for his two team members. After exiting his vehicle and without hesitation, Lieutenant Garrett closed on the enemy position and engaged the enemy with a 9-millimeter M9 pistol, killing one and wounding another. Upon discovering one of his team had been killed, Lieutenant Garrett pulled the remaining severely wounded team member to safety. Lieutenant Garrett, with complete disregard for his safety, picked up a discarded service rifle and assaulted the enemy car, and killed an enemy combatant still in possession of the stolen classified material. By his outstanding display of decisive leadership, unlimited courage in the face of enemy fire, and utmost devotion to duty, Lieutenant Garrett reflected great credit upon himself and upheld the highest traditions of the United States Naval Service. For the President, Robert C. Spencer, Secretary of the Navy."

Dan handed his father the framed citation and shook his hand. Kyle asked Lenny, "What is it?"

Lenny Wilson waited a moment and then replied, "It's Colt's Cross."

After the brunch was over and his guests had left, Colt let

the CID protection detail know he'd like to visit the National Mall. The mall was a public space that ran from the foot of the United States Capital to the Potomac River. Also known as "America's Front Yard," the mall celebrated the people and events that shaped the nation. Colt liked to stroll among the monuments that honored the country's heroes, but he also enjoyed watching the tourists and city residents that filled the mall on sunny afternoons. There was something comforting about seeing people simply enjoying themselves in the sun next to the reflecting pool.

Colt was casually dressed in jeans, lightweight jacket, and a Seattle Mariners cap, looking like the thousands of people visiting the Mall that day. Most of his protection detail maintained a discreet distance, but one agent walked at his side. Colt wandered north and soon found himself facing the Vietnam War Memorial, with its two long black granite walls joined together forming an apex. He walked to the center of the memorial where a workman sat next to Panel 1W, which listed the servicepeople lost from April 15, 1972, until May 15, 1975.

"Excuse me, Secretary Garrett, nice to see you again!" Colt turned to see an elderly man wearing a faded Army shirt and a teenage girl at his side. He remembered speaking with the man and his granddaughter just a month earlier at the Wall.

Colt offered his hand to the veteran. "Yes, sir. How have you been?"

"Just fine, Mr. Garrett. Stephanie and her parents are visiting again this weekend. I want to thank you for looking into what happened to my Silver Star recommendation. I received this last week with a nice letter from Mr. Holmes." He touched the medal pinned to his shirt with pride, and asked, "Why are you here to-day?" Colt pointed to the workman using a small tool to convert a plus sign next to a name into a diamond.

Stephanie exclaimed, "I know what that means! Somebody has come home!"

Colt Garrett nodded. "Yes, somebody has come home."

*As of October 18, 2021,
the number of Americans
missing and unaccounted-for
from the Vietnam War is 1,584*

About the author

Captain Tom Carroll served thirty years combined active duty and reserve service in the United States Navy, specializing in Special Intelligence and Surface Warfare. Colt's Cross is the second novel in the Colt Garrett series.

His first book, Colt's Crisis, was published in 2020.

Tom owns an information technology firm in Olympia, Washington, where he lives with his wife.

TOM CARROLL

COLT'S CRISIS

Purchase Book 1 and start the adventure...